THE BURNING PEOPLE

The Burning People

A novel

by

ANDREA DREILING

Adelaide Books
New York / Lisbon
2021

THE BURNING PEOPLE
A novel
By Andrea Dreiling

Copyright © by Andrea Dreiling
Cover design © 2021 Adelaide Books

Published by Adelaide Books, New York / Lisbon
adelaidebooks.org

Editor-in-Chief
Stevan V. Nikolic

For any information, please address Adelaide Books
at info@adelaidebooks.org
or write to:
Adelaide Books
244 Fifth Ave. Suite D27
New York, NY, 10001

ISBN: 978-1-956635-03-4

Printed in the United States of America

For Dad,

I miss our camping trips and your steady love.

Bunny misses running like the wind.

Contents

Chapter 1

Bent Branch Falls 1974

Mary-Frances died in the springtime, an anomaly. Her body was carried out of the house while her radio broadcast a boxing match across the murky living room. A sunflower yellow, fleece blanket hung over the only window in the room, catching sunlight in its golden weave. Thick shadows had congealed in the corners. The static roar of some distant crowd poured through the speakers and jostled to fill a house newly emptied.

The men from the county hospital moved efficiently as they loaded Mary-Frances's body onto a stretcher. Each step they took was outlined by rubber soles that fell heavily on the wooden floor. The stainless steel gurney drug its nails across the silence as they extended its folding legs, screeching- leveling its petty complaints even as the lead-bodied fog of death settled into the room. In the last weeks of her life Mary-Frances had only enough energy to tend to her own sickness. The bookshelf and the singular, crooked lamp wore their abandonment as crowns of dust.

Somewhere in a part of the world untouched by Mary-Frances's death, Muhammad Ali and Joe Frazier were preparing to fight each other. The announcers' oblong, nasally voices rambled alongside each moment of the boxing match with no direction of their own. The sound of the stadium broke open the oppressive atmosphere hanging in the room. The round maroon speakers at each end of the radio pulsed with the obscure excitement. The radio was made of blond, heavily grained wood and its knobs were polished aluminum. *A real pretty piece of equipment* was how Mary-Frances once described it.

Curtis and Abigail waited outside, afraid for the moment when the waiting would be over; when life had to move on only much emptier, flimsier. It was as though time was grinding its gears, the axle responsible for pushing the sun across the Southern sky lurching around with a stomach full of sickness. *Muhammad Ali approaching the ring very deliberately, but it doesn't matter how you go in. It matters how you go out, that's the thing.* Finally four men crossed the threshold of the house, bracing themselves against the handrails of the front porch as they shouldered the weight of the stretcher, easing it down the steps. Abigail held her breath as they passed by her. It seemed that her Mama's body was being treated as though it was extraordinarily heavy, considering all the life it had just lost.

Curtis stood alone underneath the scarlet oak tree, watching nothing. His eyes had become exit wounds for grief. Grief was a problem without a solution, a cruel taunt to a man who had always relied on his own hands to fix what is broken. Humans love to toil against their own uselessness. It is as though grief was invented to remind us of the fact that our lives are just a series of reactions in a chaotic universe. Curtis imagined that god was a scornful being. This is the only way that he could make sense of his life.

Abigail pressed her back into the shroud of kudzu vines that hung from the rails and slats of the front porch. The vines slunk around, avoiding the hard right angles of the steps, designing a life of softness for themselves while Abigail contended with a new and persistent jabbing sensation just below her sternum; the arched entrance to the cathedral of emotion that sings through the human body. The heart is the priestess, the lungs a wet pipe organ. *Frazier staying low to get away from that jab.* The four men pushed Mary-Frances down the driveway and towards the waiting ambulance, bumping over stones and the contorted roots that lunged up out of the earth before plunging back underground: tiny serpents defying the limits of their underworld. Abigail stared down at her feet and a small finch hopped up from underneath the porch, nearly landing on her bare toes. She bent down to examine the small creature and it held still just long enough for her to see a small crack running across its beak.

Joe Frazier has always been vulnerable in the early rounds, I think he lost the first rounds in every fight he ever fought. Abigail knew Joe Frazier's name from overhearing the men down at Harper's Grocery talk about him. Mr. Hodges, who ran the theater next door, Ace Ellery, Mr. Harper and Bud who never seemed to have a last name or a proper first one. Bud played the guitar, soft and mindless while the others talked, then fast and jangly when the conversation paused.

"Well, waddya think Ace, our boy Joe's gonna keep his title?"

"Course he goin' ta keep it, the man's a monster but he's still walkin' next to god. Ali don't even act like he's from America, he cain't jest come into our boxing and beat out Joe Frazier."

Once a week Mary-Frances gave Abigail a dime so that she could walk to Harper's and buy a bottle of Coke. Abigail could be a strange child. She was more comfortable among adults than children her own age and counted their neighbor, Miss Camilla June, as her closest friend. Mary-Frances, with her limitless concept of nurturing, did what she could to encourage her daughter: this surprising child who spoke the language of grown-ups. The way Mary-Frances saw it, the weekly dime gave Abigail a way to go into town and navigate the strange dusk that sits between commerce and friendly affiliation. Abigail could ape these adult actions but in the end she sat down to enjoy a soda, something sweet and pointless, the way that a child should.

When the men talked tough, Cora Harper always left her place at the register with her feather duster and walked through the aisles, spinning each can until it faced outwards, lining up the candy bars and restacking the loaves of Wonder Bread. Abigail stayed put, feeling as though she was getting away with something, using her unassuming presence to remain unnoticed as she peeked into the men's world.

Cora Harper ran the grocery store with her husband, Beau Harper. Whenever Abigail entered she did so with such regard that she barely rang the bells hanging from the door. This wisp of a child with her erect posture would guide the door back to its frame as though she already knew about the wear and tear on hinges and frames that accumulates over stretches of time longer than her own, new life. Mrs. Cora adored Abigail. She always greeted her in the same way, "What'll it be honey bee?"

"One Coke please," Abigail would respond, sliding the dime across the counter to Mrs. Cora.

Cora would then pluck a straw from a ball jar that sat next to the register and plunge it down into the thin neck of the coke bottle and Abigail would grab at it in an excitement that betrayed the careless child still vital inside of her.

As she had sipped at the last Coke that her Mama would ever buy her, Abigail was perched on a short wooden stool and leaning her back against a bare patch of wall, poking her straw in and out of the sweet nectar, pretending to be a hummingbird. Coke fizzed and moved around in her mouth in the same way that laughter did. Since her mama never bought herself a Coke, Abigail decided that she would make her laugh extra that night, so she could feel it too.

"Yep, Joe Frazier better beat that son of a gun! Ali's been goin' around callin' Frazier a gorilla like he ain't one himself. He's a damn fool, he's goin' ta get what's comin' to him."

Underneath the men's brass, the guitar played sweetly along, keeping tempo as though there was no such thing as fighting, no yelling. No dying. Bud was a Vietnam veteran, once an unwilling participant in other men's fighting, and one of the only residents of Bent Branch Falls who wasn't planning on listening to the upcoming fight between Muhammed Ali and Joe Frazier. From behind the big hollow body of his guitar he was happy to strum all that violence away.

"Now you finish up with that suga', I'm sure your Mama's wonderin' where you're at," Cora shot Mr. Harper a sidelong glance.

Mary-Frances wasn't wondering where Abigail was at. Mary-Frances was wading through fever dreams, a landscape crafted from neon colors that did not exist in Bent Branch Falls. A place populated by memories that walked around on two legs and she was wondering, more than anything else, if her own mother would cry when she died. Were there tears left for Mary-Frances, or had the crying been done when Mary-Frances was 17, and running off with Curtis, carrying his child in her womb? The fractured memories mutated into tall monsters with exposed sternums and fingernails made of baby teeth. They stomped carelessly through Mary-Frances's garden as they lumbered off into the woods and left her alone to cough herself into a deep exhaustion.

Frazier just doesn't have the power that he had in the earlier rounds. The back doors of the ambulance slammed shut. The sharp, dry sound yanked Abigail back to the present moment. She wanted to go backwards, she wanted to bring that last Coke to Mary-Frances and sugar coat her illness with it. Why did she just sit there drinking it? Why wouldn't she have just sat there drinking it? She could feel her teeth rotting in her syrupy saliva.

Mary-Frances was carried away by the ambulance in a cloud of dust. She was on her way to nowhere. The radio kept up its relentless vigil. From outside of their house, Abigail and Curtis listened to Muhammad Ali beat Joe Frazier and the cheering was an incomprehensible language. That levity, that ability to abandon yourself and be swept up in the moment at hand was something Abigail and Curtis could no longer understand. Curtis walked down the driveway unsteadily, like a blind dog, and Abigail knew that he was going to his garage. The garage sat on the road that ran by the edge of the property, set about a half mile in front of their house. Abigail stayed on the front porch, she didn't know where she was going.

Chapter 2

Caville, NC 1964

In 1929 the scientists who watched space, the ones who pulled prophecies about the universe from the emptiness between galaxies, noticed that the emptiness was growing. It was swallowing light like velvet does. It might swallow us one day. The prophet-scientists predicted that the universe was expanding, and would continue to expand throughout the future.

If the scientists of 1929 were correct, then by the time that 1964 had come around, the universe's growth had changed the entire scale of space. Relatively speaking, Earth was smaller and so were its inhabitants. Even as the human race was multiplying it was shrinking, becoming less consequential in the grand scheme of things. But since the human race needs to believe in its own importance in order to continue functioning, we don't pay attention to these sorts of things. This is why in 1929, when the people who would hear the news of the ever-expanding universe heard it, most of them accepted it and quickly forgot. They were unaffected by their relative smallness. They simply went on with their days.

The tyranny of relative-smallness causes the events that are ordinary in the grand scheme of things to seem extraordinary to the individuals which they happen to. The incomprehensible size of things does not change the technicolor way that each of us experiences our lives, and this was proven true once again on the day that Mary-Frances learned of her pregnancy, 44 days after Abigail was conceived.

When the two pink stripes that Mary-Frances's hormones had magicked into being appeared on the pregnancy test, they stood out sorely against the bleached porcelain of the bathroom sink. They materialized on the plastic stick while she sat slumped on the floor, hoping that they wouldn't. When they did, they only proved what she already knew. She was sick with the knowledge and had been for weeks.

As Abigail made her presence known, all Mary-Frances could think about was her family- mostly her ma, Caroline. Their relationship was already strained, worn as threadbare as the rugs that Caroline hung off the railings of the front porch to beat dust from each day. News of Mary-Frances's pregnancy would surely punch a hole right through the sparse fabric of their family life. Mary-Frances knew this but didn't know how she would handle it, or if she could. This new, suffocating reality crystallized around Mary-Frances. In the polished knob of the bathroom cabinet she could see her distorted reflection peering back at her. In the rarified moment this crescent shaped version of her face could be just as real as the heart shaped one that she saw in the mirror each day.

At this point it might have been nice if Mary-Frances had someone to remind her that she was small and ever-shrinking; that over the course of her pregnancy her troubles would only diminish in size. But the Christian school she attended, and all the friends that she had made there, were not interested in any sort of science that may be used to ease the mind of a pregnant teenager. The friends Mary-Frances had would refuse to speak to her in the coming months. What else was she to expect?

Caroline and her friends were downstairs, exercising the newfound independence that selling tupperware had brought them.

"Well I may just have to buy one of those plastic lids, the ones that fit right over the casserole dish, those look so nice. Now Caroline, what color lipstick do you have on? It's beautiful on you," Mrs. Stein from across the street could be heard droning on over all the rest of them.

Caroline didn't like Mrs. Stein, but like so much in life that she didn't like, she had learned to politely tolerate her loud-mouthed neighbor. Some things that Caroline did like included reorganizing her jewelry box and key lime pie. At one point, she could have said with absolute certainty that the one thing in this world that she loved was her daughter. But now that conviction had lost its simplicity. It was still love, but one that demanded patience and an amount of uncertainty, so she distracted herself by wondering whether or not she should arrange her rings according to the color of their stones rather than the finger that they had been sized for.

Caroline knew that something in her daughter was growing wayward, kind of like the one branch on her azalea bush that wouldn't stop reaching past the rest and jutting out over the edge of the driveway. Caroline relished snipping that one branch off with her gardening shears. Each Sunday upon arriving home after church service, she donned her sunhat, pastel pink gardening gloves, and began pruning back the bushes by triumphantly cutting off the offending branch. Richard blamed that boy that Mary-Frances had been seeing, but Caroline's gut told her that it wasn't about him. Her precious Mary-Frances felt confined by the life that they had provided her. She could sniff the emotion out in her daughter because it was not so unfamiliar to herself. She also felt confined.

There were probably plenty of better times during which Mary-Frances could have taken her pregnancy test, but a bout of nausea had clouded her judgement. The steaming odor of pigs in a blanket that permeated the living room where the ladies had gathered sent her running up the stairs with her stomach turning in every direction. Finally, against this background of carefully measured rebellion and brightly colored shift dresses, Mary-Frances pulled the pregnancy test from where it had been hiding underneath her mattress for three days and used it.

As she sat trying to calm herself she watched her Pa, Richard Henderson, through the wavy glass of the bathroom window. He walked back and forth across the backyard pushing a lawn mower. His blurry silhouette was like a trout bending into a river's current. But, unlike any animal, Richard was all for civility; for keeping things neat and static. It showed in his carefully ironed trousers and perpetually trimmed Kentucky Bluegrass. The bluegrass had arrived in spongy rolls that were unfurled and flopped across the yard, smothering anything that had grown wild there.

Adrift in the rising panic, Mary-Frances struggled to get a hold of her own breath, simultaneously hoping and doubting that she would be able to love this child properly. But Abigail was already raising mountains in her, uprooting everything she had known in her short 17 years. Abigail was not waiting for love. She was gathering mass. She was an avalanche.

Caroline knew that the minutes during which Mary-Frances was not in the living room talking to her friends would stand as a testament to her rudeness, and Caroline's shortcomings as a mother. Her friends would swallow any comments they may have about this along with the tiny bites of pineapple upside down cake that they took from their pastry forks. Caroline distractedly smoothed her dress down with her sweaty hands wondering why she had chosen one with such a short hemline. She did not feel liberated or whatever it was she was supposed to feel in this tiny excuse for a dress, she felt exposed. It cost just as much as a full dress too.

"Coffee anyone?" Caroline held the silver carafe up in front of her and realized that no one was listening.

"Well then, I'm jest goin' to step outside and take in some air," she said, just in case anyone was listening. The other women remained absorbed in their conversations as she squeezed between the little groups of them that had formed in her living room and went out to the front porch. She wanted to run up the stairs after her daughter and break down that bedroom door of hers, always closed now days as it was. But she would never do that, she wouldn't even let herself knock on it politely because that may inadvertently demonstrate her upset to the other women. Amidst this newly mobile class of sales women there was no room for emotion. Tupperware keeps things clean and separate; all smells and tastes encapsulated in slick plastic- a perfect tool for the modern woman.

Mary-Frances let the inertia of these outlaw minutes settle onto the tile around her. She knew she was embarrassing her ma with her prolonged absence. As Mary-Frances worried over Caroline, then worried for herself, the distance between them seemed more impassable than ever. Caroline would be most concerned with what their neighbors and Mary-Frances's teachers thought when they found out about the pregnancy. Caroline would worry that the people of Caville would blame her for her daughter's lack of chastity. But Mary-Frances had already accepted the fact that love is chaotic, ungoverned by the rules of society. She already knew that the love she felt for Curtis was as unlikely as a fire being compelled into existence by the strike of lightning. But given the right conditions these things do happen.

The bottom of her stomach broke like a thunder cloud and Mary-Frances turned to vomit into the toilet bowl once more, maybe just from nerves this time. In the tear-flooded relief that comes when the body finally stops heaving, she realized that the only sure thing in her life from here on out was the fact that she was a mother. She wiped down the toilet bowl with a gob of tissue and walked down the stairs, meeting her ma's suspicious gaze impassively, rearranging her face into an indecipherable expression, a cold chip of marble.

Chapter 3

Bent Branch Falls, NC 1974

The funeral was a carnival of despair. Flowers from the blossoming dogwood trees floated over the mourners like confetti. Women wobbled like inexperienced stilt-walkers as their high heeled shoes sunk into the wet grass. In some blessed corner of his mind Curtis had found a piece of silence for the first time since Mary-Frances's death, and held onto it by avoiding eye contact with anyone. He and Abigail held hands as they took their seats, the ceremony spinning around them in festive distortion, as though it were all a reflection at the glassy core of a carousel. But today there would be no conciliatory prizes, no second chances. The last act of the whole show would be Curtis carrying the casket down the aisle alone.

The service took place at the side of the grave. Folding chairs were arranged in rows extending back from the gravesite and a minister from Caville stood in front of the freshly dug hole without a podium or a microphone to speak into. Somebody had arranged the funeral. Curtis forgot who had arranged it all, it didn't matter. The casket would be heavy. Death, the accumulation of a whole life, is heavy. It was approaching noon and in the unobstructed sunlight the unnatural saturation of the makeup that had been smeared onto Mary-Frances's face made her seem unreal; made of plastic.

Abigail couldn't look at her own mother in a box like that. Never once in her life could Abigail imagine her mama lying down willingly in a velvet lined box like some prized piece of jewelry belonging to someone else. If Mary-Frances could have, she would have opened her mouth wide and laughed all the mourners away. Abigail could imagine her and her mama lowering the casket into the river and hopping right in, floating away from Bent Branch Falls and out onto the Mississippi River. Maybe they could make it all the way to the ocean.

Curtis was coming out of last night's drunkenness and the approaching hangover was searing, like fog burning off of the treetops in the morning. The soggy whimpering and sobbing sounds coming from the crowd descended on his head like crows and pecked at his temples. He did not feel the defeat that generally anchored death to its finality. He felt rage. The choreographed routine of sorrow that the whole town had taken up upon learning of Mary-Frances's death began with a quiet acceptance of her departure. But Curtis did not accept it, and stood alone in his refusal. The show went on regardless. The town orchestrated his grief for him, depriving his feelings of their true form. Curtis allowed himself to be puppeted through the routine for the most part, but couldn't bring himself to allow anyone else to act as a pallbearer. The death was his burden to carry.

Right away the news of Mary-Frances's death had spread with plague-like efficiency and it was only a couple of hours after the ambulance had left the Kennedy house that people started showing up, with food of all things. Food like a useless salve, so clumsy in its abundance. No amount of anything could fill the hole left by the loss of Mary-Frances. Though he wanted to hide out in his garage, sitting quietly with the desire to fold himself into one of his neatly organized tool boxes, Curtis forced himself to stay in the house, ready to greet his well meaning neighbors as they streamed onto the property. He and Abigail were forced to open the door every half hour or so to sweet potato casserole. Collard greens and bacon. One infuriating pie after another until finally Curtis lost his temper.

Mrs. Buncombe, an opressively religious woman who had never been their friend and who had always spoken ill of Mary-Frances behind her back, stood on their front porch. Curtis swayed in the doorway, Abigail faithfully at his side.

"Can I help ya?" Curtis leaned forward then reeled backwards, overwhelmed by the way Mrs. Buncombe sweated through her makeup.

"I heard the news Mr. Kennedy and I am so sorry for your loss." Mrs. Buncombe spoke in carefully ironed phrases. Her husband sat idling in the driveway, unwilling to pass his condolences on to *those people*. Now Mrs. Buncombe stood there in front of them, defenseless and fidgeting. Worried about maintaining her status among the followers of the Bent Branch Falls Pentacostal Church, Mrs. Buncombe had spent the previous hours convincing herself that bringing the Kennedy's a pie was the godly thing to do. Curtis and Abigail stared out at her blankly and she began to doubt her former conviction. The top of the door frame sagged as though even the house was furrowing its brow in confusion at her appearance on the property.

"Well here, I baked a pie for you." Mrs. Buncombe's hands shook a little underneath the pie tin as she held it out to Curtis.

"Well, thanks for the fuckin' pie." he responded and passed the gluttonous thing to his daughter who echoed him, "yea, thanks for your fuckin' pie Mrs. Buncombe."

Mrs. Buncombe turned on her heel, hoping they did not see the angry flush swarming across her cheeks like a pack of wasps. She cursed her husband for not coming with her to face those miserable people even as she resolved to show up at the funeral.

Now the day had arrived and Curtis's best friend, Jimmy, sat on his left and Abigail on his right. Across the aisle, also in the front row, Caroline and Richard sat together staring into their laps. Curtis barely recognized Mary-Frances's parents, he had only met them a few times nearly ten years ago. After Abigail was born Caroline and Richard had made the trip from Caville to Bent Branch Falls a couple of times. For a while the gleaming, opal-innocence of their new baby granddaughter was enough to wash over the distaste they felt towards the sordid affair of her conception, but eventually their visits tapered off.

Though the people of Bent Branch Falls filled nearly all of the chairs and some stood at the back, the front row, reserved for immediate family, was nearly empty. The white backs of the vacant chairs reflected the sun menacingly at the minister as he stumbled through the ill-equipped service. Sweat gathered underneath his collar. His name was Brian Hagge and he had known Mary-Frances when she was a teenager attending the Mountain Empire Baptist Academy. He remembered her as quizzical and fragile, a student threatening to collapse under the strict dogma of some of the more fanatical teachers at Mountain Empire. He also remembered that she was gorgeous and so unaware of this plain fact that it was alarming.

Brian Hagge worked as the minister and school counselor at Mary-Frances's high school and could never shake the feeling that he should have been able to save her, that he had failed her. With the combination of traits that she possessed, the teenage Mary-Frances raised two impossibly contradictory feelings in minister Hagge: he wanted to protect her, but he also wanted to avoid her- he hated to even look in her direction. He was paralyzed by his inability to ignore the impassive way that she existed within her beauty. He was completely unable to approach the path of her education objectively even though it was his job.

The changes in Mary-Frances's performance during her last year at the school were rapid but not unpredictable given her unrestrained intellect and disaffection for group activities. Brian saw her worsening attendance record as a direct result of her growing competence. Through his many friends in the community Brian had tracked Mary-Frances's course away from religion because it was unique. It was not littered with beer cans and pilfered cigarettes the way that most of his other students' rebellion was. He remembered the way that Eleanor Caine, the owner of Caville's bookstore had called him over to her counter one day as he was browsing just to tell him that Mary-Frances had begun showing up at the weekly open mic to read her poetry. She locked eyes with him over her spectacles, "She's very good. A very interesting mind."

Brian Hagge had also caught on to the fact that Mary-Frances often hitchhiked to the mountains and spent the day hiking alone when Caroline complained about it to a teacher at the school. Without clear reason to do so, both women regarded this story as a lie and a cover up. What could she really be doing all day? In the conservative community the liability of being a young woman had a way of turning any alone time into an event clouded over by suspicion and unease.

Brain Hagge refused to discipline Mary-Frances in the way that his position at the school required him to. In a way Mary-Frances had tested his faith, and its ability to supersede institutional rules. The severity of the distinction that he was to draw between right and wrong was up in the air and tied to Mary-Frances's fate. He was confident in this course of action until he heard of her pregnancy. At that moment his restraint became a grave misjudgement, a personal failure on his part. It was this history that caused the sweat to well up at the minister's hairline, underneath his collar, in the deep divot beneath his heavy bottom lip, as he offered the final rites of passage like an apology to Mary-frances.

"And so we ask you, our heavenly father, to guide this soul out of darkness and to its rightful place in your kingdom, amen."

"Amen." half of the crowd responded. The other half had lost interest in straining to hear the minister's unamplified voice and had receded into their own thoughts. But now it was time for the coffin to be lowered into the grave. It was time for Curtis to make good on his refusal to ask anyone else to be a pallbearer.

Jimmy nudged his arm, "Ya sure about this man?"

"It's cuz I have to." Curtis responded, squinting; working his mouth around the sour situation.

"Well, shit." Curtis grunted as he stood. His boozy sickness helped him to feel more distant than ever from the people crowded around and he turned to them, looking as though he was about to charge into battle.

"My wife was a good woman and most of ya'll know that. Fer most a you, that is the reason that brought ya here. If any of you're here for any other reason, than git." He spat into the dirt and began walking down the center aisle to where the coffin lay at the back of the congregation.

Mary-Frances his love, her post-death face such an abominable beacon, parted her lips just barely and Curtis heard it when she told him that she loved him, one last time.

"I love you too" he responded then let the lid of the coffin fall shut with a heavy clunk. He took a mallet from his back pocket and drove six long nails into the coffin lid, three on each side. As

Caroline watched the spectacle she couldn't help but reflect on the Curtis that she had known when he was a teenager. Before he had become Mary-Frances's lover he bagged Caroline's groceries every Saturday at the grocery store in Caville. She liked him then, thought he had a sweet and flexible way about him. He was always eager to carry the groceries out to the customers' cars for them and even had a habit of arranging the bags in their trunks.

Curtis took a step backwards, took off his suit jacket and folded it neatly over a nearby headstone. Already the button down shirt underneath was nearly soaked through and beads of sweat swelled at his temples. The casket was shiny and black with silver railings on each side. With the gaudy glint of it, he realized that it was Caroline who must have arranged the funeral. Only Caroline and Richard would have been able to afford this limousine-like vessel to carry their daughter into the afterlife. Curtis turned his eyes heavenward and muttered under his breath, "this is what you've done to me." With that he threw himself into the task of lifting the casket alone.

He grabbed the railings at one end, the end that Mary-Frances's feet rested in. He started by rocking the casket back and forth, pulling it off of the table inch by inch. When half of the casket hung off of the table, its weight suspended by his arms, he turned carefully, letting go of it with only one hand at a time until his back was to it. Then he doubled over and backed up, wedging his folded body underneath it. He snailed forward with the casket on his back, his whole torso heaving with the effort of it. In this way he began his staggering trip down the aisle. A few steps into his journey he could be heard saying, "Mary-Frances, you could kill me."

Nobody can help a man like Curtis and nobody tried to. There is a steel core in each of us and when life cuts so deeply it is all that we have to rely on. An unbreakable center made of hundreds of impacted moments. Our mettle comes from the world's unbearable pressure.

"This is an outrage." Mr. Buncombe finally declared after five eternal minutes of Curtis's painstaking progress had sweated past. He stood up and pushed his way down the row, past the knees of those who remained sitting. Mrs. Buncombe followed him, her chin pointed upwards and refusing to waver. Everyone else stayed put. Holding their breath, wringing their hands; quieting the frightened animal just below their diaphragms that was sending its acid claws up into their esophagus' while whispering *no no no no*.

When he had only a quarter of the aisle left to travel, Curtis tipped over sideways. The coffin crashed down and would have crushed everyone sitting on the right side of the aisle had they not been quick enough to move out of the way. With a disturbing serenity Curtis began taking off his shirt, carefully guiding each button through its hole. He pulled it off of himself and threw the garment on the ground at his feet. Then he stood there, holding the crowd over the edge of the world. The inconsolable rhythm of his breathing was visible through a thin, ribbed undershirt. His muscles had risen to the surface of his skin like those in an ox's body. He seized onto one of the silver railings and dragged the casket, now on its side, towards the grave. Each burst of movement came in a quick yank. Tugs that channeled every bit of strength in Curtis's body and compressed it into a millisecond packed with force. A yank. A grunt. A deep breath. Over and over until the coffin sat at the side of the grave.

"We all did this to her." Curtis growled at the congregation. Then he got behind the casket and gave it one more massive push. It rolled haphazardly into the hole, landing at a diagonal angle. Caroline flinched at the words he spoke and the horrific way that her daughter had come to her final resting place. *We all did this to her.* Caroline repeated to herself.

Chapter 4

Caville, NC 1963

Like everyone Abigail is a story of two; made of two opposing sides, slightly asymmetrical. Made from two people- Mary-Frances and Curtis. Theirs is a history that was not threaded through with an easy type of love, and maybe that is true of all that makes up the story of Appalachia. The banjo that receives the most love hums with the deepest sorrow. The unloved hit flat notes constantly.

Mary-Frances could never be sure of the exact day on which Abigail was conceived. Such is the ferocity of desire- it wraps you in the warm haze of its treacly light, and suddenly what seemed abhorrent and sticky when demonstrated between others is all that you want to tend to in your own life. When she met Curtis Mary-Frances was sixteen and had an ever-growing feeling that the parameters of existence that she had been given could turn out to be all wrong. A menagerie of lies encircled by a white picket fence. An idea of life spun from sugar and meant to be devoured in one sitting, but not preserved, and surely not lived.

For this reason Mary-Frances began escaping to the mountains anytime that she could. The life that flourishes in the forest is determined simply by what can and cannot exist when pitted against the natural elements. There is no room for hollow institutions among species that cannot lie and have no reason to. The woods preached in a language that could be understood by everything, so Mary-Frances left her textbooks at home and hitched rides into the mountains as far as she could go at every opportunity.

"Miss Mary-Frances, where have you been all day?" Caroline leaned back against the kitchen counter, arms crossed tightly. Mary-Frances felt as though the answer to this question was pretty obvious given the tessellation of shallow scratches on her calves, the chunky and unattractive hiking boots that she wore, and of course the smell that followed her through the door: a mixture of sweat and wet dirt. A dark green and feral aura that encircled her.

"Hiking Ma, what do you think?"

"I don't know what to think sometimes. I don't know what to think about whatever it is you do with your time." Caroline was working so hard to winnow her consciousness into something sharp enough to pierce through Mary-Frances's aloof demeanor that she was almost forgetting to breathe.

"OK then, I'm going to go upstairs," Mary-Frances replied, wondering what it would be like had she actually been lying to her mother. Caroline could be so terse, like a tightly woven bird nest edging itself toward a freefall, daring gravity to break it into its thousand fragile constituents.

Mary-Frances and Curtis met in the grocery store where he worked; their eyes trying to obliterate the counter that stood between them while Caroline poured all of her focus into signing her name with tight, perfectly symmetrical curly cues. You'd think that with each check she wrote Caroline was demonstrating her virtuosity to a god that suddenly cared deeply about handwriting. Which was just as well because while her Ma gave alms to the god-of-pretty-writing, Curtis and Mary-Frances cast careless wishes into the pools of each others' eyes.

The moment that they finally got to pass more than just glances between one another came about through a rare mistake made by Caroline. "Shoot. Shoot, shoot, shoot." Caroline muttered as she sat in the driver's seat of the family Studebaker digging through her purse.

"Ma, what?"

"I think I left the checkbook inside the grocery store."

"Oh, I'll grab it for ya." Mary-Frances clunked the heavy door of the car open and began walking across the parking lot towards the Piggly Wiggly. She had carefully picked out the olive green, gingham dress that she wore, and now she angled herself towards the shining doors of the supermarket so that she could look at her own reflection as she approached them. Her hair was long. It cascaded and split around her shoulders then ran over her chest while the rest spilled down to her lower back. She raked it all around to one side of her neck then nervously tossed it back the other direction, letting it find its own place again.

Curtis piled bread and bananas on the side of the grocery counter while shoving cans of vegetables and boxes of noodles down into the bottom of a deep paper bag. His eyes meandered over the rest of the store, skipping from one pyramid shaped display to the next. Whatever was on sale that week was piled up near the store's entrance and labeled brightly with neon colored tags full of exclamation points. *Is it really that convincing?* He wondered to himself.

"Hey um, 'scuse me?" Mary-Frances stood behind Curtis's right shoulder. She had been standing there for a while, debating whether or not she should just get in line behind the rest of the shoppers so she didn't interrupt anything. But she didn't want to ask the cashier for the checkbook, she wanted to talk to Curtis. He turned to her.

"My ma thinks she left her checkbook here, ya find it?" Without looking up from the numbers she was punching into the register the cashier, a heavy set woman with apron strings tied tightly around her middle, handed the checkbook to Curtis and Curtis held it out to Mary-Frances.

"Yer Mary-Frances right?"

"Yea, that's right. Curtis is it?" she glanced at the white oval name tag pinned to his apron even though she already knew his name.

"Yep. You want to go out for a shake or somethin' with me?"

"Sure." Mary-Frances panicked, not knowing what to do next while Curtis picked a receipt up from the floor and pulled a pen from the deep pocket in his apron,

"here write yer number down. I'll give ya a call."

So Abigail's untimely exit from the primordial soup began with a moment stolen from the ordinary timeline of things. If Caroline hadn't left the checkbook on the counter, she and Mary-Frances would be pulling out of the grocery store parking lot and into main street traffic in a slow arc. Once she was pregnant with Abigail, Mary-Frances often wondered if Caroline realized that her small moment of forgetfulness had become the window that Curtis slipped through and into their lives. And if so, she wondered if Caroline would ever tell Richard that this was how it happened. But Mary-Frances knew her ma better than that. Caroline would stuff the guilt down inside of herself; seal it off like some forgotten bit of potatoes sitting in tupperware at the back of the fridge, resentful mold growing where no one could smell it.

From that day forward, the thing on Mary-Frances's mind was Curtis. Curtis with knuckles like knotted rope that flattened themselves out over her waist before his hands slid down the curve of her hips. Curtis with his rusted out truck that jumped between gears, shaking Mary-Frances from the day dreams that crept over her mind like fog, cushioning the silences that settled between the two of them sometimes. Curtis lived outside of Caville, in the mountains of Yancey County and could take Mary-Frances to obscure swimming holes and lookouts; places averse to being known by outsiders.

When they went on drives Curtis's long face was a gaunt canvas for light and shadow to race across as they sped down woodsy roads. The enduring stretch of his body curved around like a hunting bow, allowing only a small portion of his lower back to touch the seat. The rest of him thrust moodily over the steering wheel as he calculated the timing of the clutch, the speed at which the next turn could be taken. Mary-Frances would turn so that she was facing Curtis, lean back against the door and let her hair whip out of the open window, riding the rush of wind as the truck sliced through air. Curtis had to try as hard as he could to keep his eyes on the road and not on her.

Curtis's name contained two metallic syllables that clattered like a dropped kitchen knife whenever Caroline or Richard spoke them. Cur-tis.

"What do ya think it is that that boy wants with you Mary-Frances?" Richard stood between her and the door with his arms crossed over his chest.

"Oh come on Pa, I don' know." she sighed and fidgeted.

"Well I do know. I know exactly what every boy that age wants, so ya better look out fer yerself." Mary-Frances suspected that he was acting on Caroline's orders more than anything, but she was still surprised at her pa's sudden impulse to become involved in her personal life.

"That boy's not from around here and we don't know who his family is," Richard continued.

"He's fine Pa, trust me."

"OK, I'm tryin'." Richard softened, it was over with. Truly he hated breathing down Mary-Frances's neck like that, but Caroline couldn't leave the matter be.

To Mary-Frances, her parents' distress at her blossoming relationship with Curtis was a barrier to her happiness. With all of the novel feelings taking shape inside of her she did not have the space to consider theirs. Maybe this is why they disliked him so much. Curtis became the inescapable mountain tops on her horizon while they themselves, their rules and their expectations, dwindled until they were broken fences that she passed through easily. One moment Mary-Frances would be quietly washing dishes and in the next she was slipping through the back door to be with Curtis.

"Your daddy do this to you?" Mary-Frances and Curtis were lying in a nest of blankets in his truck bed when she first noticed the magenta switch marks slashing across his back and ribs.

"He does that sometimes. He gets angry." Curtis didn't know where his pa, Waylon's, anger stemmed from, but his entire childhood had been steeped in it. What Waylon knew that Curtis didn't was that the anger had an origin but no end point. His anger was not his own, he was hexed with it. It ran like chlorophyll in the leaves of the trees that grew on their property, it colored in the wood grain that patterned the floorboards of their cabin- the whole place was infected. The anger was a curse.

"Well I wish that he wouldn't." Mary-Frances sat up to pull her shirt on over her head then rocked on to her back, raising her pelvis so she could pull her jeans over her hips. She buttoned them then leaned over to kiss Curtis's injuries.

"You should take me home now."

Mary-Frances's relationship with Curtis disappointed her parents though she never understood why. Their idea of Mary-Frances was becoming illusive, like a late afternoon shadow sifting into dusk. The harder they tried to influence Mary-Frances's decisions the more heavy-handed their expectations of her became. But expectations are made of nothing physical. They are like the dark spaces in between galaxies, they grow to encompass the ever-shrinking physical bodies that they stretch around as the universe expands. This is really unfortunate for those that the expectations opress. But since hope is not made of anything physical either, it's safe to assume that hope grows in tandem with oppression.

Chapter 5

Bent Branch Falls 1974

Camilla June sat in the back when she went to Mary-Frances's funeral and understood why Curtis had made such a scene. Before Curtis had wedged Mary-Frances into the dark earth with such ghoulish ceremony, she had seen the way that some of the attendees looked at him and Abigail. Some people had arrived with judgements that cast long shadows over the whole affair, reading from their bibles as though it was illiteracy that kept the Kennedys from paying for a doctor, or having Mary-Frances's lungs drained. For Mary-Frances the usual charity of Bent Branch Falls had never arrived; and the vultures circled overhead, even at her funeral. *We all did this to her.*

Camilla understood Curtis enough to be a little afraid of him too. It had been a week since the funeral and Abigail hadn't been to visit once, which was out of the ordinary and worried her- that little girl and that man made of edges all alone in a house together. A house that would be crawling through the first stages of grief. The forest had a way of magnifying emotions. Its crooked branches could grow into the shape of whatever sentiment you gave them. And now that summer break had begun and Abigail wouldn't be able to escape to school, she would be surrounded by her loneliness on all sides.

During the weeks that it took for Mary- Frances's illness to consume her, Camilla would ask about her every time she saw Abigail. She would wait until she was pouring out glasses of lemonade for the two of them, so that her back was turned and say, "Now how's your mama gettin' along with that cough of hers, honey?"

Abigail always replied, "jest fine Ms. June." She replied in that way even when she was unsure, "she's expectin' to get better any day now."

Camilla knew that she was only hearing the comforting echoes of what Mary-Frances and Curtis told Abigail to put her young mind at ease. The truth was a ball of knotty roots, tangled and tucked beneath Mary-Frances's inflamed lungs. Still, even without the ability to find the truth, Camilla could sense that things were not *just fine*. The eventual news of Mary-Frances's death provided unwelcome proof of what she had known all along.

In her small kitchen with its buttermilk yellow curtains and powder blue linoleum countertops, Camilla prepared a lunch to take to Abigail and Curtis. The smell of roasting chicken and swelling cornbread pulsed the air. The baby breath flowers stenciled onto her wallpaper came to life and vined into the kitchen's atmosphere, thick with nourishment. Camilla packed a wicker basket with the chicken, cornbread and, of course, lemonade- Abigail's favorite, and began the two mile walk to the Kennedy house.

It was late spring now and the blossoms on the trillium plants were still balled into little fists, as though they were threatening the whole world with their unfurled beauty. A cold

breeze raised goosebumps on Camilla's arms but she preferred
to let her body jolt into the small wonder of it rather than put
on her sweater. Mr. Harper's white Plymouth came rocking
down the road behind her and stopped at her side.

"Ms. Camilla June aren't you a sight fer sore eyes."

"Hi, Mr. Harper, where you off to this afternoon?" Beau
Harper hung out the window of the car, its door pinned between
his bulky torso and pink left arm.

"Down to the store, gotta help Cora out with a couple a
things."

"Alright then, you tell Mrs. Cora to drop by my house for
tea sometime, I haven't seen her for a minute."

"Sure I will, you need a ride anywhere?"

"It's alright, I prefer to walk." Camilla preferred to stay out
of any situation that required her to be alone with Beau.

"OK then, you take care."

Camilla shifted the basket to her left hand and waved as
Beau eased the car down the washed out road. Camilla wore the
same sensible walking boots that she did every day. The mountains offered that kind of freedom: no need to make sacrifices for
fashion. No need to stay in the colored parts of town or ride a
bus where she'd be sequestered in the stinking back end. When
she was young and growing up in New York City, segregation
was no longer the law, but it was still the code. In Bent Branch
Falls there was enough space for her to live peaceably alongside
people, the ones that harbored any racism did so quietly enough.
In the city, its pressure built up in the crowded public spaces and
shoved colored folks into corners. She had left all that behind in
Harlem, and she would never be willing to take it back.

Curtis's garage sat on its own little island of cement butted
up to the main road. It was just past the strip where the rest of the
businesses that made up downtown Bent Branch Falls huddled

together. He did a good business. Camilla would never know it for herself since she didn't own a car, but she had heard that he could fix anything. His skill usurped the need for him to be friendly, so he wasn't when he didn't feel like it. Still, the residents of Bent Branch Falls and the surrounding towns brought him their cars, tractors and motorcycles in all stages of disrepair and he fixed them. And when night fell and he seemed to be doing other sorts of business out of the garage, everyone looked the other direction. Even the county police needed a good mechanic in the area.

Camilla turned down the Kennedy's driveway and walked past the side of the garage where chrome bumpers, hub caps and car doors were piled up on one another behind a chain link fence. Thick stalks of milk thistle shot up through the detritus, their purple heads bobbing on the breeze like anemones that had been left behind a receding ocean. Monarch butterflies the size of her hand trembled on the ground as her shadow passed over them. Camilla paused when she had almost reached the house, stained so dark the wood was almost black. Sunlight did not illuminate its facade but burrowed into it, disappearing into a mouth of darkness.

"Abigail!" Camilla pulled open the front door and yelled into the front room after knocking several times with no response.

"Abigail, honey, I brought you some lunch."

"Miss June!" Abigail came running from behind the house at the sky-blue sound of Camilla's voice. Her bare feet pounded over the ground as though thorns and sharp rocks did not exist. She launched herself at Camilla's legs before Camilla could even bend down to receive the hug, so Abigail stood there with her face pressed into Camilla's belly button and her arms wrapped unselfconsciously around Camilla's butt. Abigail had barely seen another person for days. Curtis came and went, prowling the property and town with no agenda. Wolfing his way up and down main street; buying liquor, buying cigarettes then disappearing once again. The cars that sat half fixed in his garage were owned by people who knew better than to bug him about it so soon after the funeral.

"Ya hungry baby? I brought you some lunch."

"Yep. Yep I s'pose so." Abigail trailed off and her eyes followed after something that seemed to be moving across the landscape behind Camilla's left shoulder. Camilla turned and saw nothing. Already the heavy spring rainfall had conjured weeds up from the ground and they thronged Mary-Frances's abandoned garden. Ivy vined through rows of arugula and trails of vetch and chickweed matted over the ground.

"OK, go wash up then and bring out some plates and forks. We can eat out on the porch."

Abigail turned to go inside but Camilla stopped her, "Oh and Abigail?"

"Yea?"

"Bring some glasses out too, I brought you some lemonade." Abigail's eyes widened in delicious anticipation and she turned to the house again, letting the door slam behind her. Camilla couldn't help but notice that Abigail was smudged with dirt all over. It gathered in black lines in the folds of her elbows and in crescents underneath her nails. A tight ball of hair had nested at the nape of her neck with unruly strands spiraling outwards like the arms of some hidden galaxy. Camilla didn't want to go inside and see what the house looked like. She sat down on one of the porch steps and started pulling fragrant food from where she had nestled it into the rough, blue and white striped cloth that lined the picnic basket.

Something cold silked down her throat and settled into the bottom of her stomach as Camilla waited for Abigail to return. A displaced sense of fear, a feeling that she may not only lose Abigail, but everything, drifted over her. Everything relied on everything. The planets and stars slid around the Earth on their orbits like beads on an abacus. The calculations had to be perfect, their trajectories unmoved. As she sat on the porch engulfed in those slow moments, Camilla could feel the weight of the world shifting. Something had opened up underneath the Kennedy house, something that could cause Bent Branch Falls to fall out of orbit and deep into space. An aperture of evil.

"Miss June, did ya know that I'll be going to a whole new classroom next year?"

"I didn't know that. Do you know who your teacher will be?"

"Yes. Mrs. Cavens. She teaches the fourth and the fifth graders so I will be in her classroom with my best friend, Pansy."

"That sounds like fun. You ready for some chicken?"

"Yes, please!"

Abigail ripped into the chicken, helping large chunks of it into her mouth with her fingers. At the sight of the child's hunger Camilla resolved to leave the leftovers though it was all she had for dinner that night.

"What do ya think you'll be doing for the summer?" Camilla asked. Abigail shrugged the question away. Camilla tried not to let her worry show. The front door slammed open and Curtis stepped out of the gloom.

"Woah Abigail. I didn't know you were right here."

He bent his head stiffly in Camilla's direction. "Miss June."

"Here, I got ya something from the drug store," he began pawing around in the numerous pockets of his overalls then slapped at his chest pocket.

"Ah, there we go."

He held a bright orange kazoo out to Abigail.

"Thanks daddy." She snatched it out of his hand and set it down beside her, turning back to her plate.

"Well blow on it." said Curtis, the edge of the words as sharp as a razor and slashing into the space between them. The drumstick in Abigail's hand froze on its path to her mouth. She set it back down on the greasey plate. She kept her gaze trained on the splintering slats of the front porch and raised the kazoo to her lips. *Bwazoooooo.*

"Works." She set the kazoo down next to her, turning her attention back to the chicken. Curtis slipped back into the house; an eel retreating from the light of day. Abigail and Camilla finished their lunch in silence. Camilla wanted to leave straight away despite herself. A drop of despair threatened to run down from the corner of her right eye. If Mary-Frances were here she'd know what to do. But if Mary-Frances were here there would be nothing needing done. In a way Mary-Frances was mother to two children, both Abigail and Curtis. Curtis let Mary-Frances know him in a way that no one else ever would and Mary-Frances had always stood up for him, at times making outlandish excuses for Curtis's behavior:

Ya know he was jest joking, right?

He's jest a young man still figurin' himself out like we all haff to.

Ya don't want to see his temper? Then don't piss him off.

Most people in the town thought that Mary-Frances was a little bit crazy herself and she probably had to be, to raise a child with a man like Curtis. At any rate, Mary-Frances had done away with the social disease of caring what other people thought. *Becoming a pregnant teen in a traditional family will do that for a woman*, Camilla thought to herself. And maybe Mary-Frances liked the scorn just a little bit. She had found the freedom she needed in the mountains just like Camilla had. Mary-Frances's requirement for freedom and lack of interest in other's opinions was what Camilla had always respected the most about her.

"Alright baby girl, I should be off. But ya know you can still visit me anytime right?"

"I know that Miss June." Abigail wrinkled her nose at the comment. It was strange for Miss June to be telling her she could come visit. Abigail had been showing up at Camilla's house for years. Camilla regretted the unnecessary invitation. Abigail was clearly trying to entomb any awareness of how things had changed around her in that grave with Mary-Frances. Now Camilla had gone and spoiled it for her.

"Well, give me a hug then." Abigail sprang eagerly into her arms and Camilla held her for as long as Abigail allowed her to.

"I'm alright Miss June, I'll see you."

"OK then, I know you're a big girl. You keep the leftover chicken. The bread and the lemonade too. I'll come back for my dishes some other day."

"Thanks Miss June. I'll see ya later." And Abigail turned to gather up the leftovers and bring them into the house with her.

Chapter 6

Yancey County, NC 1963

In memory's measurement, time and distance collide and co-alesce, they become one. The time-distance contraption is what whisks you along from childhood to death; its inexorable current flowing at a pace that always seems too quick in retrospect yet painfully slow in the present. Like anyone, Waylon Kennedy grew into a person changed by an accumulation of joy and wounds, the person that he was molded by the elements into the person that he became: a gaping canyon cradled in weathered stone. When he moved with his wife, Eudora, to the unincorporated territory of Yancey County his idealism gave the land he had purchased a fools-gold sheen. This land was his now and he planned to live off of it.

Unfortunately the land had its own agenda and did not plan on being further corrupted by humans. Already it had absorbed native tears. Already it had endured the fallout of a distant war when German prisoners were held on it, the Nazis sweating the memory of unnatural horrors into its soil. The land had swallowed both their relief at being out of battle and their sorrow at being imprisoned far from home. Its waters had tongued the ragged edges of skin torn through by shrapnel as the soldiers washed their wounds in the creek. So the land learned too much and swelled with the malfeasance of humanity. It is likely that the very soil of the land was still an unhealed gash when Waylon and Eudora Kennedy arrived. But the Kennedy's thought very little of its history as they signed the title deed for it at a bank in Caville and prepared to move North.

It wasn't until 20 years later that Waylon finally gave thought to it. As day broke and the first remorseful rays of sunlight ached their shine through his eyelids, Waylon wondered how much blame could be reasonably placed on history. But the potential displacement caused him to hate himself even more, for being weak, for imagining he could cheat blame. Surely his failure was all his own. He rolled the dryness of his perpetual hangover into cottony beads of saliva on his tongue, denying himself water. The way the weight of his own breath was bearing down on him, he was convinced that it contained the whole world; its creatures and its storms. He sucked it in and blew it out, slow. Slower. Counted to 100 and back down to zero. He tried to push the memory of yesterday from his mind but the effort was useless. In the sobering first moments of the day he could not duck into the warm, chosen womb of drunkenness. So he became sure that his family hated him, and the knowledge ran its glacial fingers over the contours of his heart, pressed into the mouths of its atrophied valves.

While last night's moon had risen over chaos, a blizzard of blood matted feathers and the thick vein in the center of Waylon's forehead swelling, this morning's sun had only the void left by destruction to greet it. Their rooster had been killed off with the rest of the brood, slipping his last prideful call into the world from between coyote teeth. Waylon had told the boys to gather up the chickens and lock the hutch before the sun went down, but when he pulled the truck into its usual parking space in the driveway his headlights swept over the chicken coop and the glint of the door lolling back and forth, unlatched, caught his eye. Feathers lay in a thick dusting over the ground and were threaded through the wire sides of the coop.

Waylon jumped from the truck without cutting the engine. His heavy boots scraping along the gravel, echoing the dread in his chest that beat in rhythm with his heart. In the beams of his headlights he spotted the droplets of blood, they diminished in size as they moved away from the chicken coop. They mapped out the path that death had followed when it trotted back into the forest. In his close-hearted way Waylon loved those chickens, and his love was reciprocated in the eggs that they laid for him. In the chickens' absence he could already feel hunger sharpening its teeth on his ribcage. Fear dripped down the back of his throat. But that snake-skinned sensation threading its way through his intestines evaporated in the rising heat of his anger. *I asked them to do one thing.* He thought to himself.

"I asked you boys to do one thing for me!" Waylon screamed, kicking open the side door of the house. When the door hit the wall behind it and bounced back at Waylon he punched through its screen and stepped into the kitchen. His rage expanded and pressed up against the walls. The whole house bowed, the windows curving outwards, the timbers cracking in the rarefied air. Upstairs Curtis and his little brother Elias sat side by side on Elias's twin mattress in their shared bedroom.

"What do ya think it is this time?" Elias asked in a whisper.

"I don't know Elias. I don't know what it is. We got to think" Curtis sat crook-necked, his forehead pressed against his right fist cursing his mind as it meandered through an emptiness.

"What were we supposed to do?" He raised his head with a sharp inhale, "the chickens. Elias ya said ya got the chickens in, right?"

"Yea, yea I did." Elias's voice pitched off course, his lantern eyes scrambling to find purchase on a landscape that suddenly didn't look like his bedroom. It didn't feel like anyone's bedroom or a place where someone should sleep. It was moon-cold and desert-barren.

"OK, well I dunno why he's mad then. I dunno what's goin' on. Where's Ma?"

"I think she went to her bedroom." Waylon's footsteps fell heavy and crooked on the stairs.

"OK, well if he comes in jest let me do the talkin'. Jest get behind me and let me do it, OK."

Elias nodded listlessly. Now that he was fifteen and nearly as big as his older brother he felt bad that Curtis was still trying to protect him all the time. The distance between fifteen and nineteen seemed to shrink each time that Curtis took Pa's heat for the two of them and in that moment he wanted to tell his older brother *no, you get behind me*. He wanted to but he didn't. Suddenly the house went silent.

Waylon struggled against himself as he stood in the hallway of closed doors. He had made himself alone in this house that he shared with his family and still, the guilt could not help to cool his temper. He could not figure out how to break those barriers down, how to open those doors without kicking them in. He tried to smooth out his ragged breathing. He punched against his own chest hoping it could jolt his heart into a less furious rhythm. But the stress just spread outwards and added its weight to his fists, until they were stones. Until he was a cold cliff, ready to cast them down on anyone who stood below. His thoughts pressed themselves into that flat-line, driving anger once again and he muttered, "how dare they close their doors against me."

"You open this door!" Waylon screamed down the hallway and Curtis stepped from his bedroom with his jaw clenched to face down his pa's fury.

"You two boys been home all evening and couldn't manage ta remember ta turn in the chickens? Thas what yer tellin me?"

"No, Pa. We did. We did put the chickens in." Curtis glanced back over his shoulder at Elias in confusion.

"Well then, did ya manage to latch up the coop right like I showed ya?"

"I dunno. I mean yea, I think so."

"Well I reckon you didn' because there is not a single god-damn chicken in that coop right now. The coyotes already got to them. Every last goddamn chicken gone. In shreds."

Curtis took a step backwards. It was worse than he thought. Inside the bedroom Elias replayed his memory of the evening over and over again, but the part where he shut and latched the door to the chicken coop just wasn't there. Like a reel of film with those moments spliced out.

"Ya wanna come have a look for yerself?" Waylon was luring Curtis out of the house. Elias couldn't let this happen, couldn't let his brother charge towards the monolith of their father's violence alone, once again.

"I did it, it was my fault, OK?" Elias emerged from the bedroom and stood behind Curtis's right shoulder. "I put the chickens in, I must've forgotten to close the latch right."

Curtis wanted to disown the gratitude that swelled in his chest. He already knew that neither of them would be spared. Waylon's beatings were not actually about the events that sup-posedly triggered them, they were moments in which whatever beastly thing that stalked through his entire being night and day overcame his will power and took control of his whole body.

"OK then Elias, why don't you come outside with Curtis and I, and take a look at what a mess you've made of things."

Suddenly Waylon was self possessed. His anger had a target and was flowing from him in easy, sadistic waves. He didn't know what to do about the chickens, but he knew how to teach his boys a lesson and at this point he still believed whole-heartedly that they deserved exactly what was coming to them. He would make sure that they understood the crime of their mistake. He turned and walked down the stairs. Curtis and Elias avoided each other's eyes and fell into step behind their father.

The truck still sat idling in the driveway, its headlights turned on and pooling in two distinct circles. They would be spotlights for the horror show to come.

"Ya see this mess? Them coyotes took every last one of our'n chickens. Hope ya weren't plannin' on eggs fer breakfast tomorrow or ever again cuz there will be none, thanks to you boys."

"Pa I can git eggs from the grocery store. I have to work tomorrow, I can git eggs." Curtis knew it was a mistake the second the words left his mouth. His pa hated that he worked for a company, punched a time card. Waylon was set on homesteading, living off of the land. But his frustration at the land's difficult, clay soil had led him to drinking and left the whole farm in a constant scramble for food and basic goods. Eudora was left to pick up the scraps and try to quilt them into some sort of a life for her children. Waylon still had a knack for farming, carpentry and animal husbandry, but any money he managed to bring in with those skills was mostly poured out in shot glasses. Curtis had to get a job just to help the family stay afloat, but Curtis's insistence on working outside of the house was the ultimate betrayal in Waylon's eyes. It was proof of his own inadequacy.

"Yea you think you're a man now jest cuz you carry around groceries for housewives, huh? Don't ya son? But what kinda man cain't even take care of some goddamn, lousy chickens? Think you're gonna find good, fresh eggs in a Cambell's can? Well, do ya?"

Curtis said nothing. Curtis hadn't seen it until now- how Waylon's pride made him small, how the mountains can raise a man up until the air is so thin that his words barely make it stir. Curtis wanted to leave home right then, just to watch his daddy crumble. But then he remembered Elias and the contradiction broke open inside of him; an ooze yoked in confusion that spread and ran out towards his limbs.

Waylon bent the fresh branch of a nearby sapling in two with both his hands. He twisted the lithe, green wood at the weak point he had just created until it finally broke through. He held the switch out then slashed it downwards through the air in front of him. It made a sound like a forceful exhale, like an athlete preparing for a definitive moment. "Whatever Pa, jest get it over with already." Curtis stepped forward and yanked his shirt over his head. He turned his back to Waylon and let the switch crack open his skin.

Chapter 7

Bent Branch Falls 1974

Loneliness crept out of the woods on cat feet and gently curled its feline body around Abigail. Curtis banged through the house without any regularity, he and Abigail had taken to leaving the doors wide open. The house was becoming nothing more than a hallway that Curtis and Abigail passed through as they pinballed from place to place. Abigail's hunger came in furious waves that disregarded the three meal times that Mary-Frances had always forced her to observe. Now that she was out of the habit of eating regular meals, the loosed hunger was an unholy cavalry that Abigail would rather battle than acquiesce to. When she lost, her failure propelled her to the refrigerator to paw through the cellophane covered, conciliatory casseroles that had paraded across their front porch in the hands of their neighbors. After the sense of ceremony had evaporated from the happening of her mama's death, the pyrex dishes full of creamy foods looked like floats that had forgotten to hit their brakes at the end of the parade and crashed into each other, piling up in decadent wreckage. Some of them had begun to sour and stink.

The radio kept its vigil for five days after Mary-Frances's death. On the fifth night its batteries died, cutting out while Bessie Smith sang the blues. In the absence of the crooning the resulting silence seemed capable of taking up and leading a life of its own. It became clear to Abigail that loss was capable of growing infinitely: a nothingness that mutated and became something; then became everything. Abigail crossed the room and stared into the mesh fibers of the radio's speakers, spun its batteries hoping to spark some residual life from them and then knocked it against the wall a couple of times. The nearest radio tower transmitted Abigail's longing in duet with Bessie Smith's symphonic prayer. They prayed to the gods of flimsy existence. They prayed to the gods of broken hearts; and somewhere in the world seemingly untouched by Mary-Frances's death, a kindred heart was broken by their song.

After the five days of radio came three straight days of rain- a conspiratorial drumming on the tin roof. At first Abigail welcomed the rain, its cool thudding dispelled the silence that had grown inwards from the corners, and clumped mossily on the walls. But the longer it kept up the more its sound faded into the background, became static. Only a day of rain had passed when Abigail began cursing it, she was sure it would prevent Miss June from coming to visit her again. Miss June's visit had been the best thing to happen around the Kennedy house in a long time. But it was spring in the South and those wet curtains of melancholia would fall all around the Kennedy house for days. There is nothing like bad weather to condition a person to their own isolation.

Even in the rain, the doors to the house remained open. In her boredom Abigail had taken to standing on the back porch then winding her way through the house to the front porch in search of a glimmer of sunlight. She would push her wet, bare feet in a skating motion over the black and white tiles of the kitchen. Most people who visited the Kennedy family commented on those checkerboard tiles. Mary-Frances loved the tiles and had picked them out herself, *they're jest like the floor of the diner where Curtis took me on our first date. Imagine, sittin' down ta eat every day in the atmosphere of your first date with your husband. In this kitchen we never forget about the love that brought us here.*

It embarrassed Abigail when Mary-Frances said this, it felt like she was sharing something that was supposed to be kept a secret. In a way, it made Abigail feel cheated, like the tile became less special the more people that knew about it. Still, Abigail liked the tile and made a game of only walking on the black squares while avoiding the white squares. She too liked to imagine her young parents on their first date, fumbling to gain traction in each other's lives. It was only right that this bit of history colored the floor that she now stood on.

Sometimes Abigail laid down on the couch that Mary-Frances died on and pretended she was dying as well. The couch was full of the sentiment of fading and Abigail found peace in the idea that life had an exit, that one could find its door knob in the most unexpected ways. When she laid down, trying her hardest to take up the shape of her mama, Abigail could remember Mary-Frances's last days here so vividly.

"Abigail baby, sit down next to me for a minute."

"OK Mama. When do you think you're gonna git better?"

"Any day now. I feel like I'm almost all better right now, I'm jest tired. I'm Jest really, really tired. What's your pa been up to today?"

"mmm, I think he's been workin' in the garage all day. Some man with a nice new car been in there with him."

"Oh, ok, I see. He workin' on that man's nice car or they workin' together on somethin' else."

"I think it's somethin' else."

"OK baby, thas' jest fine. They're probably in there balancin' the books. And what did you do today?"

"Um, I watered the garden an' I went down to the river."

"Yea, our rain barrels still got a lot a water in them?"

"Yep. It rained two days ago, din't ya notice?"

"Oh oops, sorry baby I jus' forgot. Did ya go to town for a soda like I told ya to?"

"Oh yea! I did. An' then Mr. Harper, an' Mr. Hodges, an' Ace Ellery were there an' Bud too an' they said some guy named Joe's gonna fight someone and that he's a gorilla but god still loves him an' it's goin' ta be a real big fight!"

"Woah, Abigail! Those men don' know what they're talkin' about sometimes an' you don't need to go around repeatin' them. Sometimes when men talk about gorillas they're not actually talkin' about gorillas, you understand me? Some people can be real ugly sometimes so you gotta be careful about what you're listenin' to, you understand me?"

"Yes Mama." Abigail wasn't sure that she understood, but she didn't want to disappoint her ma, especially not when she was so sick.

"People goin' ta say some real strange things to you sometimes so ya gotta be careful. I'm not always goin' ta be here to set you straight, so promise me you're goin' ta be careful."

"OK, I promise."

"Good. Now, Abigail?"

"Yea?"

"Fetch me a glass of water, my throat's burnin' up like hell."

During those days Mary-Frances didn't make Abigail go to school. Abigail sure wasn't going to remind her about it, and happily passed the days caring for her instead. She watched the school bus rumble past the end of the driveway each morning, gleefully free to remain in the house barefooted, hair unbrushed, books abandoned to the floor of her bedroom. She didn't realize it, but she was attending a different sort of school, one that would teach her the wretched ways of inevitability. How full the silence between words can be: all of the muted meaning stringing together life's nonsense. Abigail would have to learn it all so early.

Curtis trusted that Mary-Frances would get better soon because that is what she told him, and that was the easiest thing to believe. In the meantime, he and his partner, Liam Fields, were collecting more bets on the upcoming boxing match between Muhammed Ali and Joe Frazier than they had ever taken on a single sporting event. Liam and Curtis had met on a clear day in June when Liam limped his cadillac into the lot in front of Curtis's garage. Curtis had seen him coming and stood in front of the garage wiping his hands on a grease streaked rag.

"Looks like yer havin' some troubles with the radiator," Curtis called out without making a move towards the pearl colored car. Liam stepped out from the gray smog rising from the hood and walked purposefully towards Curtis.

"Liam Fields," he held his hand out stiffly. Curtis noted its softness as he shook it, then wiped the beads of sweat from his forehead.

"Alright then, what can I do fer ya Liam? And how much of a hurry are you in?" In Curtis's experience the person's patience and the texture of their hands could indicate a lot about the price they'd be willing to pay. Liam took a step back, took Curtis in for a moment and began to laugh. He laughed alone with no intention of curtailing himself. He undid the top button on his shirt.

"That was good man, real good. But it's not my hurry that's gonna line yer pockets, it's the wife's," he jerked his head back over his right shoulder. A statuesque woman stood next to the car fanning herself with a wide brimmed sun hat. Two golden haired children, a boy and a girl poked their heads out of the open door. "You know how it is."

Curtis nodded slowly, "Should we pull it in the garage then?"

"Sure. Any place round here I can bring the family to first though? Let em' get some ice cream or somethin' while we work this thing out?"

"Sure. Bring 'em to mainstreet, there's a couple a places down there. Take my truck." Curtis extracted a key chain, lightly hung with one silver key. He and Liam swapped keys.

"Thanks, man. Be right back."

Liam was an accountant in Caville, and after recognizing Curtis's privileged position in the community had proposed on that first day to help Curtis bring gambling to Bent Branch Falls. Since then he had been driving up to the mountains to do business with Curtis on the weekends.

"Got a pile a money right here." Liam sorted the bills before counting them out. Laying them face up on the rough wooden table that Curtis used as a desk. He stacked the bills from left to right, ones, fives, tens, twenties and the occasional fifty or hundred dollar bill.

"Yep, people'r real excited about this boxing match for some reason." Curtis had no interest in sports, he was just interested in the money he could make off of other people's interest in them.

"Dumb mother fuckers" he snorted to himself. Liam paused for a minute without looking up then kept sorting.

Curtis rewrote peoples names and the amount of money they had put down in neat columns on a fresh page in his notebook, bloated by the years of fluctuating humidity that stagnated the air of the garage. Liam wore the green accountant visor that he kept in his briefcase. Curtis tapped on its bill, "How's things down in the grand ol' city?"

"Oh you know, hustlin', bustlin'. My boss down at the firm's still breathing down my neck. Woulda walked out of that place a year ago if it weren't fer the wife and kids."

"Shit, yea. Family's an expensive habit."

"Don't I know it. How bout you? Yer wife still battling that pneumonia?"

"Yep. Says she's gettin' better, I dunno if I should believe her, but that goddamn doctor wants to charge us an arm an a leg jest to take a look at her." Mary-Frances's cough rang out from the living room window- a hacking noise with phlegmy teeth chewing up the air between the house and the garage. Curtis and Liam locked eyes for a moment before Liam resumed his sorting.

"Look Curtis, if ya need to borrow some cash to get that taken care of it ain't no problem. Ya can git me back when the garage picks up again."

"Nah, I'm not takin' no money from you."

"Come on man, she don't sound so good."

"I said no. I don' need yer money. 'Sides the pay out that we're goin to git from this boxing match is goin' ta be a big one. Once we collect on it I'll be able to call up the doctor. Anyways my wife's a fighter, I'm gonna end up haffin to hold her down jest so that dumb doctor can get near her. She grows all those herbs out back ya know? She's convinced that she can cure herself."

"OK then, I hope she finds the cure soon. I dunno how you sleep at night with that wallop of a cough tearin' through the house."

"I don' sleep at night." Curtis laughed.

Abigail opened her eyes on the blank ceiling. In the final days of her mama's life nobody had told her that Mary-Frances was going to die. Nobody had even acknowledged the possibility of it. It was as though reality had forked and Abigail had gone the wrong direction. Down the path in the opposite direction there must be a world where Mary-Frances had stood up from the couch one day and resumed tending her garden and doing the chores. Maybe it was Abigail that had died and was now circling around in some funhouse version of her own existence. Her mama must be hiding behind a mirror somewhere, waiting to jump out and scare her. *Must be that way* she thought to herself then rolled over to nap away the afternoon on the wine colored couch.

Chapter 8

Bent Branch Falls 1964

By November the riotous forests surrounding Bent Branch Falls are already turning dormant. The leaves leak the last of their autumn colors into the dirt, while the sprawling ground cover and wild rose bushes retract their limbs and nestle down at the base of their stems. The ferns flash their brown bones as the early-morning frost bites away at their verdant flesh. Curtis and Mary-Frances knew that moving to the mountains ahead of an approaching winter would be difficult. But facing the scorn of her own family was far more daunting to Mary-Frances, so she insisted that she and Curtis leave before Christmas came, bringing its flurry of relatives and formal dinners with it.

For the people of Bent Branch Falls, the autumn of 1964 was already difficult in its own right; it was a season marked by the death of a child. When Colton Hodges drowned in the river some of the town's people surmised that god was doling out punishment to the Hodges for opening up the town's first movie theater. That portal, through which movie stars strutted, was like the eye of evil blinking open and shining its glamorous gaze onto people previously unaware of Hollywood's wicked excess. Colton was found 54 hours after he had gone missing, colorless. His body: a corporeal ghost. It was as though the frigid waters of the stream had washed the complexion from his flesh.

Despite her husband's faith in the goodness of film, Raelene Hodges's mind began to stray as the superstition surrounding the theater resurfaced in the gossip of Bent Branch Falls. As her son's death began wreathing her life with its thorny stems and brittle roses, Raelene looked back on the impromptu meeting that took place at the church two years earlier when her husband, Tucker Hodges, had decided to begin building the theater for the town. She had to sit through the ordeal at his side while half the town railed against them and their plans to bring movies to Bent Branch Falls.

"I have lived here all my life and seen this little town grow an' change, but wholesome activities have always been what's kept everyone together an' outta trouble. I don' believe that films have any place in Bent Branch Falls. Jest look at this smut," Mrs. Buncombe held a poster advertising Breakfast at Tiffany's up, her hand trembling as though god himself rushed through her body, puppeting her through her righteous speech. Cora Harper rolled her eyes, how she wished Mrs. Buncombe would just fall off the mountainside and stop stirring up trouble in the name of the lord.

"This Wo-man," Mrs. Buncombe had a way of emphasizing even the most benign words to the point of grotesqueness when she was making a point, "is half naked and smokin' a cigarette. Is this the sort of thing that our children should be seein'?"

"Dunno 'bout children but thas' what I'd like to be seein'," Ace Ellery yelled from the back. Cora ducked her head in a fit of giggles. She hoped they would end up with a theater in town, but even if they didn't this meeting was a satisfying enough show on its own. Beau sat at her side, forcibly drowning his discomfort in a lukewarm sea of fabricated apathy. Cora had dragged Beau to the meeting, they needed to show their support for the Hodges because if the Hodges opened up a movie theater then the Harpers could sell candy and soda to the audience members. Tucker had already approached her with the idea and she thought it was a good one. The theater would be good for everyone.

"I see that some of you are jest fine lettin' the morals of this town fall into disrepair, but I for one am not." Mrs. Buncombe gripped the side of the pulpit like she was about to pick it up and smash the sin right out of everyone with it. Her remark was met by a rising buzz that honeycombed the small church with the town's differing opinions.

"Alright, alright. Settle down." Mr. Bennet stood up and clapped his hands together for lack of a gavel or desk. He had volunteered to officiate the meeting when he saw the tensions rising. Bent Branch Falls didn't have any sort of local government and most people wanted to keep it that way. The town had learned how to govern itself when it was necessary. Mr. Bennet shooed Mrs. Buncombe back to her seat in the front pew and asked, "Anyone else have somethin' to say on this matter before we take a vote?"

Cora's hand shot up, "I do. I got somethin' ta say on the matter."

"Alright." Mr. Bennet cleared the stage.

Cora, who was well liked in the town, was ushered to the pulpit by the light of her agreeableness. "Beau an' I have also lived in Bent Branch Falls all our lives and, like many a you can see, it is a place of peace an' quiet. A place where people can do what they like without a worryin' that someone's goin' ta come aroun' stickin' their nose where it don' belong." Cora couldn't help herself from directing a pointed look as Mrs. Buncombe, "I do imagine that Mr. Hodges will use his good judgement when selectin' the films to be played in the theater an' we are all at our'n liberty to decide whether or not we will pay his business a visit. I don' see why we would shut a thing down 'fore it even gets started. An' besides, I don' wanna live in a town where I haff to ask permission every time I wanna do somethin' or start sellin' somethin' different, do any a you? Thas' all."

The wave of applause that engulfed the room as Cora walked back to her seat indicated that the vote had already been cast before a single hand was raised. So Mr. Hodges's theater was resurrected between Harper's Grocery and the post office amidst the tepid approval of the town.

When Raelene Hodges stood on the front steps of her home two years later, face smeared by the whirling blue and red of police lights and the news of her son's death, she replayed that scene over and over again in her head. Were they being punished for the movie theater? Could it be that her life really was ruled by a god who had time to watch movies? It seemed absurd. When Raelene had gone to see the shows at her husband's humble, one-screen theater, she had felt the same way she felt when attending church. Both the church and the theater housed a group of people, cut at awkward angles by their shortcomings, and drawn together by their need to transcend themselves. A preacher could do it, but a good movie could too.

So, Curtis and Mary-Frances arrived in Bent Branch Falls in 1964 just ahead of a cold season already frozen stiff by tragedy. Mary-Frances's pregnancy was still invisible, but her face glowed like a naked forty watt bulb, with the soft light of her fruitful womb. The bed of Curtis's truck was filled with pieces of furniture that had been saved to the side for him by his mama, and the duffel bag of clothes and books that Mary-Frances had snuck out of her house with. Mary-Frances decided not to tell her parents that she was leaving, but given her family's legacy of silence the decision was an easy one. The Hendersons kept a lot of things behind pursed lips. The emotions and events that made up the family's history floated around formlessly since no one was willing to define their edges with words. Mary-Frances was simply conforming to this tradition.

On the morning that she would discover her daughter's absence Caroline could feel a hole gaping in her heart before she knew what exactly had ripped through it. The arrhythmic jaws of loss chewed at her chest. She dulled the inexplicable anxiety with routine. First the coffee, slinking through the grounds in a black velvet rope that curled at the bottom of the tempered glass pot. Then her makeup, one layer at a time: foundation, blush, mascara, the choreography ending as always with a meticulous search for the shade of lipstick that would best match her dress. Curlers, pantyhose and jewelry were unrolled, stretched and clasped, and when it was over, and the door to her daughter's bedroom remained closed, she suddenly knew what was missing.

Caroline may have never regretted her reaction to the news of her daughter's pregnancy if Mary-Frances hadn't run away. Most likely, she would have held her daughter's transgression over her, taunting her with it like a hypnotic pendant fabricated from reproach. She would get revenge for having been humiliated. But now, as she swam through Mary Frances's bedroom, sound and light bending around her, a heavy sediment of remorse settled over her heart. She opened the closet and all the dresser drawers one by one, each missing garment further proof that Mary-Frances was gone and had left by her own volition. Caroline collapsed on the bed and the clues she had dug up fell into place around her. Mary-Frances had run away. Most likely she was with Curtis. For the first time Caroline hoped she was with Curtis, because if she wasn't that would mean that she was all alone. With this in mind Caroline bolted down the stairs to the kitchen.

She thumbed through the white pages searching for Curtis's last name. There were four Kennedys listed but two of them had addresses in Caville and two of them didn't. Knowing that Curtis lived somewhere outside the city, Caroline decided to start with the ones without Caville addresses. The first call was answered by a man with a deep baritone voice, who let her know that nobody by the name of Curtis lived in his house. Caroline hung up the phone and dialed again, this time her call was answered by a woman. The woman's voice sounded weightless, as though any emotion that was once in it had been replaced by helium.

"Hello? Kennedy house." Eudora looked out the rain streaked window over her kitchen sink and crossed her one free arm tightly over her narrow chest. She had been expecting this call and knew it was Caroline before she even picked up.

"Hello, is this the Kennedy residence where Curtis lives?"

"Well he lived here til yesterday- is this Mary-Frances's mother?"

"Yes," Caroline sighed. Apparently this stranger knew more about her daughter's plans than she did.

"Mary-Frances didn't tell you she was leaving did she?"

"No, she didn't. Have she and Curtis gone off together then?"

"Of course. Curtis loves your daughter very much."

Caroline's voice cracked, "I'm just happy that she's not out there on her own."

"Curtis would never let that happen." Eudora felt no pity for Caroline. "Those kids are in love whether you approve or not and now they're off to make a life together."

"Do you know where they're planning on going?"

"No, I don't." Eudora was used to lying for her sons.

"C'mone you have to know something. Don't you understand? I need to find my daughter." Caroline struggled to smooth the whining plea from her voice. She hated this woman, and she hated her son.

"My advice to you is this- wait for Mary-Frances to contact you. As I understand it you don' approve of her choice to be with my son, and that's hurtful to both of them. You made your choices and now she's making hers. We all do it. Your daughter's safe with Curtis whether you want to believe it or not. Now, I can't help you anymore than that so try an' calm down."

Eudora hung up. Caroline stood in her kitchen bewildered with the bleating dial tone burrowing deep into her right ear. Just out of reach of the phone line's unwavering buzz, the things she had said when her daughter had broken the news to her played over and over in her mind.

"Ma, I really need to tell ya somethin'." Mary-Frances had stood over her, sadly gazing at the stacks of photos that Caroline was sorting through.

"OK, well sit down then, what is it?" Caroline scooted over on the couch and patted the spot next to her. Mary-Frances had dropped her body onto the couch in a freefall of emotion and Caroline could sense what she was about to be told. Mary-Frances stared down at her lap for a long minute until sucking air deep into her lungs.

"I'm pregnant." The moment congealed between them, held them wriggling in its inescapable grasp. They were like two flies stuck to flypaper.

"No you're not. Mary-Frances, are you absolutely sure about this?"

"Yea, I'm totally sure Ma. I took the test. I haven't had a period for ten weeks now. I don't think it can be anything else."

"Jesus christ." Caroline let out a gasp.

"How could you do this to us? I knew you've been up to somethin'. I knew you were up to no good. What in the hell are we supposed to do now lil missy? Marry you off to that trash you've been going off with? What do you think, ya gonna raise a child on some grocery bagger's salary? Are you jest plain stupid?" As the anger mounted her voice shredded into a pissed-off rasp.

Mary-Frances was unsurprised at Caroline's reaction. At least her pessimistic predictions could work like antivenom now as her ma hurled one insult laced question after another her way. Caroline's voice pitched off into alien octaves, its volume unable to keep up with the rage swelling in her chest as the reality of the situation crystallized around them. Mary-Frances wouldn't cry until her bedroom door was shut firmly behind her. Richard didn't find out what was going on until two days later when Caroline finally found the courage to tell him.

And now, after a month of performing a carefully curated routine of reticence, her daughter was gone. Knowing her daughter, Caroline was quick to understand that Mary-Frances was gone for good.

As Mary-Frances and Curtis bounced up the dirt road towards their new home the load of furniture toppled from the truck. It was the impossible gullies that had finally loosened their precarious haul and scattered it into the ditch.

"These roads are real tricky, if ya wan' I could follow behind ya'll with some of yer stuff, lighten up yer load." Jimmy yelled at Mary-Frances and Curtis from his front porch just across the road. Their inexperience was jumbled up in the pile of furniture and embarrassed Curtis. Jimmy had known, as everyone in Bent Branch Falls always knows, that Mary-Frances and Curtis were coming before they got there. But the couple before him seemed much younger than he had expected. She seemed so delicate as though she was hewn from bird bone. Curtis loomed like a startled bear over her shoulder.

Curtis's face soured and he took off his baseball cap, held it by the bill and slapped it across one thigh. Jimmy would come to know this habit of Curtis's well, it seemed that the motion of it helped him to think. Jimmy thought that Curtis didn't like him or his suggestions at first, but eventually Jimmy would see that Curtis is just like that- a little closed off, a little bit angry. Curtis was a man who had gone about preparing himself for the world as though no one in it would like him.

"Wan' me to help you with some a this? Where ya'll comin' from anyways?" Jimmy asked as he approached.

"I'm Curtis, this is Mary-Frances. I'm from Yancey County and she's from Caville." Curtis held his hand out to Jimmy.

"Jimmy. Grew up right here." The two men shook hands and Jimmy tipped his ragged hat in Mary-Frances's direction.

"Well, what do ya reckon you'd like to do with this mess here?"

"Well what I'd like to do is set it on fire," Curtis laughed dryly, "but I s'pose what we should do is git it up to that house of ours, it's up the road a piece."

"Alright, lemme jest git my truck then. I know which place yer talkin' about, everyone already knows somebody bought it. Ya buy it outright?"

"Hell no. Still tryin' to figure out how we're goin ta pay fer it. But I've been learnin' mechanics from my Daddy since I was a young'un, should be able to make my way with that."

"Sounds like an alright plan to me, we could use a good mechanic 'round here," Jimmy walked back to his house and pulled his truck up alongside Curtis's. Mary-Frances worked alongside the two men until their possessions were packed into the trucks, secure enough to be bumped over the backroads of Bent Branch Falls. The three of them drove cautiously forward, a hopeful brigade inching their way towards a new life. Mary-Frances threw her bare feet out of the passenger side window, let the chill of autumn nibble on her toes.

Chapter 9

Bent Branch Falls 1974

Mary-Frances died two days before Virginia's birthday and she was going to have the party anyways. It's what Mary-Frances would have wanted. Mary-Frances had always been a good neighbor to the Jenkins family and though Virginia didn't talk to Curtis much, he was her boy Jimmy's best friend. Virginia had rescheduled the party to give the grief washing over the town at Mary-Frances's death time to recede. But two quiet Saturday nights had passed since the funeral and she figured people could use a little celebration to lift their spirits up. She stood in her kitchen and stirred the batter for her own cake. It would be two pound cakes, served with some of the Hawberry Jelly that Miss June made so well.

On the other side of town her son's phone rang. He lifted the receiver of the rotary telephone that sat in the middle of his kitchen table.

"Yep?"

"Jimmy it's your Ma. Yer gonna come over fer my birthday tonight?"

"Yea, course I'll be there."

"OK, good. Do me a favor an' make sure ta stop by the Kennedy's on yer way over and remind Curtis and Abigail to come. Haven't seen neither of them since the funeral an' it be good fer 'em to get outta that house."

"Yea I'll do that. I'll make sure they're comin' over."

"Thank ya son. Be here round dinner time, your aunt Ivy's cookin' up a whole mess of food for everyone and I'm baking cake"

"Oh, sounds good. I'll see ya later then."

"OK, see ya later."

Jimmy set down the phone, looked around the clutter filled trailer then crossed the threshold of his doorless bedroom. He crouched down and yanked open the cabinet doors set into the wooden ledge that held his mattress. One by one he pulled an assortment of wine bottles out of the cabinet, careful not to stir up the sediment of char that had settled to the bottom of the moonshine that they held. As he pulled each one out, he examined the dates written on the masking tape, looking for one that contained the good batch that he had fermented over the last winter. It had turned out smooth and buttery, the color of burnt sugar.

When he found a bottle of the winter batch he held it up in front of himself, remembering how cold the first months that he had spent in his trailer had been. In the winter, everything about the mountains grows sharp and still: like the difference between ice and water. Putrefaction struggles along slowly, death pulling its hundreds of hungry mouths along the frozen ground; where holes in boots let wheezing coughs and blue lips slip in. When the air is that cold, breathing in feels like sucking granular pieces of glass down into your lungs; thornier than cigarette smoke.

Jimmy had bought the trailer in October and the prideful glow of possession had begun to leak through the holes in its tin siding as soon as autumn was blown into winter. The trailer was cold. And when he was cold inside of it Jimmy would start to feel like a lifeless sardine. The two small windows in the place were dirty enough to lend the light that does creep in through them the mucky glow of fish oil. Cold fish, dead fish.

Jimmy's trailer sat on its own small lot in the midst of a whole group of trailers, without a single tree between them to temper the lack of privacy. The trailers are filled with people who already know you the second you move in. Boundaries are thin when so many people live so close to one another; stretched ever thinner by a mutual need, a camaraderie formed silently in the night as everyone wages thick-blanket-wars against the cold. They fight the same enemy separately and together. A small army whose victories are won when they are finally able to drift off to sleep.

Jimmy uncorked the moonshine and put his finger over the mouth of the bottle so that as he poured the liquid into a shot glass the flow trickled at an incremental rate. He wanted a single swallow, just enough to remember the flavor, to savor his own success. He let the liquid burn over every surface of his mouth as he combed through the different tastes that popped up on his tongue. Butter, banana, toffee. Warm colored things.

Later, Jimmy grabbed the moonshine from where he had left it sitting on the kitchen table, and hopped off the front step of the trailer. He decided to walk to his Ma's birthday party so that he could cut through the forest, move through the cathedral of trees that hemmed in Bent Branch Falls. He crossed the main road and began following the train tracks as they veered away from it.

Jimmy liked taking the train tracks, he thought of the trains as rhythmic, obscure animals. The trains held an independent and ritualistic life of their own. They shook Bent Branch Falls as they passed by, leaving the memory of their screams hanging in the air. Their metallic memory wreathing the dark pines until the needles poked holes in the clouds of burnt diesel and they deflated, lying down flat on the forest floor. They coalesced uncomfortably like aimless travelers. The regular schedules and unknowable mechanisms that governed the trains gave them a life that was entirely distinct from the towns that they passed through. The trains were like a spine, a straight line enmeshed in the tangled muscle tissue of Appalachian forest. Synapses spinning their electric cobweb away- to far flung limbs.

Jimmy veered out of the forest and emerged from the trees a hundred yards before the Kennedy's driveway intersected the main road. He stopped at Curtis's garage first, entering without knocking. At the sound of the door banging open Curtis jumped up from where he was kneeling next to his safe, and was already calculating his path to the rifle leaning in the corner when he realized it was just Jimmy.

"Woah man, hey. What's goin' on?" Curtis grinned and for a moment it was a smile that Jimmy recognized from before Mary-Frances's death. A smile that was thoughtless and spread without obstacle across Curtis's face.

"Jes' stoppin by ta see if you and Abigail are comin' up to my ma's birthday party."

"Oh, the birthday party, I almost forgot." Curtis shifted his weight distractedly from foot to foot then crossed the garage to lock up the safe- a steel ammo box cemented to the floor.

"Brought some shine for ya." Jimmy held the bottle of moonshine out in front of him, "Come on, let's have a drink."

"Alright. Thanks for that. It's a good batch?"

"Still workin' on drinkin' that winter batch, it's a good one. I got another batch in the still, think it's goin' ta be a good one too."

"Alright yea, yer gettin' good at it. Ya could be sellin' that shit an makin' some money if you stop pussyfootin' around it."

"I know it. I'm just scared of the law ya know."

"Jest sell it outta my garage, we're already runnin' the gamblin' here. 'Sides, those fuckin cops say anything to me about it I'll quit fixin' their cars. They'll have to drive clear to Caville jest to get their oil changed." Curtis grabbed the bottle, opened the front door and spit out of it.

"Come on up to the house we'll have a proper glass."

They walked towards the house and a peculiar feeling washed over Jimmy. The clouds seemed to be metallic bellies, bloated and poisoned, full of things far more noxious than rain water. The house was leering and it seemed to be taller than he remembered. It loomed over them. It cast a long shadow. Abigail fur balled out of the front door and gave him a wave. She looked dirty. Even from twenty feet away she looked dirty, her hair nested with generations of filth and dark stuff; matted with the black edges of thunder.

"Abigail, you wanna come over fer my Ma's birthday?"

"Hi Jimmy. Sure." Jimmy waited for Curtis to tell her to go clean herself up but he didn't. Jimmy turned his gaze to the glass bottle that Curtis held in his hand. Cracks seeded from underneath his grip on the green glass and spread over the whole bottle. Then they receded, disappeared. The moment hung in the air, while their surroundings became unreal. The atmosphere around them emitted a low moan. Jimmy shook his head to clear his thoughts. Abigail and Curtis didn't seem to notice anything strange.

"Ya know what, let's just head over, we can have a drink when we get there."

"alright, if'n ya say so." Curtis responded and yanked the cork out of the bottle. He threw back his head and took a swig. Abigail pulled the bright orange kazoo out of her pocket and blew on it, then sprung ahead of them barefoot, zigging down the long driveway towards the road to the Jenkin's house.

Chapter 10

Bent Branch Falls 1964

The two trucks pulled up side by side in front of Mary-Frances and Curtis's new house. While Jimmy and Curtis wrestled with straps and bungee cords, throwing half-hearted elbows at the labor that they only pretended to dislike, Mary-Frances circled around the house. Ferns and vinca, brittled by the approaching winter lay matted over the backyard like sea creatures left behind a receding tide. Something scurried through the underbrush, something that probably sounded bigger than it was among the dead leaves. She walked to the center of the leveled yard and imagined the garden she would plant there, then crouched down and sunk two fingers into the soil. Maybe this was the moment that death plunged a taproot deep into her chest: a witches finger that would suck the life from her. She never could have guessed at what colors the pnuematic cough would eventually bloom in, before hanging so heavily on its stem, bent like a scoliotic back by its own heavy blossom. Mary-Frances refocused her eyes and stood to walk towards the scarlet oak tree flanking the house, snapping open her pocket knife.

"Mary-Frances come're an' see about this furniture real quick!" Curtis's voice drifted out the front door of their new house. The dull blade of Mary-Frances's pocket knife paused at the peak of the A it was carving. A for Abigail. She was sure their child was going to be a little girl. The fetal mass inside of her seemed to be unfurling itself petal by petal. Mary-Frances stood back to admire her work: a heart as wide as the tree trunk, the valentine curves at the top rendered in short, straight little lines, with C+MF carved in the center and below that an A.

By the time Mary-Frances finished her carving and went inside, Curtis and Jimmy had pulled two chairs out of the mess of furniture and boxes lumped in the center of the living room floor. Jimmy lounged back in the pit of a deep, olive-green arm-chair while Curtis sat bent forward with his elbows on his knees on one of the straight back wooden chairs that matched the sturdy, acorn dining table Eudora had given them. The sunset tinted light streaming through the window sent boyish hues of peach across their open faces.

"What'd ya want me to do about the furniture?" Mary-Frances stood at the helm of the chaotic joy that was to be her new life.

"Here, have a sip Mary-Frances," Curtis held a flask up to her but turned back to Jimmy as he went on,

"It's ol' Jimmy here's first batch a moonshine. Tastes like shit but it's really strong." The end of his sentence cut up into wails of laughter as he and Jimmy both doubled over.

"Curtis I cain't drink that shit with a baby inside a me. You know that."

"What? You guys got a kid comin'?" Jimmy straightened up and looked back and forth between Mary-Frances and Curtis as though trying to decide whether or not it was a joke.

"Yep" Mary-Frances patted her small stomach proudly. "A baby girl."

"Well, she thinks it's a baby girl," Curtis said suddenly sober.

"No, I know it's a baby girl. And her name's gonna be Abigail."

"Hey, when'd ya decide on that?"

"Jest now. Come take a look at the tree, it'll tell ya." The three of them left the house and went to the tree to gaze at Mary-Frances's carving.

"I'm sorry Jimmy, how rude a me." Mary-Frances flipped open her pocket knife and slashed a big J in the tree next to the heart.

"Since you're our first friend in Bent Branch Falls." The three of them grinned. The shadows lengthened, inching forwards to kiss the feet of approaching darkness. Fireflies rose in a seance, sparking ecstatically in the night sky.

"Well, I reckon I ought ta get headin' home, my Ma will be wonderin' where I'm at." Jimmy patted at his pockets until he heard the jangle of his keys. A chorus of frogs rose up, a few of them distinguishing themselves from the drone of the group. A soprano croak with a glass edge, a bassy moan heavy as mud.

"Thanks for all a yer help." Curtis shook Jimmy's hand and Mary-Frances pulled him into a hug. After Jimmy pulled away in his truck, Mary-Frances and Curtis went inside and dragged the mattress into the bedroom. They fell together, their bodies intertwining easy as streams of smoke. Light and fluid. The urgency in Curtis's exploration of Mary-Frances's body had been replaced with a revery that slowed his hands and opened his eyes after she became pregnant. He cupped the shallow curve beginning to swell between her hip bones, the surface of her belly bending towards the moon like an ocean at high tide. They were so tired that they slept in their clothes on the undressed mattress, no sheets or blankets or pillows. Just arms and shoulders and a pocket of body heat held between them.

The fortress of mountains encircling Bent Branch Falls delay the sunrise and give the dawn a syrupy, slow-crawling drawl. Curtis woke up long before Mary-Frances, the crude alcohol he had drunk with Jimmy the night before was skunking from his pores and his worry over Elias was beating against his eyelids. This morning Elias would be waking up in his half empty bedroom, left to pull an ordinary day from the slip-shod structure of life on the Kennedy farm. Curtis couldn't help but anticipate the day's labor, the dull work, the toil of beating back boredom and rumination, even though he wouldn't be there to participate in it. On the Kennedy farm boredom often bred with fear giving birth to coyote-kings that ruled the landscape of the brothers' minds.

Two weeks earlier, when Curtis told Eudora that he was leaving and that Mary-Frances was pregnant she couldn't help but be disappointed in the circumstances of her first grand-daughter's birth. Mary-Frances's parents were angry so there would be no wedding, just an unceremonious departure. For a day she let herself languish in discontent. She pulled her nicest dress from the closet, laid it on the bed and ran two fingers ahead of the zipper pull, stretching the fragile lace away from the metal teeth. The dress struggled over her hips, and the breadth of her body pulled the garment in ugly, stressed lines that streaked over her stomach and waist. *It's just as well* she supposed. The last time she had worn that dress was at Elias's baptism. She sat on her bed in her underwear and let the tearful twilight clothe her instead.

By the time Curtis was packing up to leave home, Eudora remembered how to push her desire for ordinary decorum to the back of her closet. Some things just weren't for her. It hung from a bare wire hanger, next to the ill-fitting dress. More than anything she wanted her boys to leave unharmed, so she accepted a substitute for happiness: relief. She let her hope for Curtis's escape bleach all the tricky details out of the situation. It was enough for her to see Curtis go, even better that he would soon have a family of his own; undoubtedly a better one than she was able to give him. Eudora lived on the sliver of waning moon that was her broken family, and all she wanted was to usher her sons off of the dead satellite before that sliver turned dark altogether.

Curtis didn't think to worry over Eudora because he was preoccupied with Elias. Elias was young and accessible, Curtis could intuit Elias's unhappiness. He had sat on his bed watching Curtis stack up the boxes holding his clothes, books and tools and taping the dresser drawers shut to get it ready to move.

"Ya know Curtis, ya may think I'm sad cuz I'm gonna miss you, but the truth is I'm just mad that you were makin' it with Mary-Frances all this time an' ya didn't even tell me. Yer own little brother."

"Oh shut up Elias," Curtis turned and grinned at him.

"You sleep less than three feet away from me every night an' you couldn' tell me one useful thing about girls, now there you go movin' in with one a them."

"Well, it's cuz I thought you were a lost cause anyhow."

"Well maybe I am. But it ain't like I ever got any help from my family."

"Oh come on Elias you cain't say I never did nothin' for ya. 'Sides, yer only 15 years old, you'll find yerself a girl soon enough."

"Yea, an' then what? Ask her over to churn some butter?"

"Well why not?" Curtis laughed, "I 'spose ya do need money to date a girl. Hey, why don' ya go down to the piggly wiggly and see if you cain't have my job. They'll like ya extra cuz yer related to me."

"*Oh wow, thanks Curtis.*" Elias batted his eyes sarcastically and hurled a pillow that bounced off of Curtis's head.

"Why don' ya jest take me with ya?" Elias said it like he was joking. Curtis turned back to the boxes and began adding an unnecessary layer of tape over their seams.

"Ya can always come visit me an' Mary-Frances in Bent Branch Falls. You'd like her, she's real pretty but she's tough too. You can meet the baby an' everything." For the first time since he had made the decision, the definition of leaving came clear to Curtis.

Elias stood on the porch next to Eudora watching Curtis drive off to his new life. "He packed his truck all stupid," Elias pointed out. Eudora rested her hand on his shoulder. The men in her family couldn't seem to express their feelings without it coming out mean. Waylon had stopped talking to Curtis all together once he knew Curtis was going to leave. He'd barely been home for the last couple of days, he was out drinking. *Let him stay out there* Eudora thought to herself. The sentiment applied to both her husband and son. Then she wondered how many days Waylon would keep drinking, limbering his mind with liquor so that he could bend it around the fact of Curtis's leaving. How long would it take for Waylon to stop believing he could control the members of his family?

Curtis turned into a dirt driveway just before the county line. He had hours to waste before he picked up Mary-Frances and thought he should say goodbye to Preston, his oldest friend. A cloud of dust swarmed up in front of his car. It made no sense, this dry, dusty dirt that surrounded the Locklear property. A dime sized desert on the thick-fleshed spine of the Appalachian mountains. He was greeted by a pack of rottweilers. Preston and his family had been breeding rottweilers ever since Curtis met him in school. The pack shrank and grew, but was always there to patrol the property in a rumbling mass of heavy paws and black lips.

Three of the dogs bounded towards the truck, but the fourth dog dragged behind the rest, pulling a lifeless back end over the ground. Curtis remembered when it happened: he had been sleeping over and Roonie's squeals sawed through Preston's bedroom door first thing in the morning. Both of the boys shot out of bed and ran towards the sound. Roonie's puppy body sprawled and straddled like a frog boiling down into empty, leathery skin after being run over on the highway. Piss seeped from under the dog's back end. Mrs. Locklear stood three feet away, hands on the curlers helmeting her head.

"Joe! Get down here, one of the big dogs jumped on Roonie's back and he's hurt!"

Preston moved towards Roonie and tried to tuck his lifeless back legs underneath him, unfazed by the warm pee and its acrid smell. The puppy stared up through its eyebrows, its confused gaze a wordless prayer.

Joe Locklear shooed Preston away, "come on, if it's back really is broke ya could kill him, let 'im be."

Preston sniffed up the stream of snot that ran from his left nostril until he was 11 years old. Sometimes dust from the Locklear's property colored it a martian shade of red. They waited all day for the puppy to stand up. They brought it water and a deer bone. it gnawed, and slurped, and relieved itself where it lay but it never stood. It's back really was broken.

Roonie grew into his paralysis and soon the lack of mobility barely affected him. The shoulders powering his maimed mass were broad, almost bovine. His paws squared over an unnaturally long distance at the end of two short, thick legs. Curtis recoiled at the sight. The dog crawled along, happily involved in its struggle. Curtis pushed against the other three dogs' chests in an effort to get past the wall of flailing paws that they created in front of him. He walked towards the house whose raw pine board siding had gathered red dust in its veins; they ran and split along cardiovascular paths.

The weathervane at the top of the house was a strange one, it was crowned by a metal plate fabricated into the shape of a gruesomely puffy, pink pig's head with a halo hovering around it, its face painted in a cherubic smile. The effect was cloying. The pig bestowed its benign smile on the paralyzed dog that staggered along underneath it. The dog had turned and began blazing the trail back towards the house as soon as it could tell that Curtis was walking that way. An ash grey callous as big as a hand erupted from the fur on its back end where it was pulled over the ground each day. Curtis swallowed down a gag that burbled in his throat.

Distracted by Roonie and his future with Mary-Frances, Curtis let his visit with Preston become perfunctory.

"Hey, I'm leaving today. Jest wanted to stop by one more time."

"Well damn Curtis, yer really doin' it." Preston laughed and let his happiness for Curtis mask his disappointment.

"I really am. Not goin' too far, though. You should come and visit once we're all settled in."

"I'll do that. Jest give me a call." There seemed to be nothing left to say. The two men embraced, let the short conversation be a goodbye that stuck to the point of goodbye.

As he pulled his truck down the driveway Preston held the three strong-legged dogs on a rope that he strung through their collars, leaning back against their lashing power he looked like a sailor battling the wind. But he left the hobbled dog free and it drug itself along behind Curtis's truck, laughing in his rearview mirror, laughing at the mortality he cheated with his broken back and refusal to stop living. Curtis gunned it to get the sad vision out of his rearview mirror. The receding view of Yancey County felt final.

That night Mary-Frances appeared under the light of a street lamp next to his truck. Shrouded in the white light, seen through the grain of his dirty truck window, she was like a blissed out haunting. Curtis hopped out of the driver's seat to help her lift the heavy duffel bag into the truck bed.

"Good lord lady, what do ya got in here?" he heaved.

"Oh ya know, just a whole life's worth a stuff." Mary-Frances was too giddy to think about the home she was leaving. He held her door open as she clambered up into the truck. Once Curtis pulled onto the highway his nervousness leaped into excitement.

"So where ya takin' me tonight Curtis. Honeymoon in Paris?" Mary-Frances laughed and punched him in the shoulder. Her fairytale was remade as they pulled into a motel parking lot just outside of Caville. It was good enough for her. A full night next to Curtis was all Mary-Frances wanted.

While Mary-Frances slept into the second morning that she and Curtis shared, deeply satisfied on the bare mattress, Curtis struggled to decide whether he should get up or not. Curtis's past clambered and itched over his whole body, now that it was behind him he could see it all in its monsterish detail. His daddy's anger had become a thing of mythic proportions. It's pupil's stretched into amphibious ovals. Its nails clattered coldly over hardwood floors with a fleshless sound that was a rebuke to everything human. It was so vast it had to have sprung from the soil. Curtis rolled onto his side and pulled Mary-Frances's sleep-heavy body into his. He promised himself again that he would never be like his daddy, youthfully unaware of how often we are undone by our own making.

Chapter 11

Bent Branch Falls 1974

As Jimmy walked along next to Curtis the moths that were beating around in his chest exited one by one, his anxiety receding. The gloom of the Kennedy house was at their backs and they walked towards the celebratory scent of his parent's place. The joy his mama stirred up in other people floated on the air, smelling of barbecue smoke laced with the sweetness of birthday cake. Abigail slowed and fell into step next to Curtis. Unlike Jimmy, both Abigail and Curtis were unsure of the greeting they would receive. The last time they had really seen anyone they were being pushed along through the antiseptic tunnel of formal condolences. When they came out the other end could everything go back to being normal again?

Jimmy grabbed the door knob and pushed into the festive cacophony. Virginia sat in the large armchair usually reserved for her husband, Travis Jenkins, surrounded by women draped across the furniture and sitting on the floor, circling her like pretty offerings at the foot of an altar.

"Oh will ya'll excuse me for a moment, my son just got here," Jimmy could hear her saying moments before she sprung from the huddle.

"Jimmy! My baby. I'm so glad ya could make it" She pulled him into a strong hug then held him out at arms length. Jimmy raised his eyebrows skeptically.

"Well, don't know what else I'd be doin ' on my own mama's birthday." He replied. It seemed to Jimmy that ever since he had moved to his own place, less than three miles from his parents, his mama had gotten it into her head that he was going to leave for good. The notion was especially absurd given the fact that Jimmy had lived in his parent's house until he was 25, only to leave because he had no interest in marriage and no idea what else he should do with himself.

"Well thas' cuz you're a good son. Oh, hi Curtis, hi Abigail." Virginia paused, moments ago she didn't even realize the pair of them were standing there. It was as though they had materialized from their own murk, a nebulous fog preceding their sudden appearance in her house. They took her off guard.

"Um OK, well come on in then. All a you come right in," she spluttered, struggling to regain her composure. As the little group flowed past her to mingle with the party she couldn't help but notice how unkempt the little girl had become in the couple of weeks that had passed since Mary-Frances's funeral. She felt bad for Abigail and wondered if there was any way she could run a brush through her hair without making her or Curtis uncomfortable.

"Virginia, get back over here! You were jest about to unwrap the little gift Beau and I got for ya." Cora called out to her.

"Better not be another jar of hawberry preserve," Virginia joked as she was reabsorbed back into the group of women.

Curtis drifted along behind Jimmy as Jimmy meandered through the party, stopping every few feet to greet a friend or family member. Over and over again people called out to Jimmy, reaching eager hands out to shake his or pull him into a hug, only to suddenly realize that Curtis was also standing there; an apparition. Curtis didn't wait until they made it to the kitchen, he uncorked the bottle of moonshine in his hand and drank from it right there, standing in the center of the living room. He was now free to dispose of good manners, he had become an invisible man.

Apple watched Curtis from where she sat in a folding chair in the corner of the living room. She watched him pull the invisibility over himself just as she had when she arrived in America on the arm of her new husband. Bud sat at her side holding his guitar, softly plucking out a tune that he had been playing ever since she met him in Vietnam. Years ago Apple found out what Curtis was learning now: how gravely people can miscarry emotions, mixing up sympathy with fear, allowing the disillusioned cocktail to push them to the edge of antipathy so that your sorrow becomes their burden. But Curtis didn't realize that he was luckier than Apple. He could leave Bent Branch Falls and his humanity would be reset, no one would know his tragic history. Apple's pain was melted into her ethnicity, forged into a compound material in the furnace of war. Apple's burnt sienna skin and black iris' branded her pain into the consciousness of everyone she met before she even had a chance to talk to them.

Maybe Curtis realized that Apple was seeing him because he came over to her and Bud and pulled a folding chair up so that he could sit facing the two of them.

"Hey Bud, hey Apple. Been a minute, huh?" Apple and Bud were some of the few people that hadn't shown up to Mary-Frances's funeral and it made it easy for Curtis to walk up to them like that.

"Curtis!" Bud stopped playing his guitar and reached out to grab his friend's hand. Apple nodded to him, keeping her arms crossed around her torso.

"Ya hear on the radio the other day how they played the whole Rolling Stones concert live?"

"Oh shoot no, my radio's been off. Don't have no battery juice in it right now."

"Well shit, I wish I woulda known, I would a' had you over fer a listen. It was good. It was really good man, it sounded like a rockin' show. Wish I could a been there in person."

Curtis grinned. Bud liked The Rolling Stones a lot more than he did. Bud liked music more than anyone he knew. But it didn't really matter what he or Bud liked, in this moment it just felt good to be talked to by someone who wasn't measuring out their words, dragging the entire weight of Mary-Frances's corpse through the whole conversation.

"Want a swallow?"

He held the bottle out to Bud who snatched it right up.

"Yes I do." After he gulped from the bottle he dragged the back of his hand across his grinning mouth. "Thas' some good stuff."

"Yea, it's from one of Jimmy's batches. He's gettin good!" Curtis exclaimed and pulled from the bottle.

"Little lady?" He held it out to Apple. Apple shrugged and took the bottle from him. She pursed her lips tightly and took a tiny sip, not really wanting to drink the harsh liquor but not really wanting to say no.

Jimmy finally pulled himself from the swamp of relatives filling his parents' living room and appeared over Curtis's shoulder. "Curtis come grab yerself a beer. Don' kill the whole bottle in one sitting, ya gotta mix it with water remember? Jest like I told you, fifty-fifty. Tastes better that way, ya get all the flavors out of it."

Curtis grinned vacantly and stood up to follow Jimmy to the kitchen. The liquor danced behind his eyes, lending his gaze a lilting magnetism, a force without direction. The countertops in the kitchen were heaped with food. A pile of hushpuppies rose in a golden pyramid. Fried chicken- wings, drumsticks and breasts piled haphazardly on a silver platter. Greens stewed in their juices in a deep ceramic baking dish and everything spiraled outwards from two loaves of golden pound cake, one covered in powdered sugar the other in a crystalline glaze.

Abigail was being coaxed into taking a plate by Virginia's sister Ivy, "Come on now it'll be good for ya." The woman straightened up when she saw the way Abigail's eyes tracked Curtis's movements across the kitchen and asked him, "this your young'un?"

"Yes ma'am, I do claim her as my own. I'm Curtis Kennedy."

"I'm Ivy, Virginia's sister. Jest came into town for her birthday."

"Nice to meet ya," Curtis held out his hand to Ivy, figuring she already knew everything there was to know about him and Abigail. That must be why she was taking such interest in Abigail. Curtis thought that pity rained down on Abigail only because her mama had just died. He did not see the shroud of neglect that cocooned his daughter. The pity which had taken hold two weeks earlier at Mary-Frances' s funeral had only gained momentum as Abigail became visibly disheveled. Abigail, the small town debutante dressed up in communal grief, wore the town's disrupted pulse and the dischord of the Kennedy home in her clothing and hair. Each morning she awoke in the atrophied heart of a house whose love was thinning; whose warmth was leaking out through single pane windows. With everyone's unwillingness to cross Curtis the question was not how to help, it was how long they could reasonably wait until they *must* do something to help. How much misery could Abigail bear while the adults stood around being polite?

Abigail hunched over her plate at the kitchen table, her reluctance falling away as the food began to disappear between her lips. More and more quickly she shoved hushpuppies into her mouth with greasy fingers, stirred her greens into a glob of mashed potatoes. She brought heaping forkfuls of butter beans to her lips: chewed, swallowed, envisioned a strategy for her next bite. Curtis lifted the tab on a can of Busch and swayed out to the back porch where tobacco smoke curled around the rising refrain of music being played by an impromptu string band. Apple came into the kitchen and sat down next to Abigail.

Abigail lifted her head, "Hey Apple."

"Hey Abigail."

"Do you an' bud still have that raft that was tied up next to yer house when I visited you that one time? Do you remember?" Apple smiled because Abigail had come to visit her only a few short months ago and in the entire time that she was there she hadn't mentioned the raft once, but she must have been thinking about it a lot.

"Yea we still have it. You can come visit me again some time and we'll take it out on the river."

"Cool!" Abigail stood to put her paper plate in the trash. The can was already heaped up with the party's refuse so she balanced it precariously on top of the mound and walked out into the living room. Apple stood, folded Abigail's plate in half and using the side that wasn't smeared with food shoved the inflamed heap deep into the can. She sat back down at the kitchen table hoping that Bud would be ready to go soon.

Chapter 12

Bent Branch Falls 1968

The roots twisted down into the soil, forking and drifting side-ways, following jagged paths carved by the water that they chased. Each time that Cora dug up one of her hawthorn saplings she wondered at the fragility of their support system. How the tap root trickled and spread into a delicate tessellation of capillaries: roots thin and white, accustomed to the close embrace of darkness. When unearthed they languished like arched throats, offering themselves dangerously to the harsh air. *Funny how quickly things grow tough in the sun and the wind,* she thought to herself as she cradled the raw roots in the fold of her calloused hand. People and trees, their knotted knuckles and twisted burls.

Cora's Gramma Bunny had planted the hawthorne orchard long ago. Generations of trees had sprouted in the nursery before being transplanted into the orchard to replace the older trees when they died off or became diseased. In the cool temple of the grove's branches Cora packed the unearthed sapling into a five gallon bucket half-filled with soil. The black dirt clumped and broke into forms without angles; mixed with her sweat and circled her wrists like onyx bracelets. The cylinder of plastic looped around the handle of the bucket that was supposed to relieve the pointed press of bare metal into skin had cracked and was now pinching Cora each time that the weight of the little hawthorn tree shifted. She stopped to grab a hold of the sapling's trunk, steadying it as she hopped over a rivulet of water. Spring water bubbled up from the mountain at one end of the orchard and ran in small streams over the rest of the clearing. The trees provided the Harpers with enough Hawberries to sell to people from all over the county, fresh, jellied and in pies.

Gramma Bunny was a woman blurred at the edges by a pervasive softness. Soft voiced and soft bodied. After her death Gramma Bunny had only stretched further, finally untethered; her's was a ghost that haunted everything. Cora could especially feel her presence in the orchard. Bunny was early morning dew, rarifying every single surface, electrifying the forest's colors until their brightness jolted Cora into memories of her childhood. These were vividly singular moments: picking berries with Gramma Bunny and eating them sneakily until her teeth, tongue and fingertips blushed with pleasure. Carefully ladling goat's milk from a bucket into ice cube trays so Bunny could freeze it and make soap from it later.

Cora needed her Gramma Bunny now more than ever. Something in her marriage to Beau was slipping sideways but she couldn't figure out what it was. The space between them had gone cold as the space between stars, and it was growing, expanding with the universe.

"Beau what do ya think yer doin' goin' to town on a Tuesday night?" The sun was setting in layers of peachy haze over the horizon and Cora stood in the kitchen with a rolling pin in her hand. Clouds of flour had fluffed over her and caked in streaks across her cheeks and along her forearms. A line of pie tins stood ready next to a bowl of the hawberry filling that would be slopped sweetly into the crusts that Cora was rolling out. Beau stopped and turned away from the front door. Cora wondered if he had even planned on taking a minute to say goodbye to her.

"Me an' the boys goin' to play some poker down at the store."

"Ya'll been playin' a lot of poker lately. Ya gonna be plumb wore out if you don't stop stayin' out late like this."

"Come on Cora is jest fer fun anyways, an besides, what else i'm a goin' to do all night?"

"Oh I don't know, mayb be with yer wife for a change. What, suddenly none a you men got wives ya gotta please?" Cora turned back to her dough, let the conversation fall out of gravity, a meteor that would crash into something later and cause its damage. For now she didn't want to talk about it. Beau crossed the rest of the distance to the door and slammed it shut behind him. Cora worked her anger into the dough, flicking her wrists sharply each time she pulled the pin back up, moving it to the edge of the wanton expanse it was steam rolling.

For the first time since he had started having an affair, Beau felt guilty about it. When the affair began, the only other feeling that accompanied his newfound pleasure was a sense of surprise. The comfort of his marriage had curbed his interest in women and dulled his desire. So it was surprising to him when Jolene began pursuing his attention as she shopped at the grocery store each week. The first time he noticed her, the early summer heat was milking glistening drops of sweat from the creases in her elbows and wrists. Jolene had dropped her change, coin by coin into her purse, biting her bottom lip before leaning across the counter, "well aren't ya gonna offer me any help out with my groceries?"

Beau hadn't been planning to offer her any help with her groceries, he never had before. The groceries consisted of only a couple cans of vegetables, orange juice and a tin of rolled oats. Beau stared at her for a couple of moments, gradually discerning her attempt at seduction, then shrugged and walked around the counter with her small paper bag in his arms.

Beau sat in the driveway for a moment longer than usual before sticking his keys in the ignition. The old plymouth sighed as it turned over. He drove slowly towards the fork in the road where he always met Jolene. When he conjured up the image of her high cheekbones and sea green eyes he realized that he knew almost nothing about her. She lived with her family on the outskirts of town. Ever since her daddy had left all of them high and dry, rumours about her brother's criminal mischief and her mama's depression had circulated, but nobody had a thing to say about Jolene. She was mysterious and beautiful, suspended in the ether of possibility.

Beau was growing weary of keeping the affair hidden. The secret was small and overwhelmingly dense. The evenings that he and Jolene spent together were short, a couple of hours here and there- a tiny fraction of the day that soared above the ordinary rhythm. But he thought about Jolene all the time, and Cora had clearly begun sensing her presence in their lives. After being faithfully involved in the consistent and predictable pace of marriage for so long, Beau had managed to convince himself that he deserved this dangerous intimacy, at first. Now that conviction was wearing off.

When he pulled to the side of the road Jolene was sitting on a boulder, a few feet up on the steep, green embankment. She stood and gathered her long white skirt high around her strong sun-baked thighs and began picking her way through the thick foliage. When she was only a few steps from the bottom she abandoned herself to gravity, letting it pull her legs into a skipping run as she tossed her skirt up and it billowed out behind her. She was a spook as pretty as a bride. She yanked on the car door and climbed in.

"Yer late tonight." She playfully punched Beau on the shoulder, "I would a been snapped up by the devil if I didn't have a little bit a him inside me already." She fussily arranged her skirt and body in the seat of the car and yanked the seatbelt around her in a quick gashing motion. She was brazen in a way that unsettled most men- they couldn't grasp the contradiction of her delicate beauty and gruff comportment. The unconcerned way that she charged through the world suggested a life lived outside of her own gender.

Beau let out a quick laugh, "yea I figured you could hold yer own against the devil so I wasn't too worried. Hope you didn' think I wasn't goin' ta show up though."

"Oh, I wouldn' worry about that." Jolene looked up at him through her thick lashes, her lips curling at the corners into a cattish smile. Beau cranked the steering wheel of the Plymouth, pulling the long car into a sharp u-turn.

"Hang on a minute, are you jest goin' ta bring me straight to that cabin a yers again? Why don' you take me somewhere, ta look at the stars or somethin', buy me a drink fer cryin' out loud. I know I'm not yer wife but is not like I don' deserve nothin'" Beau, about to yank the gear shift into reverse so that he could give himself enough space to finish the turn paused and looked at her.

"OK, then what do ya wanna do? We cain't go in ta town, you know I cain't be seen with ya, but I could get us some beer an' we could go sit at the lookout fer a while. Would that make ya happy?" This was more than he signed up for and would keep him out far later than he wanted to be. He was a rodent caught in the talons of his own desire.

"Yep. Sounds good." Jolene stuck her newly polished boots up on his dashboard, letting the gauzy skirt fall into her lap. Her bare legs stretched into the moonlight.

Cora finished taking the pies out of the oven and stacked the dirty dishes up next to the sink. The spring water that they piped into the house would be icy cold and she knew that she should stoke the embers smoldering in the wood fired oven back to life so that she could heat up the water to clean the dishes properly. She glanced at the broad wicker basket that held the fire wood and saw that it was empty. She would have to get the wood. She paused long enough to feel the blunt ache spreading from the balls of her feet into her heels, then writhing up her ankles. She would rather shatter the whole pile of dishes with curse words than do all that work right then. If Beau couldn't even keep the firewood stocked up anymore, then she didn't have to clean the kitchen. "Screw it." She said loudly, to fortify her conviction, and all the remaining syllables of her unspoken anger crunched under foot as she climbed the stairs to their bedroom, to lay down alone.

A few miles down the road Beau pulled the car into a wide spot, parking diagonally so that the hood pointed at the full moon. "Come on." he snatched the cold six pack from the floor of the back seat and shoved the heavy car door open. Jolene tilted her head back against the headrest for a moment, wondering why she was doing this. Beau was a lot older than her and far less attractive. They both knew it, but now he seemed to be forgetting it. He was getting too comfortable, beginning to think that he deserved her, and still he hadn't given her what she needed. The first time that she seduced Beau he was awestruck by her and she lusted after the way that he wanted her with such intensity. She lusted after the idea that she could be hungered for, and that was enough incentive for her to go along with her brothers' half-baked scheme. But now the novelty had worn off, revealing the nothing that lay between them. This would be the last time, Jolene told herself as she shoved her thin shoulder against the stodgy plymouth door. She slipped out of the car and hopped up onto the hood where Beau already sat.

Cora woke up and reached towards Beau's shoulder, her hand falling onto the soft spot that he had made in the mattress after all these years. *What time is it?* She wondered to herself but beneath that line of thought there was simply a bad feeling, a knowledge that something was wrong, regardless of the time. The time was a human contraption that she was looking to for guidance as the universe weaved along its enigmatic path, completely unaware of hours and minutes. She didn't check the time, she sprung out of bed. She pulled a pair of loose-fitting blue jeans over her hips and threw on one of Beau's old flannel shirts. She didn't stop to think about how strange it would be for her to show up at the store, or what she would do when she got there, she just wanted to shove the snaking feeling of dread that was rearing its head up inside of her back underground where it belonged.

She climbed into their beat up work truck, hoping there was some gas left in the tank. The starter whined about its neglect as she twisted the key in the ignition, but finally the old engine turned over and the truck combusted in a throaty roar. She bounced down the road towards the store but slowed as she rounded the corner and saw a small yellow light cutting through the darkness. One of their cabin windows was illuminated, like a cat eye glaring out of its den at her. *Could be an old tramp that needs shooin' outta there* Cora thought to herself. She wasn't afraid of what could happen if she walked up on some lawless man hiding out, but she was afraid of what Beau might say if he knew that she had marched herself up the path of danger that way. Cora wondered at her own stupidity but turned down the driveway leading to the cabin anyways. *Besides, if Beau can't even make sure there's firewood in the house before leaving his wife alone in the night then I guess he has no right to tell me what type a problems I can or can't take care of on my own.*

As she drew closer, the truck's headlights dazzled in the white paint of the Plymouth. Then Cora's agitation turned to confusion. She parked the truck next to the car and began walking towards the cabin. The sound of tires on gravel swam through Beau's mind slowly as he pulled on Jolene's hips, guiding her through rhythmic oscillations of pleasure. Cora paused at the door but decided to go around to the window instead. Something in Beau's mind finally caught traction and he opened his eyes wide, Jolene gazed down into him either unaware or unbothered by the fact that someone was approaching.

"Hang on a minute. Get up. Get up. Come on, get off of me."

Beau began jostling around underneath Jolene, trying to get her to climb off of him. "What?" Jolene swam up from the depths of her insides. She turned her head and saw Cora, standing in the window. In the darkness Cora was ghostly, a water color of inexact features shifting in the shadows. But to Cora, the scene she was looking in on was lit up and clear as a television screen. Cora swam out of view and a stone crashed through the glass window pane.

"Uh oh." Jolene turned to look at Beau, seemingly unbothered. Suddenly Jolene seemed more like an audience member witnessing the dramatic height of a soap opera than a key participant in the scandal. She sat on the edge of the bed and flung her feet out in front of herself to loop her panties around her ankles. She pulled on her tank top and white skirt, and was already lacing up her boots when Beau whispered with his deflated voice, "I can't believe it."

"You should probably take me home now."

Beau sat on the edge of the bed, the heels of his hands pressed into his eye sockets, blacking the world out, willing the mess he had just made into oblivion. Jolene looked down at him impatiently. In a way maybe it would work out better for her now that this had happened. Now she wouldn't have to make the sticky exit that she was already planning for, inventing coddling excuses for Beau so that she could end the affair without setting off his temper by rejecting him.

Cora left the truck where it was parked and ran down the road. She cut across the front yard and headed into the stretch of woods between the house and the hawthorne orchard. She moved through the darkness under the watchful gaze of a screech owl. The porcelain berry vines trembled bitterly as she brushed past them. The owl followed from a distance, it's acute night vision coating the world with an iridescent glaze. Possums scattered in Cora's wake as her feet fell clumsily into each step. Without a flashlight Cora was at the mercy of nighttime. She came to the edge of her orchard, springing up from a whole history of love. The opening in the Appalachian canopy let the moonlight through but it couldn't illuminate the black hole of nihilism that was opening up inside of Cora. It's gravity was irresistible. It was sucking at her edges, daring her to find out what else could be broken.

She grasped the branch of a nearby tree and let its thorns dig into her hands. She ripped at it and it ripped at her. It felt good. When the roots finally popped and let go of their grip on the Earth she moved to the next tree. Blood wept down her wrists in thick rivulets that mirrored the veins flowing beneath her skin. She grabbed onto another tree and pulled. She pulled the satisfaction of destruction out of the ground by its roots, her hot blood falling onto the bark, her capillaries combining with the root systems as they were both pulled apart in shreds. Over and over Cora pulled trees from the ground. But this is exactly what she needed: the wrenching motion with which she yanked on each branch, the moment when the trunk finally came free and the tension in her body went slack.

She poured her rage over the orchard until she was empty and laid down in the mud, now fat with her blood. The tiredness that came over her was a damp cocoon- an all encompassing exhaustion. The full moon turned its rheumy eye towards her; pulled her into sleep.

Chapter 13

Bent Branch Falls 1974

When he looked at her Curtis did not see the need in Abigail, he saw Mary-Frances. He saw death. When Abigail began sleeping on the red, crushed velvet couch where Mary-Frances spent her last weeks he could barely bring himself to come home at night. Why did she insist on lying down in the depression left by the lingering past? The indent that Mary-France's fading body had left conformed so easily to Abigail's small frame. Their shared history shrouded the couch, a continuum woven from skin cells and loose hair. But Curtis could feel the soil underneath the house's foundation engorging itself on his remorse and his shame. He lost himself in the act of burying, happy to imagine that he could detach parts of himself and inter them alongside Mary-Frances, where he wouldn't see them again.

Abigail, on the other hand, thought it was a good idea to lie down on her mother's death bed. She didn't have the flaming tongue of alcohol to sanitize and separate her heartache, so unlike Curtis, Abigail dug into her own pain, pulling every vulgar specimen out from its dirt to be examined. So many creatures lead lives hidden from view; but she would not let her grief worm its way underground. It was hers to keep and she dug it up. She let the soil shove itself so resolutely underneath her fingernails that it became a part of her; her edges rimmed in black.

Abigail slipped easily into the habit of loneliness. Isolation was a willow dipping its roots into the pool of stillness that had sprung up inside of her- its cascade of foliage kept her hidden from the rest of the world. Alone, Abigail existed easily but she was empty too. She began to miss the school house that she usually detested, and the chores Mary-Frances would once force on her.

"Abigail come here for a minute and clean up this mess ya left here. Yer crayons are all over the place." Abigail borrowed Mary-Frances' s voice to boss herself around. She stood in the living room, in the early afternoon on a Tuesday. She was pretty sure her daddy was already working in the garage, but she hadn't seen him all day. Without adults around to give her limits her sprawling childishness had become joyless. So now she stood, hand on her hip, bossing herself around just to have something to push back on.

"I will not. I simply cain't, the colors refuse to be boxed up Mama."

"Abigail Caroline Kennedy, get yer butt over here to do what I say right now!" The expanse of time during which no one had used her full name stretched ever longer. In the weeks before her death Mary-Frances's words were cottoned in ailment, the syllables sloughing off into whispers before the words could be fully spoken. Now Abigail spoke all of her own syllables with the verbosity of a battle cry.

"ABIGAIL CAROLINE KENNEDY!"

"NO WAY MAMA!" She screeched, and ran across the living room stomping then jumping on the crayons that she had left there. She splintered the colored wax then spun on her heels on top of the mess, grinding it down into the floor. All of the colors smoothed into a confusing wash of motion, it was a portrait of time lately: the way that it had been moving around Abigail but not with her. She crushed and jumped and spun until she fell on the floor, dizzy and overwhelmed. The trickle of tears that snaked from the corners of her eyes reminded her that it was probably time to go to the river soon.

She walked to the river every day in the heat of the afternoon. She'd leave her raggedy tennis shoes and socks on the bank and wade into the river's cool waters. Gnats would hover around her head and neck, occasionally diving at her eyes. Still, she would let them hang in grainy clouds around her without batting them away. The river had a way of breaking up her loneliness with its dependable current. Each day Abigail stood in the current while the river's body slid past her, parted around her, begged her to come with it, and she was reminded that the world was still in motion. The river knew her and the river knew of places far from Bent Branch Falls, and this reassured Abigail that she would leave one day too, one way or another.

After a few minutes Abigail lifted herself off the floor, brushing away the tears that meant nothing now that no one was there to worry over them. In the weeks following Mary-Frances's death Abigail had begun crying like an adult. She cried when no one else would see her. She cried after a buildup so gradual that by the time the tears spilled down her face they were long overdue and triggered by something inconspicuous. Abigail's tears had become momentary eruptions of the grief that lived just below her skin.

River time she thought to herself as she worked strength back into her ragdoll limbs and climbed to her feet. The sun misted its heat down in oppressive waves, crashing through the humid air. It was air that could hold trees up until they out-grew their natural height. It was air you could chew on. Abigail slowed as she walked past the garage and heard her daddy inside of there, clanking and cussing. A metallic cussing that sounded like an ode to his love of mechanics. The driveway spilled her out onto the road and she passed by the front of the garage watching her daddy's feet twitch and flex where they tongued out from underneath the front end of a square-grilled car.

A ways down the road a possum lay dead, it's entrails vis-ible between matted fur. A buzzing cloud twitched through the air surrounding the roadkill, and maggots pearled along its gumline and on the rims of its torn flesh. The memory of crushing wheels was all that the corpse was left with, and now death consumed it, dragging its hundreds of hungry mouths across the pavement towards the possum.

Abigail smelled the possum before she saw it. The stench rode the heat in stinking waves. She covered her mouth and nose with her hand insisting that the putrescence stay out of her body, even if it meant refusing to breathe. She whipped her head around looking for the source of the odor until it came into view, sprawled out in the middle of the road. She kept her eyes trained on the thing while she passed it, taking stock of its ragged little teeth that still sawed at the air, its nails digging into nothing, paws clenched at the surprise of its own mortality. But worst of all was its curled up tail- that thin little trail of bone wrapped up in peachy nudity. Dead was the only way Abigail had ever seen possums, like they were choosing to sprawl their bodies across the roadways all the time just to rub their exis-tence in the face of a species that ignored them when they were alive. *We've been here all along.*

Abigail walked alongside of the river, pushing her way through the dense foliage that crouched on its banks. The late blooming rhododendron trees flashed their white flowers vividly against their dark green leaves, like sparks of light guiding Abigail through the dark tunnels formed by their branches. The Bennet kids were already there, playing in the water, when Abigail got to the swimming hole. They were the first kids she had seen all summer. "Hey!" yelled Forrest jumping in and out of the water, his pale torso a shock of floral white against the olive colored waters of the swimming hole. His two sisters, Lacey and April, turned to see who their older brother was greeting. Abigail paused as she bent over to unlace her shoes, poking a finger in and out of a hole that had pulled open where the canvas was supposed to be sewn to the sole.

"Abigail, Abigail, Abigail!" Chanted Lacey. Her words were careless as pollen, free to ride whatever wind may blow. In her excitement she chanted one more time,

"Abigail, Abigail Abigail!" Abigail straightened up and raised her hand in a silent wave.

"What're ya waitin' for? Jest come in!" Hollered Forrest. As the eldest and most restless one in the family he was used to goading other kids into action. Abigail waded into the water, goosebumps waterfalled backwards up her body, starting on her calves and rolling over her shoulders and down her arms. Step by step, until the chill rose up to her neck. The cold water lost its claws once it surrounded her whole body, letting her skin forget about the heat that had just left it.

"Where ya been all summer?" April asked her. April, the middle child, was quieter than the other two. She entered into conversations tentatively, scraping together the formalities that her brother and sister left behind for her own use.

"Oh jest you know, stickin' 'round my house I s'pose." Abigail responded, wondering how April didn't realize that she was busy with the death of her mama. Then Abigail wondered what her own thoughts even meant by that. Mary-Frances's death did not keep her busy in any way, it sunk her down into static, it was a predator sitting on her chest, forcing her to hold her breath and daring her to move.

"What've ya'll been doin'?"

"Not too much neither," April responded before her little sister squealed, "April kissed Jodie!"

"Shut yer mouth!" April yelled over Lacey's cackling laugh. But it was too late, Lacey had already started a new chant, "April kissed Jodie! April kissed Jodie!"

Forrest laughed at April's mortification and added, "is true I saw 'em do it. You probably been doin' it all summer long!"

"Oh shut up. Ya'll jest mad that no one likes you like Jodie likes me." But the two siblings looked anything but mad, they looked like they had come upon treasure and were just beginning to dig through its riches. Abigail glared at the three of them, she thought the whole thing was stupid. Nobody cared about April's mouth or Jodie's mouth or her own mouth for that matter. Nobody liked anyone that much and she could be sure of it. If her own mama hadn't liked her enough to see a doctor and try sticking around for her, then there was just no way that Jodie had taken any sort of liking to April that would last longer than the summer.

"Y'all are stupid. I'm goin' home" Abigail announced and waded back towards the shore. Her denim shorts rolled and stuck stubbornly on her wet thighs as she pulled them up, but she didn't want to dry off in the sun like she usually did. She yanked her clothes over her wet underwear and bare chest and tied the laces of her shoes together so she could sling them over her shoulder. She moved quietly through the forest trying to hear what they might say about her, but their voices gurgled into the river's current and flowed away with it. She told herself she didn't care. She tried on not caring; it could be like a bandage, it could stop the flow of pain.

Coming up the road Abigail braced herself for the smell of dead possum, watching for the spot where she was sure it would be laying. But when she rounded the bend there was nothing but a shadowy smear of blood where it was less than an hour ago. Abigail looked for it in the ditch at her side then crossed the road and looked for it over there. She suddenly wanted to find it, but couldn't even detect the stench that had earlier foreshadowed its presence from yards away. She grew fearful and stalked the road like something being hunted, taking in every detail of the world around her before moving forward.

Again rot deadened the air. The possum must be closer now. Abigail held her breath, scanning the landscape for the cadaverous animal. She nearly stepped into the swamp of its effluvient decay. Disgust then shock pulsed through her. How did it move up the road so rapidly? The wild roses vining down the embankment seemed to reach for the possum, yearning to pull it into a thorny embrace. It's eye, marbled over with daylight, stared up at Abigail and she ran all the way back to her house, a spooked animal tearing from its skin.

Chapter 14

Bent Branch Falls 1968

Beau's arms hung off the top of his steering wheel. His whole body was going numb. As he drove Jolene back to the fork in the road they passed the same clusters of mailboxes craning their empty heads forward like herons lost in a desert. The familiarity of the journey made him feel like a helium balloon whose string had been cut. The landscape morphed and shrunk, flexed hidden muscles as he rose towards the clouds; but in truth, his proximity to the ground was the only thing that had changed. His marriage shrunk and disappeared beneath him. Now that Cora knew about his affair with Jolene Beau felt as though he was a stranger looking on from above, watching someone else's life unravel.

Beau mistook the silence that had descended around himself and Jolene for complicity. In his merciful fantasy he was not alone with his guilt, he had a partner in crime. But Jolene did not feel guilty, she felt furious. At that moment Beau was not capable of any thought that didn't revolve around himself and Cora, but if he was he would have felt the anger radiating from Jolene. Heated friction burned through her as though her insides were rope that had been knotted up over and over again. The more that Beau tried to conjure up some feeble camaraderie between them, the more viciously she hated him.

The second that the rock Cora had thrown crashed through the cabin window all intimacy between Jolene and Beau was dispelled. Now they were just two people in a car. Bumping along the road towards two unshared destinies. As he put the Plymouth in park, Beau took one more look at Jolene, whose anger sharpened features had suddenly lost their allure.

"Things'll work out," he intoned for his own benefit as she clunked the heavy door open for the final time. She turned back after stepping out of the car and bent down to take in the full face of pathetic penance. What a luxury it must be to feel things so deeply. She let out a dry laugh and slammed the car door shut on his hangdog gaze. Things didn't generally work out for Jolene.

She set off down the dirt road that would deliver her back to her rib-thin existence. She would have to tell her brothers that she had failed. She wasn't able to find out where Beau Harper kept the grocery store's cash over the course of their affair. Beau's defenseless, well-fed face- that look of amniotic limpness, ran through her mind once more. Jolene did not share Beau's sense of shame because shame was for people who labored under the idea of themselves. Jolene was intractable, a molecule of water that could squeeze through the eye of a needle, become thunder freefalling through a gorge. But she had begun to wonder how long she could keep moving with no direction of her own, running through whichever rough, roadside gully that gravity pushed her into, before she dried up all together.

Jolene paused at the end of her driveway. It was a long and twisty stretch of packed dirt that wound its way through a field once lush with tobacco plants. The rye grass that she helped her pa plant each autumn to replenish the soil in the off season now grew wild all year long. A few tobacco plants still stood in the field, long-wilted into drooping witches' brooms. The trailer was a blocky shadow now, a house shaped hole in the universe where the world's millions of imperfections crept in. But in the daylight you could see that it was painted a cheerful blue, like a robin's egg laid in the meadow's soft grasses.

As she trudged forward in her heavy boots, Jolene accidentally kicked an empty shotgun shell and it flew out in front of her, pinging against the trailer's tin siding. Tayler appeared, moving so silently that Jolene hadn't even heard the front door open or close. He lit a cigarette and leaned against the railing to wait for her. Jolene's approach slowed, she'd been dreading this moment.

"Well, ya got the goods for us Jojo?"

"Nope. Couldn't get a thing out of him. The man's wife's got too firm a grasp on him."

Tayler snorted, "So wha'd ya been doin' all this time then, jest sleepin' with an' ol man?"

Jolene glared over his head before lowering her gaze to meet his, "What you been doin' all this time, smokin' and drinkin' up all the money we need for Ma's medicine?"

Tayler stubbed the cigarette out angrily on the porch railing then flicked it off into the field. "Done more for this family than you could even imagine while you were off on your own." He went back into the house, slamming the front door this time. Surely waking up their ma, who had taken to sleeping in the armchair in the living room ever since their pa left. Jolene would have to leave soon too. She had done it once and ever since she returned home she knew that she would do it again. But this time she wasn't sure where she'd find the exit.

"Damn, all these places 'round here are too much." seven years ago Jolene had sat at the kitchen table pouring over the housing section of the classified ads. Tallulah peeked around the back of her reclining chair at her daughter. The newspaper was rimmed by the dirty dishes, books of matches, beer bottles and half burnt candles that Jolene had pushed towards the far edge of the table before spreading it out in front of herself. The apron that she wore to wait on tables at the diner was flung over the back of a chair and leaking plastic straws from its pocket. Tallulah had always known that her daughter would be the first to leave. Though the three boys, Travis, Tucker and Tayler were older, they were easily satisfied. They were content to stay on the property all day helping Paul with the tobacco crop, and probably always would be. Jolene worked at the same diner as Tallulah did, so Talullah was able to watch the way her daughter plied the world for an opening that she could slip through, a passage way out of Bent Branch Falls. Tallulah flicked the ash from the end of her cigarette and the newly uncovered ember shone like an eye just shaken from sleep as she inhaled.

"Jolene," Tallulah coughed, "everything's too much. The world is too much. Yer gonna have to make due with what ya got like I always told ya. Ya gotta figure out what ya got and what ya can get with it."

"Yea Ma, well what exactly is it that I got? The money I make at the diner cain't barely cover a month a rent for these places. An' what else I got besides that?"

"Ya got that Richard lookin' at ya. I heard 'he's been goin' into the diner nearly every day askin' to be sat in yer section."

"Yep, there's always a Richard." Jolene shook her head and bent down to scan the ads again, a stone heavy as dark matter settled in her chest. A fresh wave of hopelessness that was only a grainy reprise of a lifetime's worth of hopelessness washed over her.

"Well if ye think yer too good fer every Richard and Dick that's ever given ya the time of day," Tallulah paused to giggle at her own joke, "I don' imagine that you'll be affordin' anythin' too quick." Jolene slammed her open palms down on the table and started gathering the sprawl of newspaper and balling it up.

"Ya know what ma? Maybe yer right. I should jest let the next guy who comes along shove me in some house so he can do whatever he likes to me. Always werked out fer us, huh?" Tallulah leaned her head back and spouted a stream of smoke.

"Jest find a way to get outta here Jolene, I don' care how you do it."

And she did. Jolene found her way out of the trailer just like Tallulah had predicted she would, in the passenger seat of a man's beat up car. The affair played out just like Jolene had said it would. It was all romance until she had walked down the aisle, but after that it was a series of fights between her and Rider, her new husband, and others. Cousins, bosses, landlords. Rider was no different than her hot headed brothers. Jolene and Rider lived in so many different rented trailers and apartments over the course of their short marriage that they stopped throwing their moving boxes out each time that they resettled. Jolene would carefully strip the packing tape from their seams, unfold and flatten them then stuff them behind the back of the couch until the next eviction notice was hung on their door.

Even though Jolene didn't make it out to Bent Branch Falls often, she knew the night that her Dad left. Rain pelted down from a black eyed cloud that hung over Caville where she and Rider lived at the time. In the city the rain was different, it turned the paved roads into slick mirrors that reflected the neon lights hanging in the bars' windows. It splashed back up towards the sky, unable to sink into all the cement and tin roofs. And in the morning there was always worms writhing on the sidewalks, unable to make it back to their small islands of dirt. The knowledge that something was going terribly wrong in her home in Bent Branch Falls cracked through Jolene, as sure as lightning. Three days later Tallulah called to ask if she had heard from her daddy at all.

Jolene was startled out of her memory by the sound of the front door opening again. This time all three of her brothers stepped out onto the front porch.

"Tucker, ya got a cigarette I can have?" Jolene asked. She knew that if any of her brothers were going to bum her a smoke it would be him.

But it was Tayler who responded, "Here little sister, take one of mine." Jolene narrowed her eyes in suspicion as he lit it for her. She exhaled a plume of smoke at the clear, star-clustered sky,

"Aright, what do ya want now?"

Tucker laughed nervously before Taylor cut in, "We got a new idea. You won't have to do nothin' hard this time so jest listen." Jolene glanced at the three shadowy figures of her brothers. "Look, we're gonna rob that mechanic's garage that's down the road a piece."

"Yer gonna rob that place? I've barely lived here for the past few years and even I've heard how crazy that Curtis guy is. Are you kiddin' me?"

"No look- just stop, don' worry about it. You won't even be involved. All we need you to do is pawn the stuff off in Caville once we get it. you got a car an' no one will suspect you."

Jolene rolled her eyes. "Great. So glad I came back home so that you could use me in your idiot schemes."

"Ah, come on, it's a good idea."

"No. It ain't." Jolene handed her half smoked cigarette to Tucker, "here finish it. I'm goin' ta bed."

Inside Jolene pulled a canvas duffel bag out from underneath her bed and fished her pajamas out of it. She stripped down and pulled the oversized t-shirt over her head. It was one of Rider's old shirts, worn soft by the passing years. The seams at the shoulders were so threadbare you could see the color of her skin through the thin cotton. On the front of the shirt there was a picture of an eighteen wheel truck with the words ABF Freight emblazoned on the side but the print was so faded that the truck was semi-transparent, a ghost truck.

She pulled on a brass chain and the tiffany glass lamp that it was attached to lit up. On the nightstand a series of school photos documented her and her brother's trips through adolescence. The same faces set beneath different haircuts, at times obscured by constellations of acne. Tucker, always the shy one, even appeared withdrawn in photographs. Each year, despite the photographer's coaxing, he managed to avoid giving a smile. It was a feat Jolene herself could never accomplish. Even though she hated her teeth and tried to hold a subtle, close-lipped smile for the yearly photograph, she cracked under pressure every time. It seemed that not responding to the hired photographer's pleas *to smile* was just as painful to her as another ugly, gap-toothed entry to the yearbook. She just couldn't say no.

Jolene hated sleeping next to those photographs, just as much as she hated sleeping under the bronze cross that was nailed to the wall above the headboard, but when she returned home the only place for her to stay was in her parents' old bedroom. The space had been entirely abandoned ever since Tallulah and the boys realized that Paul wouldn't be coming home. It was like a room in a house museum. Its dresser drawers were full of musty old clothing and pieces of costume jewelry were laid out like artifacts from the distant past. She crossed the room to turn out the overhead light and pulled a paperback copy of *Desert Solitaire* out of the duffle bag; anything to get her mind off of Bent Branch Falls. In the morning she would dress, return the pajamas and the book to the duffle bag and leave the room just as she had found it- a portrait of the past with only a thin layer of dust to attest to the fact of passing time.

Chapter 15

Bent Branch Falls 1974

Its thoughts were an empty swarm of buzz. First the vultures and crows had descended, untangling the fiber of its flesh with their sharp beaks, but now it was all maggots and flies- generations of them. The dead possum could feel its teeth grow longer as its gum line receded. Its life broke into thousands of creatures that crawled and flew and rattled their wings. Its life was emptying out into an eternal swarm of buzz. Soon it wouldn't be the victim, or the sacrifice, or anything at all. At least it was off of the hot pavement and in the shady ditch now.

The chrome hubcaps on Liam's cadillac flashed in a silver sheen across the possum's blank eyes. Inside the comfortable, air-conditioned car Liam did not see the roadkill. He didn't think about the insects convalescing in the air around him, fat on the blood of deer and possum, unless one splattered itself across his windshield. He pulled up to Curtis's garage, refreshed by his drive through the mountains. He stepped out of the cool air inside the cadillac and the heat rose in undulating waves around him. He tossed his ivory colored sport coat into the passenger seat and cursed his decision to wear new shoes. Mud as black as oil slopped over the toes of the shiny leather loafers as he stepped gingerly, crossing the swampish expanse between the cement path leading to the garage's front door and the island of pavement that served as the parking lot.

Inside of the garage Curtis grew stale in the atmosphere of work abandoned and left undone. A man from Allenstand had left his Impala at the garage a week ago and Curtis had not yet ordered the bumper that was needed to finish the job. The revelation clawed its way slowly to the front of Curtis's mind through a resin of malaise. Curtis knew he should call the owner, let him know that the job would take longer than expected, but he had forgotten the man's name. The log book with each customer's information was somewhere, but not there in front of him. He forgot when the last time he used the log book was. He creaked back in his chair, so sick of it all.

Curtis startled when Liam barged into the garage. Liam always seemed to barge into places rather than entering them, he was so at ease in a world made for men like himself.

"Curtis, what's goin' on man? It's dark in here." Liam began flipping up all four of the light switches that stood in a horizontal row next to the door as bank after bank of buzzing fluorescent bulbs flickered on.

"It's Sunday already?" Curtis seemed unable to get a grasp on the scene unfurling in front of him.

"Yep. Sunday already. You an' I got some books to square an' some shit to shoot."

"Oh gawd." Curtis rubbed his eyes vigorously then took his foot off the desk, allowing his chair to catapult him upright.

"Ya been drinkin'? Wanna drink some more?" Liam grinned as he pulled a bottle of maple colored whiskey from his briefcase. He slapped his green banker's visor onto his head like the whole scene was an improv sketch. He crossed the room to the safe, opened it and began shoving fistfuls of the cash into a bag. Curtis watched from behind the desk as this man seemed to take ownership of the garage right in front of his eyes. It was as though Liam and his confidence were large enough to pick the whole building up and load it into the trunk of the cadillac waiting outside. Liam returned and poured the mountain of money out on Curtis's desk to be counted.

"Well go on then, get us some glasses for this." Liam held the bottle up by its neck. "Jesus, I didn' come up here to wipe yer ass for ya."

Curtis shuttered into motion, found two tumblers stained with rings of Jimmy's moonshine and crossed the room to the deep industrial sink that sat crookedly against the wall on its L brackets. Water swirled through a permanent sludge in the bottom of the rough, white, plastic basin while Curtis rinsed the two cups out, scrubbing at their insides with his blackened fingers. Liam scraped his wrist distractedly on the edge of Curtis's desk, trying to rub a smear of oil off himself.

"Why is it that puddles of oil got all the pretty colors of the rainbow in them but the second it gets on me it turns the color of shit?" Curtis kept on rinsing the cups. He crossed the room and set the two glasses down on the desk heavily enough to make Liam pause, his hands hovering in mid air over the piles of cash he had begun to sort through.

"OK, let's take a second, have a drink 'fore we get started, ay?" Liam poured the whiskey out, shoving one of the tumblers across the desk to Curtis.

"Tell me honest Curtis, how ya holdin' up with everything?"

"How's it look like I'm holdin' up?"

"Not that well. Not well at all"

"I miss her. I miss my wife." Curtis dropped his head sideways onto the fingertips of his left hand. It was the first time he had spoken the words out loud. The admission sharpened the blade of his sadness and it slashed at the air between the men cutting all sense of comfortable familiarity into thin ribbons.

"That Mary-Frances was a good woman. How's lil Abigail?"

"Abigail, ya know...She's, I don' really know. She's a lil girl."

"Mmhmm..." Liam nodded. He couldn't imagine taking care of either one of his kids alone, least of all his daughter. They sipped their whiskey. A syrupy silence slunk down their throats. The fluorescent lights buzzed at an artificial pitch that made the insects outside sound as though they were moaning out a rich gospel hymn.

Abigail hadn't left the house all day, she didn't want to see those Bennet kids again. She stood at the kitchen counter, picking at the chicken Miss June left for her. The bottom of the baking dish lumped up with piles of grease and flecks of burnt skin. In the viscera of the roasted chicken Abigail could see the bodily juices of the leaking possum. She tried wrestling the image away from her thoughts, but was struck with a wave of nausea. She bent over the kitchen sink gagging in short bursts until her lunch slimed up her throat and splattered its pallid mess over the dirty bowls and spoons that lay at its bottom. She ran the water, dejectedly sloshing it over the soiled dishes. She closed her eyes and shoved the chicken back in the fridge, chipping the dish on the other pyrex baking pans and bowls still crowding the refrigerator shelves.

She would go visit the possum, put it in its place. It wasn't right for a creature that lived its life swathed in midnight to ruin her day like this. It was summer, the season ruled by sunshine, but for some reason the night was fighting back this year; sending its possums to rot in the midday heat, letting its owls dip boldly into sunlit meadows. Mary-Frances would know how to send the darkness scurrying back to the hole in which it belonged if she was still there. But she wasn't and Abigail would have to do it without her. She filled a glass with water, took a swallow and swished it around in her mouth. She spit the water, along with the last traces of stomach bile clinging to her teeth into the sink. She shoved her bare feet down into her polka dotted gum boots- good for stomping. Abigail hopped off the topmost porch step, flying over the bottom two and squelched her heels down into the mud at the bottom. She set off towards the road. She was on her way to scare that possum out of its apathetic death.

Soon Liam saw that he would have to do the work on his own that afternoon. Curtis's focus ragdolled about. His gaze dripped sloppily down the hood of the impala that had stood there bumperless for at least two weeks now, it careened through the air following the dimwitted flies that zapped themselves over and over again on the light bulbs overhead.

"Curtis, hand me yer notebook, ye been keepin' up? Ya been takin' any bets in this week?"

"Uh yea, what'd we say we're doin'? We got the Hornets on Thursday I think, an' then some kinda NBA game yea?"

Liam had gone silent and was flipping rapidly through the thin pages of the notebook. Forwards and then backwards, the sound of paper whisking the air.

"Doesn' look like you've written down a goddamn thing since we paid out the Frazier and Ali match. Ya got yourself a new notebook ya been usin' somewhere? Or the world's most miraculous memory all of a sudden?"

Curtis shrugged then flipped his empty whiskey glass upside down above one eye as if he were searching for another swallow trapped in the glass at the bottom.

"Ya listenin' to me? Ya got a plan here buddy? Ya obviously got a whole pile a someone's money here, so who's is it and where's it goin'? Can ya answer me that?"

Curtis returned Liam's questions with a vacant smile, and Liam realized that whiskey and banter would not be enough to turn Curtis right again. Liam had watched the man fall sideways at Mary-Frances's funeral, the problem was he thought he had watched him pick himself up again too. Turns out he didn't. It now seemed to Liam that Curtis was still back at that cemetery, sweat-stained and grief-smudged and out of his head with anguish. He had been trusting a hollowed out shell of Curtis to be his business partner and now the shell was caving in around both of them.

"Goddamn it Curtis, what are we gonna do here?"

"Settle down Liam, settle down."

"Tell me somethin' ta settle me down then. Tell me where all a this money belongs."

"Ya know, I'm thinkin' it'll work itself out."

"Since when has money ever werked itself out?"

"Ya better fuckin' watch that tongue a yers Liam. Ya can come up here in yer nice car, with yer city smarts thinkin' yer better than me, but you cain't run this business worth shit without me. So I'm tellin' ya now to jest calm down and drink another glass a yer nice whiskey with me."

Liam glanced around for the gun that Curtis kept in the garage. It was leaning in the far corner, out of Curtis's reach. He poured out fresh glasses of whiskey while calculating how much of the cash in the safe was his, and whether or not it'd be worth it to walk away without it, just to avoid the argument. But the thing that worried him even more than losing some money, was the people who'd inevitably come looking for theirs. If Curtis hadn't written down the bets somewhere then no one had any way of proving what was owed to them. This was exactly the sort of thing that Liam did not want to be mixed up in. If word ever got out that he and Curtis had mixed up their bets and couldn't pay out fairly, every gambler and crook in Western North Carolina would come around saying that they were owed some money. Liam took half of a swallow from his tumbler and slammed it down.

"Goddamn it Curtis. Ya screwed us." He stood and swept the uncounted money off of the desk and into the burlap sack. He poured the bills haphazardly into the ammo box safe. While he hastily repacked his briefcase, pressing the bill of his accountant's visor down flat and slamming it shut Curtis leaned back in his chair once more and laughed. It was a swelling laugh, a pointless laugh that gained momentum as it went. The unhinged laughter of a man who's decided to stop caring about anything in the world. Liam fumed his way out the door, slamming into the startling sunlight, and jumped into his cadillac. He roared hotly off down the road and Curtis didn't even take note of the screech his tires made when he had to slam on the brakes to avoid hitting Abigail.

Abigail stared into the windshield of the cadillac, her brightly booted feet planted stubbornly in the center of the road. Most of her body stayed eerily still except her right arm which prodded at the sky with a long stick that she held vertically beside her. When Liam's cadillac roared around the curve, almost mowing her down in its path, she didn't even flinch.

"Abigail!" Liam jumped out of the car, still too consumed by shock to register his relief at not having hit her. "Abigail! Thas' dangerous ta be playin' in the middle of the road that way, I almos' hit ya."

Abigail said nothing but as Liam approached her the stench hit him. Wet child and the smell of death shrouded the girl. Her hair had matted into a crown of filth on top of her head.

"Abigail what in god's name are ya doin' playing in the middle of the road like that for?" Liam drew closer in spite of the smell, his stomach churned. Abigail squinted right through him but began to strike the pavement with the butt of her stick in a primal rhythm. Liam grew closer then saw something swinging just above Abigail's fist, the one that was clenching the stick; a cadaverous strip of something. His eyes traveled up the swinging gristle and it began turning pink where it grew thicker and was less consumed by rot. It was attached to a mossy lump of something that had to be a possum's body.

"Abigail what do ya think yer doin' with that creature? Put it down, that thing's probably full a diseases."

Abigail snapped out of her trance. "Sorry Mr. Fields jest wanted ta teach him a lesson. He's been followin' me around ya know?"

She let the stick fall towards the ditch, the possum's body deflated around its hollow torso as it hit the ground, its little limbs bouncing stiffly, cuffed as they were in rigor mortis. She pulled a bright orange kazoo from her pocket and blew through it in four short blasts. A funeral dirge for the possum, or maybe herself. Liam turned back towards his car resolving to leave his money and never come near that side of the mountain again.

"Bye Mr Fields, Nice seein' ya!" Abigail held up her hand and ran off, falling back into a childish skip, a gait seemingly unweighted by the knowledge of death. It was as though Abigail could cartwheel in and out of a devilish possession. As far as he knew that's exactly what she was doing, Liam had seen too much that day to not believe in evil spirits.

Chapter 16

Bent Branch Falls 1968

When you exit sleep, folding your mind back into waking life, there is a moment when memory must empty itself of everything that isn't yours. Memory must contort itself into the ontological shape of you, so that you can fit into your own body once again; so you can leap into another day of a life in which you believe that your skin is a boundary line, that your dreams are your own. Cora waded through this moment slowly, she didn't want to remember who she was, but the whimpering bolts of pain that tore through the palms of her hands and ran up her arms reminded her. The sun leaked a watery light into the orchard, its beams clothed in the rising haze that makes the Smoky Mountains smoke each morning. Maybe the reality of last night could evaporate just like that haze.

Before she could remember her anger at Beau, Cora felt guilt at ripping up the orchard like she had. She lay with her forehead pressed into her forearms, nose on the dirt, breathing in the fecund scent of the soil: the fruit of constant death. *OK* she whispered to herself before pressing her forearms on the ground and heaving herself into a sitting position without letting the crusted gashes on her hands touch the dirt. The aftermath of crying hung heavily in her head. She looked for the destruction: naked roots gasping in shock, branches snapped in compound fractures, the tops of her little trees tilted in every direction but upwards, but she saw no ruin. The hawthorn trees huddled in their straight rows, laden with unpicked fruit, joyful in their preparation to scatter their seeds and go dormant for the season. She looked again at her hands, carrying the memory of carnage. She walked to the nursery, the delicate saplings still struggled upwards, clawing to claim their own piece of the sky.

The orchard had regenerated overnight. The trees absorbed Cora's anger, let it ring their trunks, but they wouldn't let her kill off what she needed. She pulled herself to her feet, accepting this strange truth without understanding. Her thoughts skipped from the orchard to Beau. If her orchard could withstand such a violent betrayal then her marriage must be able to as well. The process of fixing would be painstaking, but sometimes what has healed is stronger than what has never been broken.

Cora returned to the house. It had fallen into a deep quiet, as though it had become a time capsule of a different life in the six hours that it stood empty. Beau hadn't come home yet and the pies sat on the counter reminding Cora that things would have to move forward. She was grateful to have the task of covering their tops with tin foil. She pulled the shoe box full of shiny, folded squares out from under the kitchen sink. She unfolded a piece of aluminum foil then smoothed it out using the back of her finger nail. She removed the old creases then created new ones as she folded the reused foil over a fresh pie.

Flies gathered on the pile of dirty dishes left in the sink. *I'll jest leave'm be this time* Cora thought to herself. The grimy kitchen reflected Beau's neglect, he would have to figure out how to clean up the mess. In the meantime, Cora needed to lie down again. This morning would be the first that she and Beau weren't there to open up the grocery store at its usual time. She crossed the living room towards the staircase and saw that Beau had pulled up in the driveway. Through the front window she watched him, his forehead resting on the steering wheel, his shame coming up in waves, settling heavily into the folded skin of his neck.

Cora had just closed her eyes when the front door whispered open and Beau's footsteps rose hesitantly up the stairs. She didn't want to see him, not yet. She bolted from the bed, still dressed in the clothes she had hastily thrown on the night before and shoved her feet down in her work boots. She crossed the threshold of their bedroom just as Beau was approaching the last few steps. She stood with her feet planted heavily, one hand on her hip, glaring down at her husband, trying to recognize him among the constellation of features that had suddenly lost their familiarity.

"Beau, go clean up the goddamn kitchen." He turned and sighed, receded back down the stairs, his posture bent into the shape of remorse.

"We can talk later." said Cora, finishing off the interaction. She left the house and walked the half mile back down the road to the cabin. She circled around to the window that she had broken and ran her hand over the jagged edges of the glass. Looking through the window she could see the unmade bed. If it wasn't for this and the way the image of Jolene's body, taught and golden, her curved back laced over by a cascade of golden hair, was burned into her mind, Cora could almost convince herself that it was all a surreal dream. It didn't make a lot of sense, someone young and beautiful like Jolene going after Beau.

Cora used the truck to haul wood from the scrap heap to the cabin. She boarded up the cabin the way that people board up houses once their last inhabitant dies; as if we can keep the memories of what happened locked up inside. As though memory leads a physical existence like the beings it attaches itself to upon their waking. She nailed particle boards over the windows, leaving the one that she had thrown the rock through for last. She drilled nails through thick two by four boards and into the door frame. She let the knowledge of what she was doing radiate from the hammer into her bones; she was sealing off part of her life. Just like her Gramma Bunny once told her, "Cora, the past is behind ya for a reason."

"Look Beau, I don' wanna talk about what exactly you did, or why you did it, or how many times you did it- 'specially not that. I jest wanna know how it is you plan to fix it." Cora sat purposefully at the kitchen table while Beau leaned back against the counter, his head cocked to the side, unsure how to resume his relationship with Cora. Beau still felt as though his marriage teetered on the edge of destruction while Cora knew that it didn't. Beau didn't know about what had happened in the hawthorn orchard the night before and he never would.

"Cora I love you. I love you more than anythin'."

"Well ya gotta funny way of showin' it"

"I messed up Cora an' I dunno how to make it better. I'll do what I have to. I could run the store on my own for a while if ya want."

"No, thas' not what I want Beau. I dunno what I wan' but the last thing I need is days full of nothin'."

"Well what do ya think it'll take then? What do ya think it'll take for you to forgive me?"

"I already forgave ya." Cora let the statement hang in the air and felt the pressure suck out of the house, the tension deflating like a leaky balloon.

"I jest don' like ya much right now, and I think I jest need time." Cora hated to let him off the hook so easy like that, but she didn't know what else to do without the whole thing destroying her marriage. The cabin was boarded up but still standing. The orchard had swallowed her anger but only seemed stronger for it. She let the balance of their relationship shift back to where it had been. It was like finding a pretty wild flower and deciding not to pick it.

"Thanks Cora." Beau rubbed the back of his neck, felt the stress undo itself in the rippling wake of skin left by his dragging fingertips.

Cora replied and stood up from her seat. "I guess I'll go down to the store fer a while, people will be wonderin' where we've gone off to." She slammed the front door on her way out.

Chapter 17

Bent Branch Falls 1974

First we know that the universe is infinite. This is the type of knowledge that lives in your cells, rides the draft of your every breath. Most become devoted to the idea of infinity the first time that they look up and down a coastline or stand at the peak of a mountain. The infinite universe is the crux of our concept of everything that ever was. So, when the prophet-scientists surmised that the universe was expanding, they couldn't have measured its growth from the outside; even they couldn't travel past the end of infinity. Some things don't exist no matter how hard you look for them. They had to measure from the inside. The prophet-scientists ended up using density as their measuring stick and they found that density was disappearing- physical matter was scattering. We are forever being pulled towards the very edges of our existence and life is only becoming lighter. Soon this impossible effervescence will scatter our breath until it is just air, still and directionless. The lightness of being will lay us at the feet of oblivion.

In the war Apple and Bud saw this phenomenon sped up, scaled down, and used in the interest of political power: an abstraction. The bombs that ripped holes in the canopy of the jungle and everything that lived underneath it were mutilated universes. Men stole life's primary concept and distorted it, twisted it into a vehicle that could bring forth unnatural death. Bombs cause their damage by exploding outwards, losing density with such heat and speed that the resulting waves become a blunt force weapon, a molecular scythe.

Men have a funny way of understanding the universe sometimes, Apple mused as she stood over a skillet of frying eggs, listening to her own man stumble through his morning routine like he had just learned to dress himself. In his nervousness Bud had put on his boots too soon, he never wore his shoes inside and he hadn't eaten the breakfast that Apple was cooking for him yet. Now he leaned against the arm of the wing-backed chair near the front door and untied the laces. Trips to the VA's office always made him unduly nervous, the ordeal was a fanged combination of bad memories and the droning boredom of bureaucracy. Apple carefully flipped the eggs over in the skillet, the yolks could not break on a day like today.

"Bud, breakfast." Bud tossed one boot on the ground with a rubbery thud and bent towards the laces on the other. Seeing his distress made Apple soften towards him. She put the two plates of eggs down on the table and stood behind him, bending over to kiss the strip of skin between his collar and hair. It was the first time that Apple would not be going to the VA with Bud. Tension waved through the muscle fibers of his neck, Apple skimmed the tip of her finger down his vertebrae, stopping to press down on the large, knobby one at the top of his back.

"Everything will be fine," she asserted, then walked to the silverware drawer and chose two forks to set next to the plates on the table. Bud screeched a chair out, sat down, and began chopping into his eggs distractedly. The impending trip to the VA had forced him backwards and now he seized up in the excruciating ether of the past. Apple struggled to keep her feet planted in the present for him, she knew just as well as he did how easy it was to lose your grip altogether.

"Ya know I hate goin' down there, 'specially without you."

"I know, but it's better for both of us. Remember what we decided? I'm no good down there, I can't even read the English on those forms."

"I know it Apple, but yer good fer my temper."

"That's why ya need to learn to go alone."

Bud tilted his head back and planted both palms on the table. He exhaled loudly, "I know. I know yer right. You women always seem ta be right somehow."

Apple smiled at him, sopped up the last of the yolk streaking her plate with a piece of toast, and stood to clear the table.

"It's just a lot of waiting and a little paperwork. Nothing you won't survive."

"Yea OK, I'm no child. I'll get it done, and I'll be back in time fer dinner."

"OK. I'll see ya then. I love you."

"Love you too."

Apple worried about Bud. At times it seemed that the war had cleaved him into slivers.

Past versions of Bud stayed behind, stuck in eras as sticky as the hemic jungle mud of the war while her Bud soldiered on, always forced to confront the future with less of himself than he had before. Bud snatched her away from the dishes and her thoughts and gave her a long hug, as though he could feed on her serenity like a gum-toothed vampire. Apple let the house fall into a hush upon his exit and sat in the musty air thinking.

Abigail had first appeared in Apple's life only a few months earlier, on a cool Saturday afternoon in March. Bud sent her over with some eggs so that he could keep lazing around Harper's Grocery with the rest of the men. Apple remembered her surprise at opening her front door to find a small girl, out on her own.

"Hi, are you Apple? I brought ya some eggs. Bud sent me."

"Hi. Bud sent ya down here instead of comin' himself?"

"Yes ma'am."

"Alright, well thank you." Apple paused, "what's your name?"

"Abigail."

"Thank you Abigail. Would you like to come in for a minute, have a glass of tea?"

"Sure!" Abigail was bright and easy with Apple. Unlike the adults that Apple had encountered in Bent Branch Falls, she didn't seem to be bandanging over the questions she really wanted to ask with trite statements and cool distance. She bounced right into Apple's home like it was anybody's home. She planted herself in a deep armchair. Above her head Bud's military medals swung from nails in the wall, and above those the framed certificate declaring his honorable discharge hung. Next to Abigail a single cigarette smoked thinly as it burned out in the ashtray where Apple had abandoned it. The only window in the living room looked out onto the river. The slivers of sunlight that could make it through the leafy trees and into the room barely pushed back against the darkness that hung in it. The sun seemed content to leave the house to its dimness. The lithe body of cigarette smoke twisted in whichever direction it felt like, mocked the heaviness in the room.

"Here ya go." Apple returned from the kitchen with a glass of iced tea for Abigail.

"Thanks." Abigail settled back into her chair and sipped at the tea. Apple pulled a wooden stool from the corner so she could sit closer to Abigail.

"Now what do you do at Harper's while Bud's down there with his friends?"

"I drink a coke. Sometimes Miss Cora gives me a piece of candy."

Apple tilted her head back and smiled as though that piece of candy was melting on her tongue right then.

"My mama says yer not from around here. Where're you from?"

"Very far away. A place called Vietnam."

"Do they have candy in Vietnam?"

"We had everything in Vietnam. We had everything we have here in Bent Branch Falls for a time, just in different flavors."

"Strawberry's my favorite flavor."

"Mmhmm, I like strawberry."

"What's that over there?" Abigail pointed a finger at one of the only things Apple brought with her from Vietnam when she left, a silk scarf that her grandmother had woven for her when she was sixteen. A woman's scarf. It was bright and full of shapes that suggested flowers. It was dyed with tropical colors- green, purple and red. It hung above the mantelpiece waving like a bright flag staking its claim in the present for the land of Apple's youth.

"That's a scarf that my grandmother made for me when I was just a little bit older than you."

Abigail stood and ran her curious fingers over the delicate silk. Apple let her.

"That material comes from worms."

"What?!"

"Yea, they're called silkworms. They're shorter than the worms that live in the dirt and they're white. They spin a fiber that women can harvest and weave into beautiful clothing."

"Wow. I would like to have a silkworm one day." Apple smiled. It was easy to smile around Abigail. The day that Abigail visited stood out as a much needed reprieve during a long and ashy stretch of depression. It was a time in Apple's life that flickered dully, like the anemic picture on a grainy television screen. A time that left her feeling as though she was being broken into thousands of pixels herself.

Apple wanted to return the favor to Abigail but was afraid to approach the Kennedy house now that it was calcifying with despair, hardening into a lifeless fossil. Still, Apple could tell that Abigail needed someone now more than ever, so she pulled her strength together and left her house.

Camilla was surprised when she opened her door to see Apple standing there. Apple all alone. Camilla was so used to seeing her at the side of Bud she took a second look over Apple's shoulders to make sure she hadn't missed him somehow. Apple was dressed in overalls that cascaded over her tiny frame, barely touching her body. The denim pooled on the tops of her beat up sneakers. Camilla, who was working in her kitchen, boiling Hawberries down into jelly and canning it for Cora, was barefooted and wrapped in a lavender colored kitchen apron.

"Bud's at the VA."

"Sorry, Apple. Ya just took me by surprise."

"Yes, well I don't reckon I come around a whole lot." Apple tucked a strand of hair behind her ear, shrinking away from the stilited interaction nervously. She wondered at the Southern lilt that was slipping into her mashed up English. *Reckon?* Sometimes she could barely recognize the person she'd become since arriving in the states.

"Well come in, I always got some fresh lemonade to spare." The kitchen was muggy and sweet. The jelly in a large pot on the stove, boiling up in explosive pustules, looked like something geothermic. Camilla stopped to stir it with a long wooden spoon on her way to the refrigerator. She emerged from the foggy coil of cold air that drifted from the open icebox with a liter sized jar in her hands. The light yellow liquid swirled with pulp and sugar crystals as she poured it into two glasses.

"Well what brings ya here today?" Camilla asked as she mopped the sweat from her forehead and returned the lemonade to the fridge. "Wait, do ya wanna go sit out on the porch? It's a right furnace in this kitchen."

"Yea that sounds nice," Apple answered quickly and walked out of the house, holding the door for Camilla who carried both of the lemonades.

"OK, tha's much better. Now ya can tell me what's on yer mind."

Apple twisted her lips to the side, searching for the right words, "Well I'm a little worried about Abigail to be honest. I thought I'd ask you about her first because she seems to like you a whole lot. I don't know if you saw her at Virginia's birthday party, but she wasn't lookin' so good."

"I saw her." Camilla raised her eyes and stared out into the forest that walled the small clearing where the little cabin sat. "I was pretty worried myself. The child's absolutely filthy."

"So dirty. I dunno if Curtis is up to taking care of everything right now, but Bud tells me he won't accept help from anyone. I mean we heard about what happened at the funeral."

"Curtis is a hard man tha's for sure. Just before the party I took Abigail some lunch an' I could already tell things were not quite right. I'd be afraid to see what the inside of that house looks like right now."

"Me too." A silence settled between the two women, a silence stuffed with unasked questions. They let it snake around the porch, sending shivers up their ankles for as long as they could stand before Camilla asked, "what is there to do?"

"I was hoping you'd have an idea."

"Well if it was up to me, I'd move that little girl right in here and look after her myself, but a proud man like Curtis ain't never gonna let that happen."

"Well can't we at least go over and see her? It'd be less strange if you came along. She knows you better."

"You're right. let's go down there together tomorrow. You bring a side of somethin' an' I'll roast up a chicken. I'm a little lean this month but chances are that Cora would be willin' to donate a chicken from her grocery."

"Yea. I can do that." Apple's face broke into a relieved smile.

"OK, I'll see ya tomorrow then. Jest come by around noon. And Apple?"

Apple lifted her chin and looked Camilla straight in the eye. "We gotta make it seem like the visit ain't nothin'. Gotta remember to act like we'd be doin' this sorta thing rain or shine, 'specially if Curtis is around, OK?"

"OK." Apple stepped lightly off the porch and started walking away from the road and towards the river that ran through town. Camilla watched her strange trajectory, confused at first. Then she remembered that Apple liked to use her rickety, flat-bottomed raft to get around. Bud had slapped the thing together for her as soon as they came to Bent Branch Falls as a new couple and she used it to run all of her errands. Camilla laughed to herself about the strangeness of Apple. During all the years that she had lived in Bent Branch Falls quietly, moving from place to place on the veiled currents of the river, she had never once approached Camilla. But now their new alliance took shape easily. The peculiar circumstances at play during the summer of 1974 were shifting many things.

Chapter 18

Bent Branch Falls 1968

Tallulah Gray preferred to pour tang over her frosted flakes in-stead of milk. The sludge at the bottom of the bowl tasted like the last bite of a sugar cone, when the pointed tip is filled with melted sherbet. The last bite of her first bowl of cereal would be the best bite that Tallulah would take all day. The rest of the day was an uninspiring vista of mediocre bites. It really was like a drug to her, the 14 bowls of cereal that she ate every day. And the peaks of her pleasure gradually flattened out as the habit grew stale. Her taste buds sparked in reaction less enthusiasti-cally with each bowl, her satisfaction decreasing.

At least she still had her daughter Jolene, and her three sons, Travis, Tucker and Taylor. They had burst through the front door that night breathing heavily, clearly they were running from someone. And Tallulah wasn't stupid, she had heard the three raps on the side of the trailer as they propped their rifles up against it before coming through the door. It was thoughtful of them to try and hide their nefarious dealings from her, but it would never work. Tallulah saw and heard everything that went on in the house, she never left the living room. She hardly ever slept. "You wanna choose the channel?" she asked Tucker.

"No." Tucker said to the ceiling, annoyed that she had asked. Tucker was always transparent in that way, too consumed by his feelings to worry about hiding them from other people. The TV screen was broadcasting the waxy faces of two newscasters, their heavily saturated images taking on a surreal gleam. Tallulah was going to resist the urge to ask Tucker what was wrong. She knew that in order to keep her boys close she had to keep her distance. She allowed them to forget that she was their mother in convenient ways. Another thing that Tallulah was not going to ask was where Travis and Taylor were, because she had an uneasy feeling that they had gone out the back door and were keeping a lookout. And for what, she didn't have to resist asking because she really did not want to know.

"Where's your sister?"

"Jolene? I dunno, I think she went out a while ago. You talk to Pa at all lately?" Tucker asked her, finally retreating from his thoughts and returning to the living room.

"Not since Thanksgiving." Calling on the holidays was Paul's way of pretending he hadn't completely abandoned Tallulah and their kids. Tucker still refused to speak to his father but seemed to be keeping track of how often he called.

"You need me to get you anything tamorrow? I think I'll go ta town."

"My prescriptions." The pain medication that Tallulah needed to survive her MS. She wished they made a drug strong enough to take the edge off of her abandonment. It had been four years since Paul left. There was a small, weepy part of Tallulah that still waited for him to walk through the front door every evening. He had promised to return, had told her that he "just needed some time for himself," but it seemed that when he left he had become so absorbed in himself that he forgot about everyone else in his life. Most likely he had met some other woman by now. Someone who wasn't crippled by MS. Tallulah had memorized the different gaits of her three boys. She could tell by the sound of their footsteps which one was approaching the front door and whenever anyone besides one of her sons came by she couldn't help but imagine that they may belong to Paul, though she ended up disappointed every time. Usually the people causing the strange footfalls never even crossed the threshold of the front door. Her boys would meet them on the front porch without inviting them inside.

"Frosted flakes and tang of course."

"Yep." Again Tucker rolled his eyes upwards. Tallulah knew her three boys were ashamed of her, and that this was the reason that none of their visitors ever went further than the front porch. She never did try to recover from Paul leaving. The MS was too difficult to handle alone and now every remaining part of her life was worse off due to the fact of her obesity. Tallulah didn't care, caring required energy that she simply didn't have. She didn't care when she poured her first bowl of cereal and she cared even less as she finished her last. Every day spent watching television and eating was like an added segment to her endless performance of *I don't care*. And she got to continue not caring as long as that sentiment was extended to the comings and goings of her sons. So their lives together had come to rest on a tolerable ledge jutting out and over a chasm formed by all that was left unspoken. There was no use in any of them upsetting the balance, they would all fall together anyways.

Outside Travis sat on an old rocking horse in the front yard. The silent night was overripe with hidden possibility, the flesh of a peach left unpicked. In the bruised darkness he replayed the botched robbery over and over again in his head. The pounding footsteps, first Curtis's as he ran towards the garage, then his own as he, Rider and his two brothers fled. The stomach breaking percussion of bullets that flew over their heads. The sound of those bullets had followed him all the way home. His shoulders hunched together between his sharply bent knees, the flying v of his collarbone breached the torn collar of his tee shirt. He tried to rock himself into a state of calm. Back and forth, each time he shifted his weight he could hear the grasses and vines that had grown over the toy's runners being torn up at their roots. Back and Forth, its mane catching the moonlight in its golden paint.

Their secondary mistake was that they didn't turn their lantern off once they were inside the garage. Who would have thought that the little light was powerful enough to send a warning flaring through the half mile of nighttime that stood between the garage and the house, alerting Curtis to their invasion? As the three brother's fled the scene, the crack of the gun became Travis's ventricles exploding like kernels of corn in a kettle. At some point he realized he wasn't as afraid of dying right there as he was of living in the fearful aftermath. The primary mistake was the whole plan itself. Robbing someone in the same small town that they lived in was a horrible idea, it was bound to bring them trouble. They had somehow convinced themselves that it would work, but that was nothing but a whimsical measure of self-deception. Their desperation had made the brother's stupid. Travis blamed Jolene, if she hadn't messed things up with the Harper's they could have robbed the grocery store in a much more efficient manner. Instead they had to go with the riskier option of robbing Curtis's garage and they hadn't made out with a single cent.

Travis jumped to his feet at the sound of a twig snapping. The world jumped between the unsteady sights of his rifle.

Psssst... the voice came from behind his left shoulder and he turned towards it.

"Travis it's me, Taylor." Travis lowered his gun. "Goddamn. Little bit jumpy?"

"Well, yea. How else am I s'pposed ta be after a night like tonight?"

"I know, I know. Jest sayin'"

"Was a stupid idea ta go fer Curtis. I jest know he's gonna figure out it was us somehow, even if he didn' recognize us back there. Ya think ma knows?"

"I dunno, as long as Tucker's not in there cryin' on her shoulder she probably doesn't know too much. But if she does figure anythin' out she's gonna throw a fit about it. She's already convinced that the whole town's out ta get her because of us."

"Poor ma. I think the whole town may have forgot her anyways."

"Cora still comes over ta see her."

"Oh yea. Cora." Travis tried his best to forget that Cora still came over to visit Tallulah. It was more convenient for him to go about his life under the assumption that his mother knew nothing about what went on outside of their home.

"Wait. What's that." Taylor pointed towards the woods then motioned to his brother. They crept forward, rifles raised against their shoulders. Taylor had seen a flash of Mary-Frances's pale wrist as she snuck through the woods to find Curtis. Taylor and Travis followed Mary-Frances from a distance and watched as she found Curtis, crouching in a thick tangle of ferns and kudzu. She dug her nails into Curtis's arm, spinning him around to face her.

"What do ya think yer doin' here?" she whispered. She made sure her whisper came out as harsh as barbed wire to make up for the volume she had to sacrifice in the name of sneaking around.

"Mary-Frances, what the hell?"

"What the hell yerself. Yer comin' back home with me. You have a baby girl to think about now, and me."

"Mary-Frances, goddamn it. The garage was jest broken into and you want me ta jest go home and forget about it?"

"Yea, I do. They didn't get anything from you. Ya already scared them off. Those peckerwoods ain't goin' ta be comin' back around any time soon, so what's left to do? Ya gonna kill them over a broken latch?"

Curtis shook his head back and forth, dismayed by Mary-Frances's inviolable line of reasoning. As though she had just introduced him to a new dimension of reality, an unbelievable but emphatically complete new world. Curtis was frustrated by his wife's reasoning. The brothers held their breath. A moment later Curtis turned around and stormed off noisily through the woods.

Inside the trailer Tallulah poured her last bowl of cereal for the day, number 14. She had always liked numbers that ended in four. Four was safe, round, divisible; tucked under the wing of five, the more infamous and overused digit. When she still worked as a teller at a bank in Caville she had always set her alarm for 6:04 AM. Now she tuned the endless noise streaming from the television set out so she could listen for the footsteps of Travis and Taylor. Tucker's white face floated in the reflective window pane as he struggled to see past his own reflection and out into the precarious night. Ignoring her son's misguided attempts at becoming men Tallulah sunk her spoon into the crunchy, sweet cereal floating in her bowl.

Chapter 19

Bent Branch Falls 1974

Camilla would have to find another dish to use for the chicken. The one she liked most still sat in the Kennedy's refrigerator unwashed, an age-polished carcass anchored to its bottom by grease. Camilla bent over, clanking through her disorganized shelf of pots and pans, tsking under her breath at the annoying nature of things. While she went on, preoccupied by her dishes, a raw chicken sat in her kitchen sink defrosting. To think that the bumps on its skin were not goosebumps from having been frozen, but lumps left behind after its feathers were pulled out. It's death skin was preserved in one slippery sheen of unanimous color, what a different sort of death this chicken led from the possum.

She found one. A boring white one. The baking dish that she left behind with Abigail was much more appealing, it had peach colored sides decorated by stenciled, pearl-white flowers. She would have to remember to retrieve it later. She pulled a bundle of herbs down from where they were strung up on the rafters and chopped them into crunchy flecks to be stirred into melted butter and brushed over the chicken. Her nerves were like live wires sitting in the bottom of her stomach and upsetting it with alternating currents of apprehension and obligation. She pushed back on her nervousness by imagining that this time her visit to the Kennedy's house would be different. Abigail would be clean, Curtis would acknowledge her. She would be their friend again.

Apple appeared at the door a couple of hours later, holding a deep bowl full of coleslaw with seran wrap stretched over the top of it. Apple all alone. Today she wore knee high burnt-orange gumboots beneath a knee length, cotton dress. She held up the raincoat draped over her right forearm, "It might rain today."

"Hi Apple, I'm sure hopin' it won't. It won't be quite as pleasant, walkin' all that way in the rain."

"We could take my raft, it's always faster." Camilla smiled at the suggestion and motioned Apple inside.

"Here make yerself comfie an' let me stick that coleslaw in the icebox. There's still about a half-hour left on the chicken."

Apple held out the bowl to Camilla then pulled her tall boots off before leaving the welcome mat. She sat down on Camilla's couch and the cushions sucked her in so deeply that her feet hung in front of her, impotent and dangling three inches from the ground. The sound of Camilla's movements rattled out of the kitchen, the bonish clankings of pans and spatulas and the screech of an oven rack being pulled out and pushed back in. Camilla stopped short in the entrance to the living room, watching Apple study her collection of vintage tins. Americana artifacts, whose utility was now remembered only by their labels, stood like dead soldiers on the mantelpiece. Crayons long colored into nubs. Slade's toffees. Ben Hur's spices. Apple remembered the foreignness of these objects when they first came to Vietnam with American soldiers. She had followed them back across the ocean, where she had become just like them. Apple an artifact.

Apple felt Camilla's gaze and startled out of her reverie. The bright-tin boys with blonde hair and blue eyes turned their heads to look at Camilla along with Apple. Camilla cleared her throat and nervously wiped her hands on the front of her apron. She sat on the couch beside Apple, sorry she hadn't yet bought a chair for the living room.

"Well, I'm glad fer the chance ta get ta know you a little better. Where'd you get a cute name like Apple?" They sat facing forward as though talking to the tins, using their canned voices.

"It's pretty funny actually. When the American's came to Vietnam it was easier to choose a name from their language than it was to try and get them to pronounce our names right. That's what everybody did, they just chose an American sounding name. So I started introducing myself as Apple. Apple you know? As American as apple pie. Then I get here and nobody's name is Apple. People just think that it's strange. But it stuck with me, I would never be able to get Bud to call me anything else."

"Ha. That is pretty funny. Better ta have a unique name anyways, people'll remember it easier that way."

"Yea, it works out, people do remember my name."

"How do you like Bent Branch Falls anyhow?"

"It's peaceful. Do you like it here?"

"Yea it's easier than New York City, that's for sure."

"New York City?" Though it came out as a question it felt like an affirmation. Welcome proof to Apple that she was not the only oddity that had been dropped on this mountain side.

"Yep. New York City. I left five years ago and haven't been back since."

"Is your family still there?"

"Yea an' I talk to them on the Harpers' phone from time to time. My ma's always sayin' she's goin' ta come visit one of these days, but we'll see."

"But you still have their voices."

"Yea. A good telephone call can shrink the distance between us." Camilla widened her eyes in preemptive sympathy, nervous to ask the question but not seeing any way around it, "Can you reach your relatives?"

"No. I don't even know if any of them are alive. They don't know if I'm alive either."

Camilla and Apple came upon the Kennedy place as an urgent wind was picking up. A wind that carried a storm on its black breath. Every door and window in the house stood open, painting the facade with a gap-toothed grin. The torrid air whipped the atmosphere into grim festivity. The flecks of carrots sprinkled throughout the coleslaw made the dish in Apple's hands look like a bowl of confetti, and maybe this is what Abigail needed more than anything. A bowl of confetti, a pile of frivolity. But while Abigail craved something pointless and delightful, the world brought her dinner, chicken and vegetables. Mary-Frances was not around to buy her a coke.

What to do when faced with an open door to an uninviting house? Camilla yelled. "Abigail! Abigail! Me and Apple came by to see you!"

Abigail had been crouched down next to the stairs of the front porch all along, negotiating with the kudzu vines about her entrance into their soft world. She was now convinced that her future lay behind a departure, perhaps to a world that ran parallel to hers. She was sure she could find an entrance to another dimension, one where Mary-Frances baked biscuits and tended her garden. So she had been attempting to tune her cells to the natural world around her, hoping to slip sideways and into that world. Mary-Frances's death had killed off her interest in people. She stood up furtively, annoyed that the effort she was making to enter into her better world was being disrupted. When she stepped around the bottom of the stair set so that she was standing directly behind Miss June and Apple they didn't even notice her.

"Miss June, I'm right behind you." Apple jumped, her insides seizing in fear. As Miss June turned to Abigail, Apple tried her best to get ahold of herself. She was embarrassed that the presence of a small child had injected such terror into her and the resulting struggle to slow her heart rate had taken her far from the moment at hand, which she now struggled to reenter. She stood with her back to Abigail for an awkward beat after Camilla had turned around to face her.

"Abigail, oh my. I must have walked right past without seein' ya there."

"I s'pose you must have. Such strange things happen." Miss June could barely recognize the child. Abigail was sludged in grime. Dirt collected around her in such a way that Camilla was struck by the outlandish fear that the child was avidly trying to return to the Earth. Things were not better and they appeared to be getting worse.

"We brought ya some lunch, Apple and I." Abigail shrunk away. She was inflamed at the idea of accommodating the ritual of a meal time in her day for the first time in weeks, and she couldn't remember that she liked Miss June, and Apple too. The imprint of friendship that the women had once left in her life was no longer there. The tracks had been washed out in the deluge of grief. Abigail was free to act in whichever way she pleased, and in this moment she was ribbed with meanness.

"I'm sorry Miss June, but it's been a long while since I last seen ya and I assumed I wouldn' be seein' you around here again."

"I was here only a couple of weeks ago, remember? I brought you lunch." Abigail could barely remember, it was as though a century had clocked past her since the death of Mary-Frances. It was as though one errant thread had been tugged on and now everything was coming undone. The cloth of the universe was unweaving itself around her. The time-distance contraption was refusing to move in a straight line, it was failing her very existence.

"Oh. Oops." Abigail snapped out of her predatory anger. "Sorry, I nearly forgot. Thanks for comin' over. Hi Apple."

"Hello." Apple's hesitation draped her whole person. She stood there poised as though she was ready to run away. "Um, ya'll wanna eat on the porch?"

"Sure. That would be lovely" Abigail replied stiffly before withdrawing into the house and returning with plates and forks. She shut the door behind her. The three of them arranged themselves on the porch steps, Camilla next to Abigail on the same step, Apple on the top step like the tip of a triangle. Abigail barely touched the chicken and distractedly separated the orange flecks of carrot from the pallid, mayonnaised shreds of cabbage on her plate. Camillla tried her hardest to stop watching Abigail not eating. Apple had no maternal instinct and wasn't bothered by letting Abigail's emotional destitution stay outside the realm of her personal responsibility. She dug into her plate, satisfied with her choice to mix fresh dill into the coleslaw, it gave the dish a surprising freshness. Camilla on the other hand, struggled to not fuss over Abigail. She wanted to brush her hair. She wanted to wring a rag full of soapy water out over Abigail's head and run the nubby cloth over her back, even though she knew Abigail was too old to be bathed by an adult.

"Welp. We did lunch." Abigail announced abruptly and stood to take her plate back into the house. She streaked mayonnaise down her purple denim shorts as she rubbed her hands down the front of herself. Camilla looked up from her half finished plate.

"Abigail honey, ya barely touched yer chicken. Ain't ya a bit hungry?"

"Nope." Abigail pulled the bright orange kazoo out of her pocket and blew into it defensively. "It's alright. I don' want it."

"Well I'll leave it anyways, yer gonna want it later." Abigail dropped into anger: a stone chasm that was being carved ever deeper by a rageful current that ran through her. Camilla went on oblivious, she couldn't recognize such a hardened emotion stalking through the body of a little girl. Camilla stood and walked into the house, Abigail trailed behind, wishing she could yank her back out to the front porch.

"I'm jest goin' ta stick it in the icebox fer ya and where is that dish I left– last time?" Camilla expected a mess but still paused in shock at the state of the house. Knick-knacked by empty cans of busch and besotted by drops of dried up food and drink. Fruit flies massed into blackness on every surface, feeding on spilled beer and sticky-fleshed peach pits. In the center of the living room floor crayons had been dropped and crushed into a bleary rainbow. The kitchen swarmed with decay, the trash bin wore a necklace of pearl maggots around its rim. Camilla felt her heart drop into panic. She wished she had never seen it. She pulled open the refrigerator to put the leftovers inside and was confronted by a congregation of molding dishes. Rot-haloed piles of cheesy potatoes and foods blurred and into indistinguishable and leaking heaps. Her favorite dish sat amidst all of it, its sides smeared with chilled grease. The chicken carcass stood on end as though searching for someone to rescue it from its strange purgatory. She pulled the dish out and saw a large chip in its peach colored veneer.

"Abigail, this is my good dish and it's all chipped up." Camilla frowned down on her.

"Miss June, the dish is cracked because yer chicken made me sick. It sickened me with its possumish demeanor. Ain't my fault that you'd bring roadkill food over an' make me eat it." Camilla squirmed at the offense that rose up inside of her. There was no child in the world that should be able to raise the vitriol in her the way that Abigail was right now. Her lips flatlined into a bloodless grimace.

"Abigail, I am not coming over here to be talked to this way. You better clean yerself up and start talkin' more grateful. An' the next time I see you I hope you've thought about what you've done." Camilla urged the words out of her throat before her temper broke.

"I ain't asked you to come over nohow!" Abigail yelled, her eyes beading into little orbs of animosity. Camilla turned on her heel and stomped outside. She didn't want to be angry with Abigail, she wanted to sweep her from her destitute reality and into a hug. She wanted to rescue her but she had shown up too late.

As Apple waited for Camilla to return, a bleak sense of dread gathered inside of her, a sudden and unexplainable aversion to every constituent of that moment. She dropped her fork, her appetite had come undone. The feeling was wet and cold and undispersed; as though the gathering thunderstorm was going to burst forth from inside of her. The air hissed with anticipation. The horror crackled out, all the way to the tips of her hair. Thunder broke the sky and heavy raindrops rasped through the air but they weren't falling down. They were flying upwards. They were being spit from the ground and racing towards the clouds.

"Apple, we need to get goin" Camilla rushed down the steps of the porch. Apple was ready. Before she could even register the urgency in Camilla she had set her plate to the side and stood to follow Camilla down the driveway. Moments later Abigail burst from the house and hopped around in a feverish dance, chanting in a schoolyard rhythm:

Apple, Apple, all alone. accidental Apple a far ways from home.

Abigail, Abigail stayin' at home. She doesn't need no one comin' round.

Specially not Miss June!

She emphasized the last line and hurled the words at Camilla and Apple's backs. "I'm so sorry about this." Camilla muttered, wondering even as she spoke the words why she was apologizing for the child. Abigail was not her child.

Chapter 20

Bent Branch Falls 1968

Enamored with infinity and desiring desperately to feel the contour of its edges, the prophet-scientists began searching for a way to exit the space-time continuum, they began searching for a tear in its fabric. But they didn't consider that death was constantly ripping holes in the fabric, creating portals for those that it claims right in front of their eyes. The dead remain motionless while the world continues to move around them. Everything else ticks along, moving through time and space while the dead stiffen, inuring themselves to total stillness. The answer that the prophet-scientists were looking for is something that their sense of mortality urged them to turn away from. The answer is grotesque so they refused to find it. But if it is true that the dead slip through a tear in the space-time continuum, gaining entrance to other dimensions, then it is possible that our Mary-Frances and the possum are space-time travelers. The dead could simply be dwelling in a different dimension, one that doesn't require bodies; quite possibly a heaven without judgement.

When Mary-Frances opened the front door, like the myopic eye of her crouching house, and Elias was standing there she didn't recognize him as one of her relatives. At this point they had never met, to Mary-Frances Elias was a stranger. Elias regretted letting this be his first trip to Bent Branch Falls since his brother had moved away four years ago. After Curtis left the family farm the whole thing fell into a stubborn inertia, one that somehow made broken fences both impassable and irreparable. After driving distractedly through the darkness, Elias felt exposed in the light of the doorway. The mechanics of human interaction evaded him. He struggled to stay present behind his face.

"Can I help ya?" Mary-Frances was already weary of him, though she didn't know why.

"Yea, is Curtis somewhere 'round here?" Elias grimaced, "Sorry I'm Elias, I'm Curtis's little brother." Mary-Frances stepped back to reassess Elias. Her eyes traveled from his wide-brimmed hat, the one that he had laced through with his favorite bird feathers, down over his untucked flannel shirt and dungarees to his heavy, worn out work boots. Abigail appeared at her mother's side, excited into curiosity by the strange visitor.

"Oh is that yer daughter there? She's a pretty one."

Mary-Frances looked directly at Abigail as she responded, "yea, well pretty's fer dolls and flowers," then turned back to Elias, "It's nice to finally meet you Elias. Curtis is in his garage at the end of the driveway if you want to go say hi to him." She pointed over his shoulder then closed the door.

Elias turned and thudded down the wooden steps of the porch, walking into the aperture of light that the undraped front window opened up for him in the darkness. It couldn't have been too late, around six in the evening, but it was winter; the time of year when the sun tilts through an apathetic course, slinging low across the horizon and dipping below it before evening can even get started. This time yesterday, just as the grey dusk crystallized into complete darkness over Yancey County, Eudora Kennedy's feet hung in tense sickles four inches above the carpeted floor of her bedroom and below her thrashing hips. As her heart churned into the static honey of death, the rest of her body was permitted to go limp. She hung herself from the highest rafter in the bedroom, a thick oak beam that runs across the ceiling just below the roof's peak.

This is how Elias found her: motionless and big headed. The skin surrounding the rope was a feverish color and the stricture ran angry veins of magenta up and down her neck. Her bedroom slippers had dropped off of her feet at the initial jolt and lay at odd angles below her suspended body. At the sight of her Elias backed through the bedroom door and closed it quietly, as though the gruesome scene was a sleeping child that he didn't want to wake. Eudora's suicide did not surprise him, and this made him feel even worse about it. But it wasn't his fault that despair resided on the Kennedy farm, as entitled as a mean barn cat. Failure and despair were laced through the very Earth that they had dug into to lay the foundation of their home, like a curse. Of course Eudora Kennedy killed herself.

Waylon didn't come home that night and Elias sat waiting for him. He didn't think to call anyone for help now, because it was not something he had ever done before. Much of the inexplicable strangeness that enveloped Elias's life stemmed from a lack of ordinary things. Phones and friends. Calendars. He didn't understand the full utility of ambulances, that they were not just for people who were still alive. He sat by the window and watched the night fall down on him. In her undisturbed bedroom Eudora couldn't help but let darkness congeal around her, it was thick now, a viscous ink that could usher her out of the life that had killed her. Elias stood to get himself a glass of water and let his thoughts wander for the first time, towards the possibility of leaving the farm for good. He dreamed of folding it up on itself, like a big piece of paper with something unsettling drawn at its center. Maybe he could tuck the ragged edges into smooth seams; an origami bird ready to fly away with no intention of returning. But first he would have to find a way to move her, his mother's stony body. A gradual anxiety crept into his chest, a feeling that she was waiting on him impatiently.

The hours passed, their weight accumulating on Elias's eyelids, and still Waylon did not appear. Elias stayed at his post in front of the window, wanting to protect his father from stumbling into the scene of Eudora's death unprepared. Maybe Elias knew well enough that Waylon deserved no such consideration, but this act of waiting was all he could conceive of doing. Any sadness that Waylon felt would only serve to sour his blood until it was nothing but a raw, pulmonary anger that would rain down on Elias, but Elias didn't care about that anymore. Eventually he couldn't stop himself from slipping into a somniatic ravine, a deep well of sleep. He didn't wake up until the next day had nearly come and gone.

Before opening his eyes he sat listening. Maybe he would hear Waylon's footsteps or even better yet, those of his mama. But the nightmare couldn't be dispelled by stepping back into consciousness, it only hardened into truth. This is when Elias decided to find Curtis. He drove to Bent Branch Falls in Waylon's truck, the thing was hemorrhaging oil the whole way, leaving a slick mirage behind its unsure path. The edge of the little town was marked by a standard issue highway sign, green with white lettering: Bent Branch Falls Population: 1,764.

There was one open business along the main road so Elias went into it. On that night inside of Harper's Grocery, Cora stood at the counter with a crossword puzzle set in front of her. The unmarked squares stared up at her. The clues listed down the side of the page langoring in the thoughtless vacuum of her gaze. It had been one week since she caught Beau cheating on her with Jolene and the image was engraved in her mind, it was all she could see. It would have to be eroded away by time, she needed the floodwater of tears without their accompanying misery. Cora was grateful when Elias entered the store, glad to be rescued from her own thoughts.

"Hi, what can I do for ya?" The fluorescent lights buzzed out the soundscape over which Elias's uneven footsteps added a percussive line. Stuck amidst the confrontation between his inner-torpor and the situation's demand for interaction he lurched towards the counter. Cora inhaled and pushed her crossword puzzle to the side. Of course some strange man would come rumbling into Bent Branch Falls on a night like this. She reached underneath the counter and rested her right hand on the barrel of the gun they kept stashed there, trying to derive some sort of comfort from its cold metal.

"Hi, what do you wan' round here?" Elias stopped short, surprised at the harshness of the woman's tone.

"I'm sorry, I didn' mean to frighten you. I'm looking for Curtis Kennedy? He's my brother. There's been a death in the family and I need him to come quick. I was hopin' you could direct me to his place." Cora gave him a long look then decided that if the man was any sort of trouble it was probably something that Curtis had brought upon himself anyways.

"The Kennedy place? Yer gonna head up the road a ways an' when you see a mechanic's garage turn right into their driveway. The sign's bright red, you cain't miss it."

"Thank ya. Thanks fer all yer help." Elias turned on his heel and exited quickly, leaving the queer dischord of his presence hanging thickly in the store. Cora narrowed her eyes as though zeroing in on a target that was taped to his retreating back. Beau's unfaithfulness had let loose an anger inside of her that seemed willing to aim itself at anything. The whole world was in her crosshairs. While once she may have discerned the affliction emanating from Elias and felt bad for him, she now just felt annoyed at his strangeness.

Elias clunked through the gears clumsily as he drove away from Harper's Grocery and towards his brother's house. He hadn't realized how worn his nerves were until being confronted by human interaction. The woman behind the counter clearly thought the worst of him. Over the dark road he flew, as though driving upon the thin tongue of hell. When he came to Curtis's garage he didn't notice that the light inside of it was still on and he drove past it, towards the tired looking house at the end of the driveway. After talking to Mary-Frances, he left the porch of that little house wondering if the whole world had made some leap of evolution without him. The people of Bent Branch Falls were treating him as though he were terrifyingly alien.

Elias walked through the garage's front door, just like a customer would. His senses adjusted to the dank air but did not perceive Curtis among the wreckage of half-fixed cars. On the broad rough table that served as a desk sat a concierge bell, it gave off an anemic ring when Elias touched the little button on top of it. Curtis emerged from the dust, streaking grease across a rag that was once white but now colored by oily streaks of brown and black, momentos of its years spent in the garage. Elias's familiar face jolted Curtis out of his preoccupation and stiffened his posture with attentiveness.

"Elias. What're you doin' here man? Ya could've given me a heads up or somethin'"

"Hey Curtis. Nice little setup ya got here."

"Yea, still workin' the kinks out of it but it's gettin' there. Should work out alright fer me. How ya been? How's things on the farm?" During Elias's pause Curtis's face drew downwards, falling towards the recognition that something horrible had happened. Elias shifted his weight, immune to the onset of worry in his brother after having been sunken into a steel-nerved languor himself for the past day and a half.

"Not good." He announced. Though the impact of his announcement had already been sucked from the statement itself. "Ma's dead. She hung herself."

Curtis was not surprised. Of course Eudora Kennedy killed herself. For the sake of politeness he emitted a shocked sounding "Seriously?" Elias saw through his brother's attempt at normalcy but appreciated it nonetheless.

"Well, yea. Ya know, Pa's not been any better since ya left so…" He shrugged the rest of the statement into a vague conclusion. Of course Curtis knew, he understood perfectly.

"So, when did it happen?"

"Just now. I mean ya know, last night but it's still happenin'."

"What do ya mean by that? It's still happenin? Elias, our mama's dead right, thas what's yer tellin' me?" Shock without pretense. Curtis was so stupefied he was questioning his own assumptions about where the line between life and death lay.

"I mean yea- she's dead." Elias stopped short, wide eyed, chewing on his bottom lip. "I need yer help. She's still hangin'. Pa hasn't been home all week, ain't nobody around to help me pull her down. I cain't do it alone." The damn broke, Elias began sobbing. Gasps and tears that involved every fiber of everything in his chest. Heart and lungs. His mother's whole life was now turning into memory.

Curtis pulled him into an awkward embrace, patted his back. Still numb to the news, his first reaction was to wonder what he had done to deserve a week like this- first his garage was broken into, and now this. As Curtis climbed into the truck

Elias released the brake, it lurched forward just enough to slam the door shut behind Curtis. listening to the engine strut haphazardly through its combustion, Curtis sighed, "God Pa's kept this thing in awful shape."

They eased down the rutted out driveway and Elias swung the truck around as Curtis ran inside to tell Mary-Frances that he needed to make the trip back to his family's farm. Regret at her initial reaction to Elias spread through her as Mary-Frances walked up to the driver's side window of the beat up truck to offer her condolences.

"Hi Elias, I'm Mary-Frances." She wished she would have said this to him ten minutes ago when he'd knocked on her door. It's strange how other people's misery can so easily elicit alarm rather than empathy. Elias offered her his hand at an awkward angle through the rolled down window.

"I'm so sorry to hear about your Ma. You take care now, I'll be thinkin' of you an' Curtis," and Mary-Frances turned and retreated back into the house. Elias revved the sputtering engine and bumped down the driveway. When Curtis left Yancey County four years ago and that crippled dog was chasing him, dragging the dead parts of itself up the dirt road, he had felt bad for the creature. Now the disaffection and pity that held the creature at arm's length was retracting and Curtis could see the dog in a different light; he fell into pace next to it and they ran side by side. He and the dog were not so different, with their willingness to run when there was no real possibility of escape.

Chapter 21

Bent Branch Falls, 1974

The season called for wetness and the clouds answered. All week the rain came down. Soon Cora felt as though the drops were passing through her skin, churning her insides into a puddle of mud and bone. Today she would rather be inside her grocery store, counting the backstock and making change, but she couldn't let a week pass without paying Tallulah a visit. So she was driving the Plymouth up the perilously rutted out roads in the middle of the downpour to see her friend. The car moved forward and the windshield wipers waved their frantic arms back and forth across the windshield. At this point, many of the abused oak trees had dropped some of their new leaves and they papered the ground with their small and desperate handprints. With the untimely ripping from their branches they wouldn't live long enough to feel autumn's cool release. They wouldn't get the chance to flutter on the wind waving goodbye.

Visiting Tallulah wasn't something Cora did out of pity like everyone else wanted to believe. Tallulah had always been one of the most interesting people that Cora knew and since becoming nearly immobile, her mind had sharpened and hardened in so many ways that her body wasn't able to. Cora twisted the radio dial but the signal seemed to be drowning in the rain like everything else. Static drops shredded John Denver's voice into an unreliable warble. Cora had her own thoughts on Tallulah's particular brand of strangeness: living apart from everyone else, removed from their opinions, had let Tallulah cultivate a world-view that was wholly unique and completely unaware of its own remarkableness. Alone, we take up the form of our own minds.

The slice of hawberry pie that Cora was taking to Tallulah, as always, jumped on the seat with every gully that the car splashed through. Sitting on a fence post up ahead a crow, confused, maybe senile, sat in the downpour unsheltered. Its body remained motionless while its eyes followed Cora's progress up the road. Glancing in the rearview mirror, Cora ran her hand over her hair, smoothing down the halo of flyaways that sprung up on humid days. She caught the crow's eye in the mirror, its penetrating patience was odd amidst the raucous storm.

While most people in Bent Branch Falls had forgotten Tallulah's existence altogether, those who were close enough to Cora to know about their weekly visits seemed to have dismissed Cora's motives for remaining friends with her as pity. Perhaps they did this to veil their own guilt. Most of them hadn't even tried to take up pity, the most phony form of caring, as a reaction to Tallulah. It was as though Paul was the only person who ever lived in that trailer.

The front door opened as Cora climbed out of the car and Tallulah's hand, like a small white dove, flapped about momentarily in the threshold. By the time Cora stomped onto the welcome mat and bent down to pull off her muddy hiking boots, Tallulah was settled back into her armchair. Her cereal bowl with the strange nuclear-orange sludge pooled at the bottom sat on the side table next to her chair.

"Hi Cora, how have you been?" Without waiting for an answer Tallulah continued on, "I have a question for ya, do ya'll sell frozen peas down at Harper's?"

"Hi Tallulah, we sure do, why're ya askin'?" Cora doubted that Tallulah was planning on eating them herself, maybe she was asking for her boys.

"Tell me then, why are they all the same size? How do they make the peas so perfectly uniform?"

"I haven't the faintest idea. What made you wonder about frozen peas?" Cora often fielded Tallulah's strange questions about food products. She would never understand that Cora's expertise lay only in selling the food, not how it was made, grown or packaged.

"Oh who knows where these thoughts of mine come from? Well actually, it's likely the majority of them come from the television. But it does seem to me that this country has a problem with distinguishing what's supposed to be natural and what should be synthetic. I would be frightened to learn how they take a pea, something that grows on the vine, and standardize it until it's just as uniform as boiled candy. Doesn't it bother you? This is why I stick to tang. If I wanted pulp I'd drink natural orange juice, but I don't, so I drink my tang. It's delicious and it's completely manufactured. You wouldn't catch me dead with pulp free orange juice- it's an abomination. Oranges have pulp, when you remove it you are manipulating nature's creation. It's a pack of lies. We live in a society where people happily consume lies, Cora. That's why peas are on my mind I suppose."

"Ah. Well darlin', at least canned beans come in different lengths, huh? I can't restore sanity to this world, but I can point out some places where it's hidin' fer ya if ya ever need. How're the boys doin'?"

"They look fine, jest like they always do. The real question is what are they doin'? Won't tell their ma a dang thing about their days when I ask, but maybe that's for the better." Tallulah raised her voice as she said this for Tucker's benefit. He stopped in the hallway between his bedroom and the bathroom. He hooked his thumbs in the waistband of his jeans and paused, listening for Cora's response.

Cora agreed, judging by the many rumors, it was for the better that Tallulah didn't know what her boys got up to. "I wouldn' worry too much about those boys. Here I brought ya some pie."

Cora set the seran wrapped piece of pie next to Tallulah's cereal bowl. Tallulah said nothing but her hand strayed to the spot of the side table where the crude wood showed through the polish and resumed its scratching. Flecks of blood had settled into the wood's grain, marking the days that Tallulah had spent giving herself over to this room, staining it with her nervous habits. At times it would seem that her damaged nerves were wired into the walls of the place, coming alive in burning gasps at the flip of a light switch, her bones groaning and settling into the foundation itself.

"Really, the talk of the town right now is Curtis." Cora reassured Tallulah.

"Poor man, I know how it hurts to lose your love. I mean, Paul's not dead but sometimes I think it would be easier if he was. At least death ain't a choice. But, Paul made a choice."

Tucker's heart sank. He hated his pa for leaving just as much as he hated his ma for talking that way. He reached for the bathroom door and pulled it shut, assuming that the women would go on talking freely if they thought he couldn't hear them.

"Paul made a terrible choice," Cora sighed, "but the problem about Curtis is he's going crazy with grief. His is a sadness that's about as flashy as a burning rose. Almost unnatural."

It was true, Curtis was self immolating in his hysteria. His despair was louder than most- a feeling that sucked the oxygen from every room he entered.

"The other day I overhead some a the men sayin' that he's gone and lost track of all the bets that were placed on some basketball game and now he cain't pay out fair and square. I dunno what's gonna happen to poor Curtis but it would seem he's gone and dug himself into a deep hole."

Tucker opened the bathroom door noisily and turned back down the hall. He tossed his head to the side, shaking his mop of blond hair out of his eyes, and went into Taylor's room.

"Hey, come outside with me real quick, I got somethin' to tell ya. I got an idea."

Taylor raised his eyes from the comic book in his hands, set it on the floor and stood to follow Tucker outside. The comic book lay face down and tented at its spine, its cover featured giant man-eating flies lifting their victims into the sky. It's title, *Tomb of Terror, was* spelled out in large yellow letters. The compound eyes of the giant flies were trained on the brother's heels as they left the room and walked out the back door.

"Cora's in there talkin' to ma. But I jest overheard her sayin' that Curtis lost track of all the bets he's been takin' in. Which means-"

"A whole pot of unclaimed money." Taylor cut in.

"Yup."

"How're we gonna get our hands on it though? Remember what happened last time we tried to take stuff from Curtis? Do you think he still remembers?"

"Yea, he probably still remembers, but it's different now. Ya know his wife died recently right?"

"Mmmhmm."

"Well Cora's in there sayin' that the old man's gone off his rocker since. It ain't the same Curtis anymore. He's wide open. 'Sides it ain't all his money, an' someone's gonna end up makin' off with more than their fair share. Might as well be us."

Taylor ran his tongue over his teeth, "We should tell Travis soon as he's back, see what he thinks."

"Yea. Where's he gone off to anyways?"

"I think he's off chasin' Mary Ellen." Taylor rolled his eyes up at the tall dark pines.

"She don' want nothin' to do with him." Tucker laughed.

Inside Cora's gaze had strayed to the high school diploma that hung on Tallulah's living room wall. Caville Highschool, Class of '54. Tallulah's mom, Jane, had worked at the same bank that Tallulah was eventually employed by and was able to drive her into town so that she could attend public school all the way through high school. Bent Branch Fall's local school house could only educate kids through the eighth grade. If they didn't enroll in a high school in a different town, the children of Bent Branch Falls were left to cobble together an education through homeschooling, or more commonly, the lessons handed down by their parents who recruited them to work at the family businesses as soon as they were old enough. Most people raised in Bent Branch Falls were destined to become farmers, grocers or moonshiners, occupations that were not learned from textbooks. Tallulah followed Cora's gaze to the diploma, sitting in its dusty frame, "Seems like a million years ago, doesn't it."

A million miles away from Caville Highschool was where the time-distance contraption appears to have dropped Tallulah. Her life, once the colors of lipgloss and fireworks, had ashed into a single room existence. Despite their life long friendship, she and Cora's lives had not paralleled each other, their trajectories only crossed as Cora scoured a comfortable life from the hills and Tallulah fell from one. At one time the waterfalls from which the town of Bent Branch Falls got its name were used to execute the prisoners taken by the Cherokee natives that originally inhabited the land. At the bottom of the deep pools that catch the crushing falls, the prisoners were suffocated by their executioner. The water punished them, cleansed them, ushered them to their graves. Tallulah's fate was not dissimilar to those of the prisoners at the bottom of Bent Branch Falls, pushed from a precarious ledge by Paul's two hands and then ravaged by elements lying in wait for her.

"Sure does. Lucky one of us got to go to public school. If it wasn't for you being my friend I never would have met anyone outside of Bent Branch Falls. I probably wouldn't have met Beau. Remember that sock hop? Who'd you go with? It was a Steve or somethin'".

"Yep. Steve Heagle. Should a stayed with him."

"Oh come on, Steve was a jerk. Remember how he almost let ya drown on that one fishin' trip? He got you drunk an' convinced you ta go swimmin' with him. Had Beau not been there you would a drowned in the pools of Bent Branch Falls."

"Yea lucky me, now I get to sit here and worry about peas."

"You did lotsa stuff besides that. Ya still could too. I could take you somewhere if you'd ever leave."

"Don' know if I could fit through the door at this point." Tallulah laughed, but she might have been right. Maybe she laughed because she was right.

"Alright darlin', well I'm going ta get goin'. Got lotsa stuff to do at the store."

"OK, thanks fer stoppin' by Cora. And thanks for the pie."

Cora left the house and spotted two of Tallulah's sons standing at the edge of the yard. By their outward appearance they had grown into men, but as far as Cora could tell they were still young boys. Tucker raised his hand to wave at Cora while Taylor mindlessly tossed a rock up and down catching and throwing it with his right hand. Cora got into her car as he pivoted, hurling the rock high into the tangled branches of the forest's trees. A cardinal let out a dissatisfied squall and flashed red across the open sky, its whole body a blaze of motion.

Tallulah hoisted herself to her feet and her bones groaned in chorus with the pinewood floor. From the window she could see the plymouth's tail lights like two eyes peering at her through the mist. She closed the curtains against its penetrating gaze. She went into the kitchen. The kitchen was more the boy's place than hers anymore, another bit of displacement that separated her from her former life. She used to cook. All of the cabinets stood open to some degree and she could see them, the bowls and dishes that she once used in rotation, depending on what type of food she was making. She would serve beans and rice out of deep bowls, layer meat loaf on mashed potatoes at the center of wide plates. But she had lost her appetite for all that now. She opened the chest freezer where stacks of frozen pie rose like stalagmites from cavernous depths. She placed the newest slice on top of a column made of other slices just like it and let the freezer lid fall and seal shut.

Chapter 22

Harlem NYC 1969

A person is made of the wind in their sails, the forces filling them out. Though we imagine ourselves free, carving wide circles in the sky, the truth is that many of us are more like canaries, confined to one heroic act- one collapsing coal mine. But as Camilla June watched her lover, Reggie, die in his own coal mine she resolved to fly away from Harlem. Like so many people before her, Camilla June would end up in Bent Branch Falls after searching for an escape from her present reality. Camilla June's journey began with an ending, one that was drawing in around her as she sat under a night sky punctured by fireworks. The decorative fire shot out of its bright, papery cannon to live out its single moment; burning off its impurities then flashing out of existence before fading to grey and raining its ashes over Independence Day.

On July fourth of 1969, there was only one more thing that Camilla knew she could be sure of: by the morning everything that made Independence day a little bit better than all the others would be burned up. And since this was East Harlem, what had been burned to a pile of uselessness would be left in the streets; devoured by rain, bit by bit. The thought delighted her. But as she gazed from her balcony onto the chaos that ruled the neighborhood, her pride turned in on itself and fizzled out in the dregs of the beer she was drinking. Her fingers tapped on the side of the red solo cup in rhythm with the syllables as she yelled "Reggie!"

She watched as Mrs. Rodriguez locked up her flower shop across the street, her shadow recognizable by the soft droop in her spine that began between her shoulder blades and climbed, with an intensifying curve, to the base of her skull. It had the effect of putting her head at a forward angle, and because of this, whenever she turned to greet people as they entered her shop, it seemed as though she was a bright, open sunflower turning to sun her face in the momentary radiance of the open door. *Girasoles* is what we call them, she would inform Camilla seriously as she trimmed the ends of her heavy bouquets.

Lately Camilla had gotten into the lonely woman's habit of stopping by the businesses in the neighborhood to chat a little bit too long with the clerks who ran them. Mrs. Rodriguez's store was her favorite. The floral weight of the air inside always calmed Camilla, and Mrs. Rodriguez didn't seem to mind her constant presence despite her lack of purchases. Mrs. Rodriguez's dexterity was concentrated in the tips of her fingers. While she and Camilla talked she would shuffle painfully amongst the display stands crowding the tiny store while she arranged roses and lilies, fanning out sprigs of baby's breath and branches of myrtle among their velvet petals.

Mrs. Rodriguez had a way of looking straight down into you, like she was reading tea leaves at the bottom of your eyes, and she was always too honest about what she saw there. While Camilla sat on her balcony she remembered the way Mrs.

Rodriguez had pointed out her own unhappiness to her the day before.

"Camilla, you get yourself a good man."

"I got a man, Mrs. Rodriguez. You seen us together- Reggie?"
"But is he good to you? You don't seem that happy."
"He's good enough for now, I suppose."
The conversation had trickled into a silent drought. Camilla was too worn down to jump to Reggie's defense like she once would have. Reggie was using heroin again. Camilla knew it. Everyone knew it. The air in their self-made mine was growing noxious, and the biggest city in the country seemed to be shrinking around her throat, threatening to strangle her. Mrs. Rodriguez let herself drift into song, a song that stretched its disconsolate melodies over words like *amor* and *la tristeza*. The tune sewed rough sutures through Camilla's heart, like hearing someone let out a sigh heavy with pain that you know yourself.

Camilla didn't expect him to respond but she tried one more time anyways "Re-ggie!" But there was no Reggie inside of their apartment- just the crumpled ridgeline of the body that usually houses Reggie. Like one of those mountain ridges named after Native American chiefs who lay down to sleep and never wake back up. That was her Reggie now- drenched in distance and fog; a bit of history that should be photographed and written about in books. At least that way the world could know him how he was before he turned to stone. How he was before he rocked up his insides, only leaving a couple of open veins for the rest of the world to trickle in through.

Camilla knew from browsing through the bargain books down at the Doubleday Bookshop, that the short and long of history is that people can be horrible to one another. But living in terror- under all that pressure can create diamonds too. In Harlem it created people who fed one another; free breakfast and new ideas. People who made a whole movement out of caring for one another properly in the face of others' hatred. And since the rest of New York neglected the neighborhood, the blazing white, summer sidewalks had begun to crack as the tree roots that they smothered grew stronger, the shadows cast by the trees that they nourished grew darker.

"You can't separate peace from freedom because no one can be at peace unless he has his freedom." Louis would say at the beginning of each meeting from behind a veil of smoke that unfurled from the tip of his hand rolled cigarette. And once everyone had made some sign of agreement, they could truly begin. The chairs that everyone sat on during the Black Panther Community Meetings were made from a cold plastic that never seemed to warm beneath the spread of Camilla's thighs. She knew somebody had stolen them from a dumpster behind an Upper East Side school because the men would speak so boldly about details like this that you might end up with the idea that the revolution was going to be extracted, piece by piece, from garbage cans. Camilla really didn't understand why they were debating the merits and methods of self-determination from the seats of salvaged chairs, but it seemed that there were a lot of things going on around the center that she didn't quite under-stand, so she kept her mouth shut.

"OK, next order of business then. The breakfast program. How's that been goin'? Hey Camilla you got the inventory for that?"

Camilla jolted out of her day dreams at the sound of her name. "What? Oh yea the inventory" She fumbled through her messenger bag until she found the list of foods that were still in the kitchen and amounts that were left of them. She held the piece of paper out to Louis who looked past it, leaving her hand hanging stupidly in the air.

"Just tell me what we're short on and I'll get it for you."

"Oh, OK. We're short on juice. We could use some cartons of eggs to get us through the week. Other than that, we're pretty well stocked."

"Alright. Thank you Camilla. Next item on the..."

Relieved, Camilla retreated back into her own thoughts. She hated saying anything during those meetings, she was always afraid of making a mistake. She liked that the revolution was feeding people, she liked serving up breakfast to hungry kids in the mornings, but she wasn't like the other members who needed to rationalize each action with big ideas. Camilla was like most people in Harlem, just trying to get along and helping out when she could. So, while Louis and Reggie and the other men running the chapter expounded on ideas about peace and freedom and the mechanics of power, Camilla tried her hardest to get comfortable in her chair and avoid being a distraction.

The way Camilla saw it, no one would ever fix Harlem because Harlem has a way of fixing itself. And what can't be fixed waits patiently for a rain whose cleanliness can be believed in; for it to wash away all the blood still gushing from the wounded past. But it's hard to know if anything will ever fix the people who carry those wounds. Like Reggie- pulping his heart with drugs. Reggie who seemed to swell with the setting sun each evening, it's gold becoming trapped under his skin and in the shine of his hair. At times, Camilla felt that she was merely a sliver of light, a twinkle held captive in the iris of his eyes. And that feeling became a soft folding in on herself, a collapse into depths that she wished didn't exist inside of her.

In the tepid manner that most young women, new to the multiplying complications of their bodies and hearts possess, the second that Camilla met Reggie she tried to convince herself that she did not like him. The easy way that he carved his way up the street, a low-slung saxophone note, made her feel edgy. She wanted him to trip. She wanted circumstance to require him to acknowledge her- sheepishly, clumsily. But all he ever did was follow his deliberate path up the street, stopping at each front door. He would sell newspapers and talk to everyone about the neighborhood. She languished in her usual place on the front porch, arms curled around the railings like innocuous vines. Sometimes melting like the popsicles she liked to eat, sometimes just looking hazily into the distance, eyes purposefully focused on nothing.

Reggie and his singular intelligence made Camilla's whole life look like a babyish squall. Her mediocre grades despite her voracious reading. Her desire for ice cream and corn dogs, and entire days spent rollerblading through the neighborhood. Once she met Reggie, all these habits that made her grandmother's face break into a wide smile and sent her Mama's eyeballs rolling around in her head, suddenly seemed like the symptoms of true, bone-deep immaturity.

Reggie was only two years older than Camilla and possessed an encyclopedic knowledge of radical politics. He had read *The Communist Manifesto*, he had read *God and State*, and with the unwavering faith of the youngest altar boys at the church Camilla believed that he understood all of what they had to say. He walked like he carried all of the New York Public Library's archives around in his head. No silky swagger or slumping waistband of nylon basketball shorts interfering with his steps. He was all efficient motion and tightly fitted black jeans. And during the hottest months of one particularly restless summer, he became all that Camilla wanted.

When Camilla was a child, her neighborhood was a landscape cratered by virile pitfalls. Fallout from the unspoken methods of making childhood friends and enemies had left the few girls in the neighborhood separate and unwilling to make the effort required to change that. Instead they unquestioningly pursued, with stolkholmish blindness, friendships with the boys.

The only thing that Camilla had ever wanted from them was to be included. To feel the same sense of brotherhood that they floated between themselves, but always, above her head and impossibly out of her reach. The group of kids that she hung out with took to hiding in alleyways chosen for their strategic distance from each of their houses to experiment with homemade explosives. Camilla would deny the urge to flinch away when they went off. She knew that any misstep on her part would never be forgiven. She was the girl, the youngest: the liability. Those boys could cry and tattle and scrape their knees all they wanted, but everyone knew that the second that the girl got hurt, the fun was over. She couldn't help who she was or how everyone thought, but if there was one thing Camilla could help it was the fact that she would never be caught crying.

The explosions that the neighborhood kids could create grew bigger and louder. Each success brought them closer to trouble and they knew it. That's why they finally let Camilla light one. The lighter that they had used all summer was bright red, coveted, and had been stolen from the corner store. They all knew the explosion was going to be a big one and Camilla ran as soon as she lit the fuse. Still, its sound caught her like a wave that topples you onto the beach. And in the ringing silence that followed she realized why the boys had let her light this one. She stood isolated and stunned, staring at her friends as though from the inside of a fish bowl; biting her lips bloody just trying not to cry.

Camilla was stunned into the same sort of inertia when she first met Reggie. But this time the accompanying sense of betrayal was directed towards herself. She had never felt so confused but so sure of anything in her whole life. She was pretty sure that Reggie liked her but was constantly being reminded that he liked his work with the Black Panthers more. She was pretty sure that Reggie stared at her when she wasn't looking, but as soon as she tried to catch his eye his gaze would slide listlessly away. She felt stupid standing there in front of him. She felt like she was nine years old again, stunned and a little sad, love ringing in her ears and drowning out the rest of the world.

So Camilla began volunteering at the Black Panthers Community Center. That way she could be closer to Reggie while still feigning disinterest in him. She made him reach for her. He was like a dying star then, growing brighter and hotter; burning up at an unsustainable rate. He was fierce when talking about political theory and humane when giving out food, or helping the neighbors pay their electricity bills. But Camilla didn't know much about dying stars then. She'd have to learn the hard way about the black holes that follow them.

When something grows and swells quickly it is bound to run up against something else. Like how all of the puddles strung along 126th street become one during rainy weeks. As Camilla and Reggie got to know each other, all of the different currents running through East Harlem grew and converged, creating a river that swept everyone along. It exploded into riots on the streets, cutting through the nights with broken windows and police batons. Camilla and Reggie tumbled against each other like worn out stones, until what surrounded them pushed them together; later dropping them on a bank and curving away- leaving them to dry out side by side.

The sulphuric heat that lingered in the last hours of July 4th had forced the beer-heavy bodies of its celebrants inside. Camilla imagined everyone connected by the frantic pulse of their box fans and the hushed-over words of what couldn't be said out loud: *why are we celebrating the birth of a country that hates us?* But on the other hand, why refuse a perfectly good excuse to cut loose? Why not send up anger in howling displays of sanctioned fire? It seemed better than saving it up until it exploded at the wrong time, getting everyone arrested once again.

At that point, if Reggie had been the same person that Camilla had met long ago he'd have barely been able to tolerate the celebration of the fourth of July. They could agree that symbols of patriotism were symbols of oppression, but everything was a symbol to Reggie. When Camilla collected them and added them all together the only thing she found them to be symbolic of was an angry man ascribing meaning to everything; just to beat back the all-pervasive fear that their lives in East Harlem meant nothing. That they were all just ants dodging the impassive soles of human feet. The ones who stood out might even garner the attention of cops: sadistic little boys with magnifying glasses. It could be that they were all just scurrying around without a plan, going off of instinct and chemical trails.

Still, Camilla loved Reggie true enough to forgive his intellectual armor, his constant dissatisfaction. After all, this is what is required of a radical- to be living on a razor's edge, too aware of everything, too ready to unearth the insidious nature of our lives. Camilla couldn't help thinking that those who truly possessed wisdom passed through life absorbed in its small pleasures. Like Mrs. Rodriguez, singing to her flowers.

When Camilla fell out of love with Reggie she also became disenfranchised from political work. She contemplated her laziness and her happiness. And still, sometimes she wished for the stubbornness she once had, the will to divide everything into good and bad, black and white, because it made things simple;

it was easy to know what to do. But after all her disappointment, so many years of bearing witness to the brief explosions of fireworks, Camilla no longer knew what to do or how to be in love.

Camilla was happy with Reggie for a long time, until she wasn't. The distance between them grew and solidified more each day, the resulting chasm becoming uncrossable. Six months earlier the Black Panthers had been ordered to purge members that weren't following their code of conduct and Louis had shown up unannounced at their apartment.

"Hey Camilla, Reggie around?"

"Yea, let me grab him. Just give me a second." Camilla knew what was coming and already felt embarrassment climbing towards her hairline.

"Reggie get up, Louis is here to see you." Reggie rolled onto his side on the bed to look at her. He heaved his body into a sitting position and pressed his hands against his temples. His head was heavy. The air was heavy. His future rose up in front of him in black waves of tarry heat.

"Alright give me a second." Reggie rubbed his bleary eyes into focus. Camilla sat down on the other side of the bed, picked a book off of the night stand and opened it. She was not going to face Louis and drag some small talk out of the air just to buy Reggie time. He would have to deal with the situation on his own.

"Hey man, I just dropped by to talk to you for a second." Louis's gaze drifted across the living room avoiding Reggie, as he came rumple-faced out of the bedroom.

"Seems like you been using again and some of the party members are real unhappy about it ya know?" Reggie said nothing, just tilted his head and stared down the spectre of accusation.

"Maybe you should take some time to clean up, man. Come back when you're doin' better."

"You kickin' me out then?"

Louis shifted his weight uncomfortably, let a couple of drenched seconds wash up between them.

"So yea? You kicking me out now." The shock of anger that pulsed through Reggie reminded him how to feel something. The grit that rubbed his insides raw, the anger at everything that had pushed him towards radical politics in the first place was stirred up. A sediment swirling in a current of rage.

"Naw man, I'm asking you to be better. Get your shit together. That's all I ever asked from you." Louis turned and slammed out of the apartment. Reggie laid back down on the bed and Camilla burrowed deeper into her book.

That door had remained closed on Reggie for almost half a year and still his mind was stuck in the work that he could no longer do while his body cycled through the addiction that had stopped everything short in the first place. His whole life trembled with the contradiction.

If the Black Panthers had taught her anything, it was that there is something rich, a salted marrow, hidden in sorrow's bones. On that night of meaningless celebration Camilla pulled her answers from the bottom of a solo cup: Reggie could have her heart but she was going to take her life back. With Reggie inside, sleeping away his junk-sickness and herself stuck outside trying to push away her love-sickness, Camilla realized that they had been separate in this way for a long time. Once in a while we get the chance to burn through someone else's atmosphere carrying them back down to Earth. We all get a chance to create the fire and the fallout. But like any good feeling or drug it comes with its own price. Its virtue is diminished by its departure; a come down; an absence left. Before all of that, Reggie's love was as large as the full moon. Round and bright, that's how she would remember her Reggie.

Camilla knew that she had already said goodbye to him, but upon leaving she wondered how long it would take him to notice that she was gone. She packed one bag and shut the door on their life together when he was high so the feeling would come at him slowly. By the time it hit she was on her way out of New York City, with no destination in mind. She boarded a bus heading South and figured she would know when it was time to get off.

Chapter 23

Caville 1974

It was three days ago that Betty Fields began to feel repulsed by the sight of the wallpaper that hung in her living room. The art nouveau flowers pressed heavily against her field of vision, the thick petals like hot-house labia. And the colors, so bold, so matte. In fact, the more she remembered about the last few days of normalcy the more she recalled a rising feeling of discontent at all the domestic trappings that caged her days. Did this sheen of mild nausea actually glaze over those moments as they happened, or was it a feeling that came over her as she revisited them in her memory knowing, as she did now, how things would begin to fall apart?

Now, as the ease that once flowed through her marriage was being washed away by distrust, she had begun to cultivate a resentment for Liam and the home-making routines that had defined her existence as his wife in equal measure. She resented her absurd habit of sucking dust from the curtains with the extendable attachment for her vacuum cleaner. She resented having asked Liam to buy the attachment for her in the first place. In totality, she resented the time she had given to the dull occupation of being Mrs. Liam Fields. Liam clearly hadn't bought into their domestic invention the way she had. But she never had any other choice, it defined the limits of her life. It was true that Betty Fields was angry, maybe angrier than she had ever been, but the rage was tempered by regret. If she could unlearn what her husband had been doing in the hills with Curtis, she would. She'd give anything to return to her former, blissfully ignorant, cake-battered existence.

Mr. Fields could not come to the door right now and Mrs. Liam Fields was not there to answer the door and tell you this. Betty and her family were being pushed into hiding by Liam's indiscretion and the facade of his straight-laced image was crumbling just as quickly as Betty's will to be his sweet-as-pie wife was. Two days ago, three strange men had knocked on their front door asking for Liam. Betty was not completely sure what the men said to her husband but the upshot was Liam breezing up the stairs while announcing to her that she was not to answer the front door for anyone. It seemed that he thought walking past her as he delivered this bit of news could somehow give the statement a casual tone rather than the grave and terrifying one that it quite obviously carried.

"Excuse me? Liam, what did you jest tell me?" Betty was met with silence- the sound of her husband pretending not to hear her. Their daughter, Lainey, sat sprawled in front of a puzzle on the living room floor.

"Lainey go outside and play a while, I need to speak with your father." But then Betty remembered that they weren't safe anymore, "Ya know what, I'm sorry honey stay right there. I need to go get your brother inside."

Betty stood in the threshold of her front door and yelled at the rough-slatted bottom of her son's treehouse. "Chase come inside for a minute!"

Chase popped his head out of the structure, "Ma come on, it's not even lunchtime yet."

"No it's not, it's time to come inside. If you don't like that, then you can ask your daddy why he's been goin' around ruining your outside time."

She let the door slam closed behind her but stood next to it waiting. She needed to see that her son was inside and safe. Chase came through the door bewildered, trying to figure out what he had done to make his mother angry, and sat down next to his little sister to comb through the cardboard puzzle pieces. Betty deadbolted the door, turned to face the stairs then smoothed the skirt of her dress down before walking with a singular focus towards her closed bedroom door. As she entered Liam jumped and slammed the top dresser drawer shut.

"What's goin' on Liam? Why did those men come to our house and what did they say to you?"

"Nothin's going' on Betty. It didn' mean a thing. Don't go worryin' that pretty little head a yours. Those men just needed to talk some business with me."

"And what type a business would that be? Why does this business of yours got you tellin' me that I cain't answer the door to my own house?" Betty's expression was as blankly maniacal as that of a plastic doll's.

"Baby it's nothin'. Nothin' that ain't gonna blow over. Please, jest give me a minute to sort through things and don' make a fuss."

"Liam, this is not about jest you an' I anymore. We have two beautiful children and if you put them in the way of danger I will never forgive you." The plastic cracked and fell away as her face gave in to tears. Tears making round marks on the front of her dress, like punctuation to end the exchange. Her tears sent her running down the stairs, not wanting to be seen with the dark mascara-lined rivulets falling from her eyes, by the man who knew her better than anyone. Now the man she thought she once knew but didn't.

Betty remembered how after that conversation the blooming flowers on the hateful wallpaper began to look more and more like mouths gaping open in laughter. They peeled their lips back in ridiculing gasps, alive with humorless humor. Upstairs Liam plummeted into a cauldron of anger bubbling at his core. Curtis had given him away. Curtis must have given those men his name, probably just forked over his address too. He let the books get away from him and now had no way of paying anyone's bets out honestly, so he sent them to Liam. He opened the dresser drawer again and fumbled six bullets into the spinning chamber of his revolver. He had never shot it before, he had never shot a gun in his life. The Sunday afternoons he spent at Curtis's was just him playing at being tough. The revolver looked good in his briefcase. Their business was supposed to stay in the garage, tucked into the glooming fog of the mountains. But now the mountain had followed him in an uncontrollable rumble to his home in Caville, like a landslide.

It wasn't bad like Liam thought it was, Curtis hadn't given him away. But Curtis hadn't protected him either, he had mindlessly abandoned all caution, and in his fog-brained disregard for himself, he had put Liam in harm's way too. When Tucker, Taylor and Travis arrived at the edge of the Kennedy property, they froze like stick figures in a shadow box, light parted from darkness by their sharpest angles. They watched as Curtis left the garage. The lantern hanging over the door wobbled its salty illumination in an uncertain orb when Curtis slammed it shut. He walked towards his house, intent on pulling some sort of dinner from the mausoleum of an ice box. The latch on the door remained unlocked; slack jawed at Curtis's negligence. The flame of his grief was melting him into a pool of his former self. A wick burning ever deeper into self-destruction.

Travis and Taylor went inside the garage and Tucker circled around the back of it to keep watch. As Travis and Taylor struggled to find the money they knew was hidden in there, their fear rose in phantom waves from their bowels.

"Godddamn it, we gotta hurry up. We get caught in here again an' Curtis is gonna skin us alive."

Travis was crouched down next to the table that Curtis used as a desk. Opening and closing the two drawers in the filing cabinet tucked underneath it over and over again. Panic was a white wall separating his mind from logic. Inside Curtis stood at the kitchen counter, spooning up slimy greens from a baking pan. Abigail was refusing the glass of milk he had poured out for her. Instead of drinking she spun. She spun around the kitchen until the grease in her hair caught a diamond colored light in its slicked down facets. And Curtis watched her spinning away, like a star unmoored from its place in the sky, spinning out in search of a new constellation to join.

Tucker's back absorbed the chill emanating from the cinderblock wall that he leaned against while staring through the Kennedy's living room window. The backlit room stood empty like the set of a cancelled sitcom. For all he could see the facade of the house could be a painted backboard, something you could push over with one finger. Inside the garage Taylor spotted the makeshift safe: the ammo box with a heavy padlock hanging from its latch, cemented resolutely to the floor. *Damn* he muttered under his breath over and over as he examined the setup. Travis stood and began shuffling through the paper and envelopes littering Curtis's desk.

"Hey, Curtis's partner in all this is named Liam, right?"

Tucker looked up from the safe, "yep I think I heard that, seems about right."

"OK, then let's go. We need ta get outta here. You're not gonna get that thing open but maybe this Liam fellow can." He waved an envelope with Liam's name and address scrawled in the left-hand corner in front of him. It sliced through the air, created a new opening for the three brothers to clamber towards. They would grasp onto anything that could make them feel as though they were moving out and away from the trailer. It's emptiness. It's horrible heaviness. They needed to expand the liminal space in which they lived their lives- that dusk in between society and the hideout that their mother had cultivated for herself. With her insistence on a repetition so dull Tallulah was approximating absolute stillness while the world moved by, just outside of her windows.

When they left the garage Curtis watched them lazily through the kitchen window, unperturbed by the intruders. He immediately assumed it was the Gray brothers and this was confirmed by their number, height and the direction they went as they ran back into the unwanting arms of the trees. The brother's decided to head down the mountain to Caville, to find Liam and blackmail him. The slope was slick with the possibility of mistakes, but they were desperate, they were men being pressed into animosity. Fangs ripped from uncut gums. So while it wasn't bad in the way that Liam thought it was bad, the truth didn't make the situation that much better.

Betty resolved to never let anyone call her Mrs. Liam Fields again; not after she had been forced to drive herself and her two children to a motel in Sleyton just because her husband had put their lives on the line playing some demented game, running books like some hobby-mobster. She stared between the two raised ridgelines of her knuckles, hands at ten and two, while she replayed the last conversation she had with Liam in her mind.

"Liam," Betty hissed. "Liam are you out there?"

She was very visible to Liam, standing in the warm oval of light thrown on the cement stoop by the open front door, but since he was hiding in the treehouse like a prepubescent sniper, he was not visible to her. "Yea? I'm up here."

She had laughed then, a short derisive laugh: the first burst of air that hisses through a pressure valve. Liam sunk deeper into his embarrassment. "OK. I guess I'm coming up, then."

Betty bunched the wide skirt of her dress into her left fist and clenched the fabric as she climbed the ladder. She was careful to find solid footing in her low-heeled patent leather pumps before shifting her weight and pushing herself up to the next step. At the top of the climb she launched herself clumsily onto her knees. "Liam," it came out as a grunt while she hoisted herself into a sitting position, grappling with the impossibly undignified circumstances. "Do you know how stupid you look out here?"

"Yep. I sure do. But what exactly do you suggest? You want me to wait for those men to make it to the front door? You should appreciate that I'm trying to protect you here."

"Well maybe you could have protected me by not getting involved with a bunch a criminals in the first place. Ya ever think of that? What's worse is I still don' really know exactly what's going on here and you expect me to jest look the other way? Wait for you to protect me?"

Liam sighed. "Betty I know-"

"You don't seem to know nothin', but I'll help you out and tell ya somethin'. I'll tell you exactly what we're goin' ta do. You're goin' to give me enough money ta take our children out of this mess you've made and to a hotel somewhere far away from here. I'm goin' to protect them by keepin' them out of harm's way rather than leading it to our front door, and when you've fixed things up and gotten out of whatever trouble you're in, we will come back. And I may consider forgetting this ever happened. Ya hear me?"

As she drove Betty was deciding whether or not she would divorce Liam and assessing the likelihood that he would get himself killed. Whatever the next phase of her crumbling life looked like, there would be no gaudy art nouveau wallpaper in sight. There would be no flowers. There would be no empty sitting rooms, no decorative partitions. There would be only solid walls and useful things. Simple logic and clean lines. It surprised Betty, as her initial rage cooled into resolve, that she turned out to be so unattached to her former life. What makes a life anyways? As far as she could tell it was an ether of elements that flew around, capable of reassembling themselves at random. Her, Liam and the kids, their house on Clingman Place, was now an oldsmobile with her children in the back seat. In the midst of her own personal, cataclysmic event she was floating in a reality made of confetti that would soon solidify and take the form of a different life around her once they reached the motel.

Chapter 24

Bent Branch Falls 1969

Camilla June arrived in Bent Branch Falls on foot, her hair wild: a crown of tumbleweed. It was July 7th and her gaze swam through the miasma of green that colored the hills all around her. There was every shade of green in these mountains, a palette so pervasive that it even came to characterize the smells and sounds that hung in the thick air. The birds sang in the key of green. The heat sweated the scent of green from every pore on its corpulent, deep-summer body.

For three days Camilla June had sat on Greyhound buses. At first she passed through big cities frequently, Philadelphia and Baltimore, places that looked almost like New York City, almost like her home. Places that shrunk the people that lived in them as they grew, the iron arms of cranes rearranging the skyline above them. Then the space between the cities grew and the cities themselves shrunk. Eventually the bus passed through towns. In the less developed stretches of the world people get to pretend they are giants. They become famous for their home cooking. They are able to assert claim over the world's best pie or chicken fried steak and post sign boards outside of their diners telling outsiders about their preternatural inheritance. Camilla could feel herself growing too, growing into herself and becoming a spectacle, a roadside attraction in her own right.

As the bus traveled further from the big northern cities, less passengers left and entered it at each station. The remaining ones began to talk to each other but not to Camilla. The hours spent on the bus pulled them closer together at the same rate that they pushed her away. The reflection of her face in the bus window tinted the glass with its caramel color, a burnt sugar pane. Her reflection rode next to her, told her what she needed to know about herself. It was a sweet blur of ancestral history coloring the landscape that she saw as she made her pilgrimage to the South, undoing the miles that her great-grandma Hattie had traveled a hundred years earlier.

At the bigger bus terminal in Winston-Salem a woman ran alongside the bus as it began to pull out of the station. The driver either didn't see her or didn't care. Camilla watched her through the window as her arm jerked through its waving motion ever more desperately and still, the driver kept the bus moving through the parking lot. The rest of the passengers began turning their heads to stare at the running woman. Camilla June hated the thought of calling attention to herself and waited for someone else to speak up. The rest of the passengers began to set their eyes forward on the seat in front of them as though they could pretend themselves out of the collective guilt settling around them. Camilla June sighed and waved her hand in the driver's rear view mirror.

"Excuse me? There's someone trying to get on the bus."

The driver tilted his head back a little and caught sight of the woman in his side mirror. She was still running, now red in the face and beleaguered by frustration. The driver brought the bus to a stop and yanked back the lever to open the doors, the woman clambered breathlessly aboard.

"Sorry 'bout that, didn' see ya there."

"S'alright. I'm on now. The woman flashed a grin that was contoured by one missing tooth. Her suitcase looked like a boulder hanging at the end of her rope-thin arm.

"Ya can jest put that suitcase in an empty seat fer now, an' I'll throw it down in the cargo carrier next time we stop."

"Thank ya kindly." The woman paused to take in a bus load of people making a concerted effort to avoid looking her in the eyes. She caught Camilla's gaze and started walking down the aisle towards her. Her ragged blue jeans slung low across her hips where the bones protruded and her tiny tank top had knots in its straps so that they would stay up on her slender shoulders. Even with the weight of her suitcase threatening to wrestle her to the ground, she swaggered down the aisle like a country music star. Her attention slid over the placid faces of the other passengers; the ones who pretended not to see her. She saw them, each and every one of them.

Camilla pushed her eyebrows together and cast a slanted look over her fellow passengers, emboldened by the woman's obvious distaste for them. The woman sauntered slowly towards Camilla slinging her hips from side to side for all they were worth. Camilla knew before the woman sat down next to her that she was finally going to have someone to talk to. She was some sort of bus stop saint, nearly martyred by the apathy of human kind.

"Scoot over darlin' it seems that both you an' I could use a friend. I'm Angela, call me Angie. Where ya comin' from?"

"I'm Camilla. I'm from Harlem." Angie squinted a little and her eyes went unfocused as she tried to place Harlem.

"It's a part of New York City."

"Oooh. I see." Angie tilted her head back looking impressed, taking in all of Camilla with one long look. Angie saw Camilla's stained canvas tennis shoes, her purple denim cutoff shorts and her baggy yellow t-shirt. "Ya don' look like yer from the big city."

Camilla smiled, "not everyone in the city's all fancy ya know. All types of folks live there."

Angie looked happily surprised to be understood so easily by this stranger from a place so foriegn to her that it might as well be on the other side of the world. She laughed at herself, this time covering her fragmented smile with her hand. They had nearly made it all the way to Caville before Angie asked Camilla where she was headed. Camilla froze up searching for the words to explain herself.

"You don' know, do you?" Angie prodded.

"No, no I don't. I just needed to get away from the city. I just want to be as far away as I can go."

"Huh. I can understand that. Well I think if you're tryin' to get away from everything you're headed in the right direction. If ya keep on this bus past Caville yer gonna find yerself in the middle of a wilderness that could swallow New York City whole. If ya find yerself in Bent Branch Falls see if ya cain't stop by Harper's Grocery. It's a real nice family what runs the place, known em since I was jest a young'un. Tell 'em Angie sent ya, maybe they could help ya out a little."

"OK thanks, maybe I'll do that."

"Oh an' one thing is, jest don' get bit by those panthers or bears they got up there."

Camilla's whole face dropped, her eyes became headlights, shining with terror. Angie cracked up at her expression, letting her triumph roll out in gales of laughter.

"I'm sorry it's a joke, jest a bad joke. Nothin's gonna get ya there in less you go trompin' through its territory. Jest stick to the roads an' you'll be fine."

When Angie stood up to get off the bus in Caville she gave Camilla a quick hug and stone walled her face in a disinterested expression as she once again walked past the people who had refused to help her. In the wake of Angie's certitude Camilla didn't feel so bad about being ignored. In fact she wanted to confront the cold crowd of people, make them talk to her. She would like to make them tell her what in the hell was wrong with them. But Angie was white. Angie had skin that left a little bit of extra room for brazenness, and Camilla did not.

By that evening Camilla was walking into Bent Branch Falls on her own feet. Not chasing after Reggie, not pushed along by Louis. Her two strong thighs were sunlight in liquid motion, pulling her forward just as much as they were pushing the world backwards. It had been five hours since she got off the bus. After they left Caville she worked up the nerve to ask the driver which stop was the closest to Bent Branch Falls.

"Well the closest this bus can bring you is to Wildacres. After Wildacres there's jest not a whole lot out that way."

"Well how far's the walk to Bent Branch Falls from there?"

"Quite a piece up the road. I wouldn' advise it, I'd try to find a ride if I were you." The bus driver took his eyes off the road for long enough to confirm the obvious, "Ya don' have anyone up there to ask fer a ride do ya?"

"I'll be fine. What roads should I take?"

Camilla repeated the directions back to the driver just to be sure that she had them right.

"Yep. that'll get ya there. Move quick an' ya might make it before sundown."

Camilla moved as quickly as she could, passing her blue leather suitcase back and forth between her two hands. She began counting the number of steps she took between each switch just to keep her mind occupied and ther arms evenly worn out. As she walked stones turned into lizards that ran with a mechanical precision just in front of her feet until they stopped and melted into new hiding spots. The heat on the mountain was heavy but not stale. It did not carry the smell of burnt rubber and traffic, or ooze into melting squiggles of tar patch the way that the heat of New York City did. Whenever she found a wide spot in the road with a good view, Camilla sat on her suitcase and took in her surroundings, she had never seen so many trees and plants in her life- so much visible earth.

By the time Camilla June finally saw the town of Bent Branch Falls lining the county highway, she felt as though her throat would crumble away through cracks opened up by the deepest thirst she had ever known. Her tongue was glued to the roof of her mouth. She scanned the signs of each business that she passed, but before she could even read the sign labeling Harper's Grocery the door swung open and a commanding, square jawed woman with a knot of brown hair at the nape of her neck was waving Camilla over. When the woman disappeared with the clap of the slamming door Camilla wondered if she was hallucinating.

Cora bent over in front of the soda cooler and snatched out a cold coke for the sweating stranger walking up the street. She heard the bells over the door tinkle as Camilla entered the store. When Cora straightened up and turned around to greet Camilla, she felt as though she had been caught, like a river trout pulled along on the invisible line of Camilla's steady gaze. Cora paused for a moment with the bottle opener lipped over the top of the coke cap, the rough tool suspended on the fulcrum of its leverage. But then Cora felt herself spread into the quiet moment that Camilla had ushered into the store with her. She let her thoughts unwind in the topaz tones of Camilla's eyes, the easy angles of her full cheeks. Camilla's entrance was a welcome reprieve from the occasional tourists that entered, glancing wildly around the store as though they could take everything in at once, or the traveling salesmen who had time for nothing but their own pitch as they tried to wrest a deflated sense of power from the material world. Camilla's soft-bottomed suitcase made a muffled thud when she set it down on the floor.

"Little hot to be walkin' around all day, isn't it?" Cora held the cold coke out to Camilla.

"It is a little hot, but I'm alright." Camilla replied before taking a long drink from the coke bottle. Camilla lowered herself onto the stool that Cora had pulled around the counter for her, careful to keep her back straight and her eyes alert. If she relaxed she was afraid she would collapse into her bottomless exhaustion and wouldn't be able to get back up.

"Well, what's the story morning glory?" Cora cracked a playful smile, "Ain't no one just wanderin' into this place by accident, 'specially not on foot."

Camilla let out a dry laugh while trying to conjure up the right words to wrap around her unlikely story. She realized how silly she looked without a plan. Since she left Harlem she had been running on pure emotion, building momentum from her desire to get away from everything, but she had never figured out exactly where she was going.

"Yea, I know. It is a strange situation I've gotten myself into. I'm from New York City and I just wanted to get out. I bought a bus ticket for a line headed to North Carolina cuz that's where my great Grandma's from, even after she fled from here she still thought it was the most beautiful place, she always told me so. Along the way I met a woman named Angie who told me about you, and told me that Bent Branch Falls was a good place to be if you wanted to be nowhere. Really I'm just running from a man and the fact that the only love that I've ever had was with him, and I don't want that love no more. So…" Camilla stopped herself short, worried that she'd said too much. "So anyways, I'm Camilla June, nice to meet ya."

"Cora Harper, nice ta meet you too. So this Angie, was she a skinny little thing? Blond hair, bad teeth, a spitball?"

"That's the Angie I met."

Cora threw her head back and laughed, "Ya know her when ya see her. How is Angie been doin' then? Ya get a chance to talk to her much?"

Chapter 25

Bent Branch Falls 1974

Thadeus Harper believed in the value of patience but was beginning to wonder if patience was making a fool out of him. It had been nearly a month since he dropped his impala off at Curtis's garage in Bent Branch Falls. All it needed was a new bumper, so he couldn't imagine what was taking so long. What Thad didn't want to admit to himself, was that his patience stemmed more from his aversion to conflict than anything else; that his cowardly nature wore the virtuous trait like a cheap costume. He had simply never developed a taste for confronting people.

He ran his finger across the telephone number embossed on the plain business card that he had taken from the garage when he dropped the car off. *Curtis's Garage*, the card announced in blocky lettering. The longer the stupid blankness of its design stared at him the more he resented the card for its obvious lack of trying. Leave it to Beau to give him some crap recommendation. Maybe this Curtis fellow *could use a helpin' hand* as Beau had phrased it because he didn't know how to use his own hands to help.

Annamae appeared in the doorway of their living room with her arms crossed over her chest. Even on Sundays, Annamae rose with the sun and dressed herself immediately and without ceremony. She dressed herself in shades of grey and brown, colors that were easy to keep clean. She knew she wasn't pretty and didn't try to circumvent this truth with makeup or delicate clothing. She shifted her weight from one foot to the other. The sharp line of her jawbone paralleled the flat grimace that her mouth was set in as she watched her husband flail around with his habitual infirmity.

"Ya gonna give that garage a call today, or do I have to do it for you?"

"Well, it's Sunday. Maybe I should wait til tomorrow, give the man his day of rest."

"Seems as though he's takin' plenty a rest for himself. He's had the impala fer nearly a month now. I'm plumb tired a drivin' that ol' jeep a yers all over the place."

"I know, I know. I'll take care of it." Annamae snorted and walked past her husband and into the kitchen. Visible tendons sawed up and down around her sharply protruding ankle bone with every careful step that she took. As she measured two cups of water to cook the morning's grits in, she swelled with pride at her relentless dedication to correctness. If only she hadn't fooled herself into believing that Thadeus could learn from her when she decided to marry him, her life could be perfect. She resented the sloppiness of her husband's timing and attention. The date upon which this Curtis character had promised to return their impala was buried ever deeper in the X's marking days gone past on their hanging calendar.

Still in the hallway, facing the rotary telephone mounted over the thinly striped yellow and green wallpaper, Thadeus fed the vicious thoughts that were battling each other in his mind with the raw meat of his indecision. There had to be a good reason that his car wasn't fixed yet, and he really shouldn't place a business call on a Sunday. He could tell Annamae that he had called and no one picked up, but she would detect the lie. She would hold onto it as further proof of his weakness. At the rate that they were going, Thadeus wouldn't even get the relief of dying at the end of his life, he would simply waver from existence, rendered substanceless by his mounting failures. He was becoming a ghost. Thadeus grew more and more transparent under the menace of his wife's disgruntled gaze with each passing day.

Annamae whisked a cup of grits into the boiling water, listening for the whir of the telephone dial. She heard the receiver leave its place on the cradle only to be banged back down a moment later. She added a dash of pepper, one pinch of salt. Soon the day would turn into one more X on her calendar.

"Thad, have you gathered the eggs up yet?" Relieved to be pushed along to his next duty, Thad turned without saying a word and left the house. Outside, the suffocating nature of the day sifted down through Thad's chest, then gathered in a thick silt that lay over his heart. The stranglehold of his marriage cinched more tightly around him. In a moment of detachment he drifted off the course of his chore and sat down at the base of a virginia pine tree. Its needles cut the sun into ribbons that hung off of them: a small celebration. The bark gave off a cool, umbral-edged scent. He loved the tree, he loved the dirt.

He loved Annamae too. When he met her she wasn't disappointed in him. Expressing approval was as close as Anamae ever came to expressing love. Even as a teenager Annamae used predetermined and specific metrics of success to determine what she liked and did not like. She liked usefulness and precision. She liked things with a purpose like hens that lay and dogs that helped run herds. She struggled with human nature, its need for disorderly sparks of joy and sadness, the inconsistency that it allowed as an ordinary part of its ups and downs.

Thad had easily accepted Annamae's rigidity. Ironically, Thad thought of Annamae's disavowal of anything quirky as a manageable quirk itself. They had met at a county fair where Annamae was competing for the Miss Henderson County crown. Her simple features were overwhelmed by the mask of makeup that she sulked behind, but Thad was drawn to the lonely teenager and had approached her to ask if he could buy her a lemonade. Her response- "guess I could use a drink," came with a hasty addition, " to quench my thirst."

He returned with two drinks in his hands and they chose a plastic picnic table to sit down at. Annamae's thin frame sunk into the layered ruffles of her pink dress.

"Ya win the crown?" Thad asked squinting in the midday sun.

"I haven't competed yet but I don't plan on winning."

Thad laughed at the strange statement, "then why compete at all?"

"My ma. She forces me to compete. I keep telling her I'm not that pretty." Annamae shrugged, seemingly unbothered by the admission.

"Yer pretty. Yer real pretty," Thad ventured.

"That's not necessary. I know what I look like and it is not like a beauty queen. I'm just waitin' to move out on my own so I don't have to do this anymore."

Annamae left the table to attend the beauty contest and Thad stayed around to watch. She didn't place at all and as the first, second and third place sashes were being draped around three other contestants a busty woman in the front row let out a wail and flung herself onto the shoulder of a man sitting next to her. The small crowd felt the woman's embarrassment for her, she felt nothing but her own outsized disappointment. When Thad noticed that Annamae was blushing so furiously that the rising color could be seen radiating through her thick makeup, he correctly assumed that the woman was Annamae's mother.

When the competition was over Thad walked Annamae to the winnebago trailer that she and her mother lived in. It was hitched to a rusted out truck.

"Home sweet home." Annamae announced sarcastically as they approached.

"You live here all the time?" Thad asked, confused.

"Well in the trailer, yes. My ma drives us from place to place. We attend every county fair in the East. Went all the way to Minnesota once." She kicked an empty beer bottle out of the way as they approached the trailer.

"Well I'm gonna change and wash this gunk off my face but if you want I'll try to find ya later."

"Yea. I'll be around." Thad replied eagerly.

"K." Annamae banged open the door of the trailer and awkwardly hitched up her layered skirt so that she could climb into it.

For the reason of her fickle childhood, Thadeus's patience, and his aversion to conflict was disproportionately doled out to Anamae. What most people saw as proof of Annamae's cold-heartedness, Thad saw as proof of her unwavering intelligence, replete with air-tight logic. He often wondered aloud how Anamae thought of everything. And she did think of everything, she was exhausting with her everything. Thad sat under the pine tree, momentarily freeing himself from her expectations, remembering that life could contain joy and emotions resistant to being tethered to their utility. For that moment the sun was just the sun, warm and unbroken.

"Thadeus! What in god's name do you think you're doin' lazin around like that? I need the eggs, that's why I asked you to gather the eggs." Anamae's voice broke in exasperation. It felt like a punishment to her: having such an incapable husband to look after. Thadeus's anxiety swarmed in like locusts. The first insectile blots that burrowed into his brain were only omens of the impending doom. Then more arrived, crawling in piled mounds, devouring any sense of well being that he possessed until his mind was blacked out by their dense mass. The rib-boned reprieve that he had created for himself under the pine tree collapsed under the weight of its own illusion. *Why did she hate him? What did he do to deserve a wife that hated him?*

Thadeus jolted into motion despite the rusted-gear sensation that swelled in his chest. His heart banged around like the second hand on a clock that was too dilapidated to keep proper time. He lumbered towards the roost, now impatient with the hens. and pushing them aside roughly before snatching their eggs away. Their clucking sawed at his ears, they sounded like complaints. In his haste he dropped an egg on the ground, the yoke burst and ovaled into a scrutinizing eye. The chickens rushed at the mess to peck it up. It was sickening, the urgency with which they ran forward to devour one of their own. The narrow headed beasts churned into a sea of gluttony at his feet.

"Get back!" Thadeaus yelled. "Get back!" and he started kicking at the chickens, consumed by repulsion. He cleared enough space in the squabbling mass to cover what was left of the egg by kicking dirt over the top of it. The clutch retreated in a dissatisfied huddle; all the hens except for one. She lay on the ground with her beak shoved into the dirt. Her neck rose in a broken pinnacle then angled downwards to where it met her body. Her belabored breathing sent small puffs of dust up on erratic bursts of air. Thadeus stood over her immobilized form. He contemplated cracking her neck back in the other direction to put her out of her misery, but instead turned and retreated back into the farmhouse. Misery loves company.

Before he could even cross the living room Annamae appeared and tersely snatched the bucket of eggs from him. He kept moving forward until he was faced once again by the telephone. The vertical stripes on the wallpaper meandered downwards, the lines wiggling in his blurred vision. The numbers on the phone swelled and shrunk, pulsed with wicked bemusement. He picked up the receiver and dialed his little brother, Beau Harper.

"He-llo" Beau answered in the same way that he had ever since Thadeus could remember. Stretching the first syllable with anticipatory brightness.

In the kitchen Anamae began dropping the eggs carefully into a bowl of water, one by one they sank to the bottom and stood on end, still fresh enough to eat.

"Beau. I'm havin' a bit of a problem over here."

"Oh hey Thad, wha's goin' on?"

"That joker of a mechanic that ya sent me to has had our car for a month now an' I haven' heard a word about it."

"Oh," Beau paused, "Well I s'pose that is a problem. Ya give 'im a call?"

"No. I shouldn' have to. He told me it's be ready two weeks ago." Thad shrunk down into himself. He probably should have called Curtis, it just felt safer to be angry with his little brother.

"Well, I reckon ya ought to. An' Thad, jest somethin' to keep in mind, Curtis lost his wife recently and isn't doin' so good. Don' be too hard on him."

"Oh. OK, I didn' know. Thank ya fer that Beau. I'll see ya soon, OK. Take care." Thad floated happily in the relief that the phone call had brought him. One egg bobbed on the surface of Anamae's bowl of water, something half formed and supernatural keeping it afloat from the inside. Beau returned the phone gently to its hook.

"Annamae, I figured out the problem. That fella, Curtis, jest recently lost his wife. He's probably fallin behind a little cuz he's sad. He's in mournin'" Thad pulled a coffee mug from the cupboard and filled it. Now that that was taken care of, he could sit down and enjoy his breakfast.

Annamae set her spatula down and turned to Thad crossing her arms over her chest, "Ok, but you didn't figure out nothin'. Did ya manage to call him yet?"

"No. I was thinkin' I'd jest wait til tomorrow. It will be Monday then."

"Why is it that this husband a mine can be taken for a ride by every pig-headed loser in the county? Goddamn it Thad, if you cain't get anything done then I guess I'll have to." Annamae tilted the skillet erratically over just one of the two plates that she had set out along the counter top and let all of the eggs heap up on top of each other in an oozing mountain. "Here ya go," she snapped" as she dropped the plate onto the table in front of Thad and walked to the phone. Thad heard her dialing a number with swift jolts of her pointer finger before the house teetered into a tense silence.

"Hello Cu-rtis," The two syllables shattered in her throat. "This is Annamae Harper. My husband, Thadeus Harper, dropped our impala off at your garage over a month ago to have its bumper fixed. It is now two weeks after the date that you told him it would be ready by, an' we still have not heard a single word from you. Please do us the courtesy of callin' us to let us know jest what exactly is goin' on with our car. Thank you so much." The accusatory tone of Anamae's voice fogged the air in the minutes after she slammed down the receiver. Thad sat in front of the mucus yellow mashup that his eggs had become shaking his head.

"There we go." Annamae blazed into the kitchen in a righteous glow. "Anything else I need to do for you today, *Thad?*" She said his name the same way she had said Curtis's name. Thad was terrified at the prospect of hating his wife, but what else was there to feel after years of living with Anamae? He stood up from the table and scraped the mutinous pile of egg off of his plate into the trash. He pulled silence around him like protective armor and left the kitchen without trying to find an excuse.

Chapter 26

Bent Branch Falls 1969

Matter will go where there is none. Need is a chasm that will be filled. During her first minutes in Bent Branch Falls, as Camilla sat in Harper's Grocery talking to Cora, she realized that she was at the whim of everything. It was a peculiar, loose-legged feeling; one whose full implications dangled her haphazardly on its silken line. Leaving home required a fearless deference to gravity. From such heights the omnipresent possibility of falling down is inescapable. And she stood on this ledge wondering if her bravery was a misstep, trying to pin down the difference between leaving and running away.

Cora had sensed Camilla's need in the same way she had sensed her presence the second she arrived in Bent Branch Falls: wordlessly. The way mycelium archives the foot falls of every animal in the woods. Her years of running a grocery store on a mountainside well acquainted with hunger had given Cora the ability to understand the pulse of people. It was the simple inevitability of death that gave all life the courage to move forwards. If not for death, then why scramble to satiate hunger? The forest surrounding Bent Branch Falls occasionally gives way to granite outcroppings, as barren as rib bones picked clean, jutting out of the vivid landscape. Chips of rock occasionally fall from their faces. What can't give nourishment crumbles.

When the small talk between Camilla and Cora was nearing the point of exhaustion, Cora just came out with it, "Camilla, it seems to me that yer goin' ta need a place to stay 'round here. I have a cabin on my property and I could use yer help with a couple a things. You could stay fer a while, see if ya like it. The cabin's not much and needs some work done, but we could make it nice inside a there for you."

"Really? Yes, thank you. That would be wonderful." Camilla could barely believe Cora's immediate kindness and trust; extending an invitation like that would be seen as too risky in the city. Cora drove Camilla to her and Beau's place in their white Pymouth. She arranged a stack of folded blankets on the couch and removed the back cushions.

"You'll have to sleep here for tonight at least, the cabin's all boarded up. We'll have to work on it tomorrow so you can start movin' in." Cora was suddenly impatient to give the forgotten cabin a purpose, to give it new life sheltering a woman who seemed immediately trustworthy to her.

Camilla stood in the unfamiliar living room quietly, exhaustion was dragging at the corner of her eyes and the impossible task of figuring out how to express her gratitude kept her tongue paralyzed. She was unnerved by the intimate paths that her journey towards a new life was taking her, but she couldn't see a way out of depending on others. Doing so would be like asking for a life lived floating above the face of the Earth.

Despite her exhaustion Camilla struggled to drift off to sleep in the strange new environment. A clock sat on the mantelpiece voicing the movement of the night as it stretched its back and stalked slowly past her. The velvet mouth of darkness sucked away layers of reality as though it were a piece of boiled candy. The true nature of things changed shape in its mouth. Camilla wasn't used to a world that could hunch so fully into stillness. The city never let the night be complete. With their human density cities poked holes in the natural order. After all of the time she had spent on the bus, plumbing the depths of single mindedness, making a pure and unswerving effort to avoid thinking about Reggie, her will power collapsed amidst this bone-deep silence. Reggie was there with her. His hands were crawling up her stomach, stopping to weep along the winged curvature of her collarbones. Knowing her. Savoring her.

After stretching her heart along a famished line of thinning love for so long, Camilla could now feel the entire history of her and Reggie's passion convalescing inside of her body. As though the years had wound themselves up inside of her, a distillation of all the scattered moments that they had lived together. Reggie was lying with her, on the couch of a stranger. Reggie breathed through her in soft, undrugged gasps.

"Breakfast for ya dear." Cora stood over Camilla cautiously rubbing her shoulder. The smell of eggs and bacon fattened the air. Camilla felt as though she had only been asleep for one minute and an unsated exhaustion settled heavily on her head. As she stirred, Cora walked back into the kitchen. Beau sat at the table with a full plate and pad of yellow paper in front of him. He hadn't spared a thought for Camilla, he was distracted and dwelling on Cora's insolence. She hadn't asked him about moving Camilla into the cabin. She was a stranger, a colored one. It could bring them trouble. And still, Beau knew that he had no say in the matter. He had relinquished authority over the cabin the day he got caught sleeping with Jolene, he didn't have to be told to see that.

Beau's unjustified anger mixed with a regretful self-aware-
ness. The whole situation pushed him towards the cusp of self-
pity: such a worthless emotion, barely worth feeling. He kept
his head down and continued listing the supplies that he needed
to fix the leak in the roof of the store. Shingles, nails, sealant.
He chafed at the bind he was in, Cora's wifely grasp had vined
around him. And now that the blossoms hung heavy and were
beginning to unfurl their little fists, he was going to pay for his
past mistakes. He went back to pondering the leak in the roof
and realized he would have to find someone other than his wife
to hold the ladder for him.

"Beau, you're gonna have to go ahead an' run the store
without me today. Camilla and I will clean the cabin up so she
can have her own place as soon as possible." She lowered her
voice and intoned the importance of her words with an intense
look "that little girl needs a place to rest."

"Alright, s'all right with me. I s'pose I can fix that leak
tamorrow then."

"Yep, I s'pose you'll do it tamorrow then." Cora pulled a pie
from the icebox and cut it into eight pieces with four, succinct
flicks of her wrist. She pulled its tin foil top back over it and
turned to Beau. "Here ya can take this pie down to the store
too, I'm thinkin' we only have a couple a slices left in the display
case."

"Alright. Jest remind me to stick it in the car when I go."
The foil covered pie cackled in response as Cora set it down on
the kitchen table next to him.

Camilla wandered sleepily to the bathroom, hating that
she would have to make conversation with Cora and Beau. Her
mind lazed in a kittenish fog that refused to be washed away
by the palmfuls of cold water that she splashed onto her face.
In that moment she wished she could follow the water down

the drain; she could travel without consciousness through a pipe that did not present her with any choices. The small bathroom had a window next to the toilet framed by blue and white checkered curtains. On the wall hung a needle point that read *Gone Hunting*. A vase stuffed with fake, yellow roses sat on the back of the toilet. Camilla hated it.

The kitsch was drizzled over the bathroom as thick as maple syrup. Camilla felt she ought to be able to look out of the window and see the cartoon of farm life, a sunlit meadow with a milk cow, two pigs and a rooster, like the pages in coloring books that she filled in as a child, wondering what kind of world she was illustrating. But instead, the view out the window was an impenetrable fortress of foggy green.

Cora heard Camilla's bare feet patting across the floor towards the kitchen and scooped two eggs and some bacon onto a plate for her, then plucked a piece of toast from the oven and balanced it on the plate's edge. The table was already set with butter and hawberry preserves. Beau raised his eyes from the list and looked wearily in Cora's direction.

"Plate's on the table for ya." Cora told Camilla as she entered the kitchen. It was a well established kitchen. With jars labeled for the spices they held and salt and pepper shakers- too many sets accumulated throughout the years, next to the stove top. It reminded her of her mama's kitchen, full of the ephemera collected by a life-long cook. Spoons and spatulas of every size, and ceramic spoon rests. The wood piled up in a wicker basket caught Camilla's eye, yet another indication of how far she'd come from New York City.

"Thank you, smells delicious." Camilla pulled the chair out and sat down. "Morning Beau."

"Good morning Camilla." Then after an awkward pause, "Well ya better eat up. Cora's got quite a day planned fer the two of ya, and take it from me, Cora makes her plans with no room fer negotiatin.'"

Beau finished his statement with a wink, Camilla laughed half-heartedly. Her hunger made it easy for her to push the faint glimmer of marital discord lacing the conversation to the back of her mind. She crunched into the strip of bacon and immediately began spreading her toast thick with butter and jam as she chewed. She gratefully smudged out the sharp-toothed edges of her appetite with the dense, hearty food. Cora watched her appreciatively. A couple bites into her toast Camilla paused, "What sort of jelly is this?"

"Hawberry. Isn't too common around here but it's easy to grow, so my Gramma Bunny started cultivating an orchard of hawberry trees long ago, and I still keep it up. It's actually one of the things I was hopin' you could help out with if ya stay. The trees need tendin' and their berries need to be jellied and baked in ta pies so we can sell it down at the store. It's a lot of work when the season comes aroun' but we'd find a way to pay ya for yer help if yer interested."

"Yea, if you teach me I'm sure I could help out. I've never done anything like it before but I could learn."

Cora was lit up with satisfaction. Camilla seemed to be the perfect salve for the unsolved difficulties plaguing her life. "I'm jest happy you wandered into town Camilla June. I'm thinkin' you're jest what this place needed. Now when yer ready we'll go out an' I'll show you the cabin. The sheets and blankets need to be washed up but there's even a bed an a table in there fer you. We'll jest have to keep our eyes open fer a couch and a chair or two. Maybe a rug to throw on the floor."

Needing to change her clothes, Camilla opened her suitcase and stared down into it. All of its contents seemed wrong. The Camilla that would have worn these clothes, clothes that once hung in her small closet in Harlem, was not the Camilla that would have left. These were clothes with a specific conviction. Bright and unhumble, her old clothes were the colors of metropolitan tenacity. Clothes that said *I'm gonna make you look at me because I know you would rather avoid it.* But here in Bent Branch Falls things were so different. She didn't need anything but her own novelty to cause people to look at her.

Without context, her former self was a passing phase, folded up and shoved into a suitcase. So, it turns out she was susceptible to becoming anything. She allowed her mind to wander to Reggie; what would he be doing, now that he realized she probably wasn't coming home. If he was counting, he would know that they had passed through three nights apart. But how could a feeling of freshly applied loneliness break through the isolating haze of the heroin? What would the feeling even be once it reached him? Camilla wanted to know but she also wanted to stop thinking about it.

When they arrived at the cabin Cora gave Camilla a hammer and showed her how to use its head to wrench the nails out of the wood and pull the boards off of the windows. They started with the windows that sat on either side of the front door, then Cora instructed her to do the same thing to the boards over the door and left her, circling around to the side of the house. When she uncovered the bedroom window, the hole in it was just as jagged as Cora remembered. An accurate imprint of rage.

The edges of the broken window were sharp enough to surgically extricate those feelings that had been long buried, to cut the foriegn object out of her marriage even though time had calloused over it with protective flesh. She smashed the rest of the glass from the window pane with the head of her hammer. The imprint of rage became a blank square to be filled in. She used caulking to secure a square of plywood inside the pane. At least this could keep the cold out until she and Beau could afford a new piece of glass to install.

The two women worked around the house until they met in the back. Camilla was circling her tentative future, peering through the windows as she uncovered them, and into possibility. But the future remained precarious. Thick rooted saplings jutted from the hard packed dirt around the house and reached for its foundation, pulling it towards collapse. Layers of old paint and varnish peeled and oozed. Weeds had seeded in the gutters and poked at the sky. Camilla could see that the future would need a lot of work.

There was a strange feeling at the heart of the cabin, and Camilla could sense it. She could tell that she shouldn't ask too much about the boards over the windows or the way the cabin's rooms seemed to hang inside of a single moment; a flash of the past halted in its tracks and kept away from the light of day. At the center of the single bedroom was an unmade bed. As though someone had just woken up and rushed from the place only a minute ago. A half-full glass of water stood on the nightstand next to two cans of beer. Camilla sloshed their contents across the dirt outside the front door, turning her head away from the pained, mildewed scent that rose up from the mess.

Chapter 27

Bent Branch Falls 1974

Abigail awoke in the humid ether burning off of Curtis. While she was asleep he had pulled the green armchair up to the side of the couch, sitting in the same position that he had during Mary-Frances's last hours alive. He watched the undulating form of Abigail rise and fall with her breath as she slept, and decided that he didn't mind her sleeping there so much anymore. The past seeped into the present. Mary-Frances's blood-soaked cough still rattled in his ears. Abigail's lungs expanded and he could hear that macabre gurgle, the sound of Mary-Frances drowning in the fluids of pneumonia; being carried away by the riotous protests inside of her own body. And finally, for the first time in weeks, he was able to sleep. His head tilted back sharply as he sat at the side of his sleeping daughter, his dying wife.

Abigail was surprised to find her dad sleeping next to her and she hurriedly pushed herself upright. She stood over him, watching the way that gravity kneaded his features, leaving elliptical paw prints in the hollows beneath his cheek and collar bones. His skin had grown tan and loose in the weeks since

Mary-Frances's death. Melancholia hung on him from little hooked claws, dragging him downwards. There it was again, the persistent hunger. Abigail was not sure she could contend with such an implacable force. It felt as though the acid sloshing undiluted could burst out of her stomach and devour her insides until she was hollow, she was sure of it. It was possible this was already happening. Abigail contemplated the option of surrendering to the hunger, but couldn't fathom the length of time that it would take for the acid to steal away with her body altogether. After all, she was still a child. She was impatient.

Brought to the kitchen by her untamed appetite, she stood in the threshold and it dawned on her that the household objects had stopped making sense at some point. The pots and pans, the large wooden ladle, the knobs on the stove, they all had lost the meaning that their utility once ascribed to them over the course of their dormancy. Without Mary-Frances there, everything had lost all reason. Abigail recoiled at the realization then raged forward to challenge it.

As it grew, her anger demanded a physical outlet. She macheted her arm through the dishes piled up on the counter, catching a ceramic bowl on its lip and flipping it to the floor where it broke into uneven thirds. She swept her arm towards a glass, still half full of molding juice, and it toppled. The beveled glass shattered into sharp teardrops on the floor. She yanked open the fridge and began dropping the ceramic baking dishes, still crusted in putrescence, on top of the mess. A piece of glass stabbed into the arch of her foot, grinding its sharp edge deeper with every step she took. She danced through the act of destruction in a gleeful rage, the ruin ricocheting around the kitchen like a perpetual echo.

A metal pie tin fell on its rounded edge, orbiting against the tile floor until its sustained ringing flattened into a shushing noise and Abigail stopped short. Beneath the elongated ringing of the pie tin's wobbling she heard Mary-Frances comforting her. Her pinched breath collapsed into sobs. She was still hungry too. Abigail opened the fridge while tears fell down her face. Once again the only edible thing in there was the last chicken Miss June had brought over. Abigail hated it, she hated the chicken. She took the dish from the shelf and slid to the floor with her back against the cabinets. The dish froze her thighs as she rested it on her lap and tore bite size hunks from the chicken's bones with her fingers and shoved them into her mouth. Her tears fell into the pan and separated from the grease- small inland seas dotting a coagulated landscape. Blood pooled around her right heel, parting around the piece of glass that still sat in the ragged wound.

The womb of sleep delivered Curtis back into the world before he was ready, the light that entered the front window fractured into a kaleidoscopic pattern on the back of his eyelids. The splintered pattern emulated the noises that were coming from the kitchen, but he ignored the commotion, unsure if it existed outside of his mind. There was an ache in his neck after having slept for hours sitting upright in his green armchair. He was caught between the pain urging him to lift his head and his desire to languish in the moments before opening his eyes. He wanted to stretch those seconds into an infinity of annihilation.

If the ever-expanding universe suddenly reversed its course, sucking backwards into absolute density, Curtis would happily crush himself at its center; to be among the first to lose autonomy in the mash. We have seen the way that the growing space between people forces them to differentiate themselves from one another; to define the bounds of their person. Curtis had lost all ambition to continue the project of being himself, now alone. Staring into the fuzzy fibers of the red velvet couch,

Curtis forgot why he had fallen asleep in the chair pulled up to its side like that in the first place. The only memory that lingered from the night before was the haunting feeling that Mary-Frances had been next to him, sleeping at his side.

By the time Curtis opened his eyes the sounds he heard shredding through the air earlier had ceased, maybe he had been imagining it all along. He stood up from the chair, his body reanimating begrudgingly, cracking and popping in protest. His boots, unlaced but still on his feet flopped their tongues out loosely with each step that he took. He staggered towards the front door for a few steps then paused for a moment, staring at his hands. He felt that he had forgotten something and the vague sensation pulled him towards the kitchen, but he stood conjuring a mental picture of the room as it had been when he last saw it. No, he had nothing to do with the kitchen anymore. There wasn't even any coffee left to make, he had run out the week before. He continued walking and passed through the front door and made his way out to the garage.

The cicadas chirped at the late morning sky, churning the air until it rose up in a wall of noise. Their song dug its pincers into Curtis's ears. His feet drug along the muddy driveway in their loose shoes. This was the only direction that he seemed to be capable of finding in the world anymore: that short walk to his garage. He crawled through the journey knowing that once it ended he'd be faced once again with the question of what to do. Who to be. He wished more than anything that he could just curl into the subconscious world between the arms of the chair again.

The garage lazed around under its blanket of dust as Curtis entered. The dust motes milled about the air in an irritated swarm as Curtis shut the door and moved towards his desk, disturbing the atmosphere. Now in the swiveling chair, he pivoted to squint at the cars parked inside the garage. He reached across the desk and turned on the tabletop lamp, spotlighting the cars as though he were about to interrogate them, ask them what they thought they were doing there anyways. The leaden weight of his perpetual headache grew heavier. The fucking cars. Out of the corner of his eye he noticed the red light blinking on his phone. He picked up the receiver to listen to the message and was confronted by the voice of a woman. The woman's voice whipped her undisguised anger at him. Before Curtis was even sure what she was talking about, he was infuriated. It was the tone of her voice, the way it took aim at him as though he were stupid, a nobody standing in her way.

He came to the end of the message and replayed it. The Impala that the woman was so upset about sat bumperless against the far wall. He remembered now, he did have the bumper, it was delivered a while ago. In fact, he had a lot of bumpers in the makeshift junkyard behind the garage. He pulled the receiver off of its hook and set it on the desk. The dial tone bleated unswervingly, weeveling its way into any unperturbed corridor of his mind. He reached down and yanked the phone's cord from the wall. He was sick of the intrusive noises pushing into his day. Then Curtis began clanking haphazardly through his tool box; a symphony of purpose. He unboxed the bumper from where it sat in front of the impala and reattached it. The job was finished in a matter of minutes.

Curtis exited the garage and circled to the back of the building where the metallic mountain of unused car parts rose towards the sky. The luminous blossoms crowning the tops of the milk thistles slammed to the dirt as he walked towards the pile, stepping on the base of their stems to clear his path of their thorny leaves. He spotted the end of one bumper and yanked it from the stack. Another sat near the peak of the mound so he scrambled up the side of it, lunging forward as pieces of debris fell behind him, pushed into gravity's downward spiral by his heavy steps. He set the two bumpers on his shoulders, curling each arm around them and marched back into the garage, opening the door by kicking it flat-footed, out of his way.

He yanked on the rope attached to the garage door's pulley system and the paneled door raised and bent along its tracks. The shrieking metal rollers reminded him of the message left by the shrieking woman. He pulled the dark-lensed welding mask down over his face and in its reflection the flame from his torch climbed over his eyes and towards his hairline as it combusted into life. This was the end of dealing with people. Curtis welded the first junk-heap bumper onto the one he had just attached. The shrieking woman's voice became the fated fist that had knocked Mary-Frances from her perch on mortality. The shrieking woman's voice became the willow branch switches that had clawed through his childhood at the command of Waylon's hands. He smirked and reached for the third bumper, also adding it to the front of the car so that all three of them accumulated in a tumorous beak.

Curtis cut the gas on the torch and threw back the welding mask to admire his handy work. For the first time since Mary-Frances's funeral he felt excited. He laughed a cynic's laugh that carried in its sound the affirmation of his own darkening nature. What had slid along the foundation of his parent's house, sporing into slick, green colonies that ate at the walls like mold, had followed him to the garage. Curtis jumped into the mutant impala and backed it out of the garage. He turned it around, yanking the gearshift back and forth between reverse and first gear with triumphant jerks. He stopped the car once it was parked with its front end facing the road, its clownishly extended front bumper on full display for everyone who would drive by. He had given the woman a dunce cap.

Chapter 28

Bent Branch Falls 1973

The ease with which her parents defined and lived inside of their own narrow boundaries had given the young Mary-Frances the idea that adulthood was a fixed state that you would easily pass into at a certain age. At this point the trappings of the middle class would fall into place around you. Each year that went by made the whole idea seem sillier, and still there was a part of her that continued waiting for the power of mortgage payments and inherited pearls to reveal itself. Long ago when her mother dodged questions by telling her that she would *understand when she was older* she had proposed a result but no method. How was one supposed to reach these certain understandings?

Mary-Frances now stood, 26 years old, on bare feet in front of her bathroom mirror as the sun rose. She remained still, empty handed, contemplating the miracle of her bare complexion after so many hours spent working in the garden. She should look ragged like she felt inside. Her body should be missing pieces of itself after so many years of giving herself away just to survive. She should somehow look as though she was being deflated and then filled back up again, with the warm down of her daughter's love every day, because she was.

Abigail was growing up quickly, becoming wilful like Mary-Frances wanted her to be; and hopefully prepared, as she was not, for time's graceless stagger. The way it can pass you by if you don't pay attention, then return to yank you along. She would not let Abigail grow up thinking that she was not the architect of her every moment. No, she would have to take responsibility for everything, the way Mary-Frances had been forced to when she conceived Abigail. And Abigail would know this in advance rather than being blindly led to the precipice of so many devastating truths the way that Mary-Frances had been.

Mary-Frances's mother, Caroline, was glamorous in ways that Mary-Frances knew she would never be. The cultivation of glamour requires a disinterested passion, a preoccupation with things of a fleeting nature. Fashion trends, seasonal color palettes, the most modern appliances. Of course Caroline had inadvertently revealed the task of making a life to Mary-Frances through a series of things rather than ideas and lessons. But here Mary-Frances was, an infinite sixty miles away from Caroline and Richard Henderson's idea of life, and she was suddenly sure that there would never be any expensive perfume to apply, no polish to brush over her nails. Though at the same time she had also come to understand the purpose that these sorts of things served in the lives of women.

Beauty routines gave women an approved way to focus on themselves. A moment all their own amidst days planned around the needs of others. To be able to stop being a wife and a mother for just one second while you let yourself expand, becoming both the product and the process. In these moments, women got a rare second to be principally themselves; themselves becoming even more beautiful versions of themselves. With the foundation and then the blush they unpacked their desires, with the flick of a mascara wand they simplified them, and let their condensed energy stream into the effort of creating the image of a beautiful complexion, plumper lips and shinier hair.

Staring through the mirror, over the shoulder of her own reflection, Mary-Frances saw herself sitting on the couch in her childhood home, she was seven and clutching a pink backpack to her chest. The backpack was made of plastic and smelled freshly manufactured. There was purple plastic where the seams on it should be and each time that Caroline took a step in the master bedroom directly over Mary-Frances's head she imagined that it was the same sound the machines made as they assembled the plastic panels of her stitchless backpack- a muffled clumping noise. Mary-Frances remembered the exact smell of that backpack because it was this, mixed with the anxiety of her first spelling test that would make her throw up all over her desk in the first grade classroom, on a day that she would always remember as one of the worst in her life. Clump, clump. Caroline moved forward through the vigorous choreography of "getting ready". Mary-Frances sat below her, feeling completely unready, and stalled out on the side of the road to basic competency because her mother was clearly not remembering that she had promised to help Mary-Frances practice her spelling one last time before she took the test. Caroline had a way of making Mary-Frances feel completely smothered and abandoned all at once.

"Mary-Frances," Caroline sang out when she finally descended the stairs.

"Darlin', are you all ready to go? Stand up then, let me see." Mary-Frances stood up then slowly turned around.

"OK, very good. *Very* pretty. Aren't you glad we took all that time to brush your hair out today?"

Mary-Frances squinted up at her, "No, Mama. My head hurts."

"Oh, I'm sorry Mary-Frances, but you just have to get used to it. Grown women deal with all kinds of little pains, all the time." She leaned down and pinched the suspicious Mary-Frances's cheek, "But one day you're going to grow into a *very* beautiful young woman and you'll see why all the little pains are necessary."

Mary-Frances always hated the way her mother did this, dangling some vague concept just out of her reach while promising its utmost importance.

"Now let's run along and get in the car. I don't want you to be late."

"But we never practiced my spelling Mama."

"Oh," Caroline's concern was a momentary glimmer. "Oh well. I'm sure you'll do just fine."

And that was how one of the worst days in her life started. The fresh sense of anxiety at the amount of things in the world that she did not understand only grew, the test loomed over her. The night before her father had told her that spelling was so important that he refused to do business with people who made too many spelling mistakes in their correspondence with him. Because it was *sloppy.* And not only did Mary-Frances struggle to understand how spelling was so important, she also struggled to pin down the word correspondence. *How does one correspondence?*

And all this was racing through her mind as she took her seat in her first grade classroom during the second week of school. There was also the prospect that she might confuse her left and right when she went to place her *right* hand over her heart, which was supposed to be in the *left* side of her chest, when she stood to say the Pledge of Allegiance. The classroom was hot and sticky, and this seemed to make her backpack fume its plasticky, mass-production gases even more intensely. And there was the bell and the screeching of chairs; then the beep of the intercom. In the moments that everything went silent before the principal's voice crackled through the speakers to lead the school in the Pledge of Allegiance, the excitement welled up inside of Mary-Frances and made her throw up. You could see half chewed cheerios floating in the mess. It ran over the top of her desk and dripped on the floor as her classmates ran for the far corners of the classroom, shrieking. And there she was, stuck in the middle, shepherd of the vomit, source of the sweetly-sharp bile smell. On the drive home she cried and Caroline patted her knee.

As an adult Mary-Frances was coming to understand Caroline, and to understand that she had been the best mother that she could have managed to be. There is no accounting for the way that somebody thinks. She shrugged sympathetically at herself in the mirror. It was Halloween of 1973, the time of year that the dew froze in an icy lace over the tree branches and blades of grass in the morning, dazzling under the first rays of sun in the moments before it melted away. Nine years had passed since she left home, a couple less since she had last spoken to either of her parents, and still Mary-Frances was sure she'd have more things to disagree about with her mother now than ever.

Caroline had Richard had only ever visited her home in Bent Branch Falls once, after Abigail was born. Mary-Frances remembered with brief fury the way that Abigail's birth was able to reignite some maternal sense within Caroline in a way that Mary-Frances's initiation into motherhood had not. Caroline had shown up only for Abigail, never for her own daughter.

On the day that Richard and Caroline drove to Bent Branch Falls to sit stiffly on the couch in Mary-Frances and Curtis's living room, Caroline had made a key lime pie for everyone and prepared for the occasion by dressing in the same color palette as the pie. Her white stockings matched the collar and cuffs of the bright green, A-line dress that she wore. She had spent so much undue effort polishing its brass buttons that Richard broke from his characteristic aloofness to tell her that the dress looked lovely on her. This expression of the last grasps at control within a context where she had none was the only thing that Caroline could do to comfort herself that day. The meringue peaks on her perfect pie even held up for the entire car ride as she and Richard drove into the thin mountain air, ears popping in a way that somehow gave the silence between them a muffled voice.

Over and over Caroline pinched the crimped edges of the pie tin that she held in her lap, rotating it slowly. As they passed Curtis's garage and turned into the driveway that ran past the side of it and towards the house, she couldn't help but comment on the numerous potholes that bounced the car on its shocks as they approached. The potholes, the bugs, the mud; they all conspired to devise an unruliness that Caroline had no place inside of.

"Well, put on a happy face." Caroline sighed as she exited the car, hopping over the more soggy looking patches of black mud. Richard allowed himself a moment to exhale and roll his eyes at his wife and his daughter. At the unseemly schism within their family. It would do everyone some good if they could both be a little less extreme in their opposition to one another.

Mary-Frances opened the door with baby Abigail in her arms. Abigail, who came from the pregnancy that tore Mary-Frances, Richard and Caroline apart was now the only thing that could bring them back together.

"Hi. Come in, come meet Abigail." Mary-Frances looked down into her baby's eyes which still swam around the room, marbled and unfocused; as though she was a star that fell from light years away, and was trying to put together the scene of her new life now that she crashed down into the center of it all.

Caroline immediately reached out for baby Abigail, her steely expression running sticky-sweet, a face turned to honey. She brushed past Mary-Frances with Abigail in her arms and sat on the sofa smiling and cooing at the baby. Mary-Frances, Curtis and Richard were left awkwardly in the doorway. Had Caroline not just abolished all formalities by rushing into the room, Mary-Frances could have said something like, *Come on in and make yourselves comfortable,* but now she stood defenseless, looking nervously at her father, "Hi Pa."

"Mary-Frances," he reached for her and pulled her into a hug.

In the bathroom mirror Mary-Frances admired the way her cheekbones and the slim ridge of her nose absorbed the soft glow of the morning light. This was one of the privileges that she had fought for by leaving home: taking a moment to look herself over and decide that she was beautiful. She was just as beautiful as the people in her life expected her to be.

Outside of the bathroom Abigail zoomed around the house in her homemade pterodactyl costume. Mary-Frances suspected she would be jogging behind her on their way to school that day because Abigail loved the way the wings on her costume flew out behind her when she ran. The thought made Mary-Frances feel exhausted and delighted. Abigail's excitement made it possible for her to break away from the mirror, and the thoughts of her estranged parents and exit the bathroom.

"Caaaw!" Abigail screeched before slamming into the side of Mary-Frances and wrapping her arms around the top of Mary-Frances's hips.

"Abigail! Yer gonna end up knockin' me over one of these days. Yer gettin' too big to be beatin' on yer poor mother."

Abigail heard her mother's smile and nothing else. She ran off down the driveway to show Curtis her costume. Mary-Frances hoped he was in the mood to pay attention to Abigail because it was only these moments of exuberance that made the cost of all the fabric and materials they had bought to make the costume worth it. Every day with Curtis was different from the previous one. Mary-Frances didn't mind that she was the only one who seemed able to handle Curtis's mood swings, except for when she thought of Abigail. Other people could walk away from Curtis but Abigail would have to navigate his storms, as his daughter she didn't have a choice.

Mary-Frances paused in the doorway listening, as still and stiff as a doll framed by its packaging. Then she heard laughter, high and low. Abigail and Curtis. This was a life that she wanted; one that was as disorderly as her and Curtis's love. A hot, vivid life. Abigail came flying around the corner of the garage, held by Curtis above his head. She forgot herself in the excitement of it all and went floppy, forcing Curtis to crouch down and lower her onto the ground.

"Abigail! Come on, yer goin' ta be late fer school!" Mary-Frances yelled then turned to grab her boots and jacket from inside the house. Mary-Frances insisted on walking Abigail to school, it took her twenty minutes each way, and she completed the trek twice a day. Forty minutes just for Abigail, and forty minutes all to herself. The time Mary-Frances spent tending to Abigail were like little bits of supplication laid at the feet of her younger self, they made up for the attention she hadn't received as a young child. They made up for Caroline's habit of spending hours staring at herself in the mirror. Still the tradeoff came with a contradiction the Mary-Frances would never resolve. Mary-Frances was an adult who thought every woman had a right to pursue her own happiness outside of her marriage and home life. But Mary-Frances was a child who felt robbed of love when her mother did just this, in the way that is easiest and most common to the women of her generation.

The anxiety that Mary-Frances had felt at seven years old over the unseemly amount of things that she couldn't understand only grew with every new thing she learned. The best thing to do was to rely on only the simplest things. She held onto Abigail's little hand as they walked to school each day, they ripped the hulls of grass seed from their stems and threw them in the air, leaving them in their muddy tracks along the way.

Chapter 29

Bent Branch Falls 1974

During the summer following Mary-Frances's death the universe reversed its course and began to shrink around Abigail. Expansion became retraction. Rain fell upwards. Molecules of oxygen were pressed into diamonds that couldn't pass through her lungs, they accumulated on the ridges of the soft, pink tissue and turned it to glass- so breakable. Now she knew how her mother's pneumonia must have felt in the days before it killed her. The whole world poured into her and made her so heavy, like an adult crammed into a child's body. And somehow everything was fractured and broken. The whole world was not whole after all, it was a broken thing. She too, broke things. Her crayons. Miss June's casserole dish. Nearly all of the dishes in the house until she realized that no one was going to stop her.

She had exhausted herself breaking things and lay back down on the red velvet couch. She felt the lingering effects of Curtis's presence at her side and realized that she hadn't truly been seen by him, or anyone else since the day Mary-Frances died.

When Curtis looked at Abigail he saw Mary-Frances; everyone else looked at her and saw Curtis's grief. And when they talked about her, it was about the sweat and grime smeared over her. The grime became their pity. So unsightly and needless; so easily washed away had anyone figured out how to pull Abigail out from underneath it all. Abigail didn't need pity, she needed someone to find her, and make her real again. She needed a coca cola.

Abigail contemplated leaving. It would have been an easy thing to do, since everyone was busy looking away. But where would she go? She didn't want to go down the road to a different town; she wanted to follow the possum. But the possum did not choose its own course, fate chose it. Fate seemed to have overlooked Abigail so all she could do was wait. She longed for a pure emptiness. A vacuous nothing that would transform her in the image of itself when she entered it. To be a gossamer beam of light, so effervescent that the universe could no longer lay its heaviness on her chest. This is what she wanted.

She sat up and thought about walking to Harper's Grocery like she used to. But it would be different now. Cora wouldn't want to shoo her off. So there would be no fun in trying to see how long she could linger unnoticed when the men got careless with their conversation. Cora would want her to stay in the store and eat, and the food would be the same sort of vital mess that all the adults had been trying to feed her since her mother's death. Chicken and vegetables and everything she was sick of.

She swung her legs to the side of the couch and pulled on her gumboots. Clumps of earth and grass were still deep in their treads and the slick rubber was flecked with dried mud: drops that once tried to flee in the wake of her footfalls. She followed Curtis's large, oily tracks across the sticky floor and out the front door which now hung on one hinge. It swung back and forth, the whining pitch of its rust and crookedness laid itself over a low, cavernous hum that rose from the forest. Abigail paused, it was as though every cell in every bit of life out there had begun vibrating until their tiny reverberations coalesced in one dark cloud. A plague of locusts that swarmed but went nowhere. The omnipresent sound reassured her that it had always been there, that her finally noticing it had nothing to do with its existence. She was now so lonely that she could notice things outside of the range of ordinary human experience. *Yes* the forest sang back to her.

As she walked down the long, unpaved driveway she made no effort to swerve around the puddles. She looked down into them, these swellings sitting atop the places where the Earth decided that it could take no more. She stepped directly into the reflection of her pale face, it floated like a buoey unchained in the moments before its stark color rippled outwards from the yellow toe of her boot. Her face floated like the saddest planet, leaving its orbit for another unknown universe, as she approached the garage. From a distance she saw a car she recognized but couldn't place, a white plymouth like a dead albatross flattened by its fall on the pavement of the garage's parking lot.

As she came closer, passing alongside the junkyard that sat behind the garage, a hesitation crept into her step. Her strides became shorter. Suddenly voices cut through the dome of hum that held the sky, shattering it into particles as small as silica grains washed from granite. Just like that the sound was gone, as though it had never been there at all. And in its place, voices arguing, sharp as knives.

"Do you understand why she was impatient though? People jest cain't be without their cars for that long."

"I don' give a shit about her or her car. You heard the message she left. If she goin' ta talk that way she can figure out how to fix her own damn bumper. An' now she has three of them to try an' do it with."

"Curtis, this is ridiculous. This is my brother's car and I was the one who sent him to you. I shouldn' haff ta see his vandalized car sittin' in your lot when I drive by it. I know his wife can be kinda unpleasant, but is this really necessary? Don' you want to keep your business runnin'?"

"Don' tell me about my goddamn business! Go on an' mind yer own."

The argument burst out of the front door of the garage, the two men were pieces of shrapnel flying forth from the explosion their tempers had created. It was then that Abigail realized where she had seen the white car before, it was Beau and Cora's car, always parked in the lot in front of their grocery store, in the space furthest from the front door. Beau turned on his heel and pointed his finger in Curtis's face,

"You listen, this is not the last you've heard from me about this."

Curtis looked skeptically at the red faced man. To him Beau's anger was annoying, a gnat that had died in his eye. What was an all consuming fire inside of Beau, was no more than an uncomfortable poking sensation to him.

"OK, see ya later then." He gave Beau a sardonic, two-fingered salute then turned and went back inside the garage. Abigail walked from the edge of the lot towards Beau as he marched over to the car that must have been the subject of the argument, yanked its door open, pulled the keys from the ignition and made a show of pushing down the locks on all four doors. When he stood to close the car's door and walk back to his own, he was stopped short by the appearance of Abigail. Like a tiny ghost, she was made fearsome by the fact of herself. The silver car keys dangled around his middle finger as he held up his hand as though to ward her off.

"What's the problem here?" She inquired, just trying to make conversation. But Beau didn't see Abigail when he looked at her, he saw the many unhinged facets of Curtis. He saw a tiny menace that should be blamed for her unkempt hair, her fraying clothing and milky breath. In response to his startled silence Abigail turned and assessed the car herself.

"Oh, I see. Looks like there's a few extra bumpers on this car. This your car? I've never noticed it before" He stood stock still except for a telling twitch in his left cheek.

"It's my brother's. Didn't have so many bumpers when it got here." Beau could not stop the blame from flowing through his voice.

The fact that Beau could not see that Abigail was a child, simply made him no better or worse than anyone else in Bent Branch Falls at that time. The town's strength had always been derived from its people's instinctive deference to the majority. It was a network made stronger by a preference for the ordinary; by lives lived as amoral tributes to the norm. This was the best that could be hoped for, it was what held Bent Branch Falls together. Over the past month Curtis's emotional excess had begun to be perceived as worse than others and this would not bode well for Bent Branch Falls. Surely this would wreak havoc on the natural order of things. Beau could not help but feel that Curtis's worseness had somehow rubbed off on Abigail. He was offended by the well-meaning little girl despite his better intuition. Ultimately the death of Mary-Frances had triggered an imbalance that was larger than the town itself.

"It's OK Beau," Abigail pressed on, trying to cheer him up. "A few extra bumper's much better than having no bumper at all. Right?"

Still her attempts at conversation could not break through the chill of the situation at hand. Beau merely turned and stalked away, mumbling *Jesus Christ* under his breath as he went. He climbed into his own car and roared off towards town. Abigail turned to look at the car with three bumpers and began to laugh, imagining all the bumping that could be done in a car with such a ridiculous front end.

Why Beau cared about this absurd car parked in her daddy's lot she had no clue. Then the levity of her laughter was confronted by the memory of Beau's anger and suddenly she felt peculiar, like her laughter wasn't allowed until his anger had been reckoned with. Her laughter turned into a battle cry. She walked around the front of the car with its three bumpers and jumped on top of them. They held her weight easily though a part of her wanted them to fall off and break. She wanted to break something, for fun this time. But no matter how hard she jumped and stomped down on the bumpers they held fast, didn't even dent. So she went for the headlights and kicked them squarely with her heavy rubber boots. Over and over. It was her only version of fun so it was OK, and she needed this: the whole tension of her body whittled down and aimed at the headlights, all of her unmet needs forgotten and replaced by the desire for shattered plastic.

The shattering, when it finally happened, could have also taken place inside of her crystallized lungs as the laughter ripped into howls and converted her: from a child carrying a communal sense of grief and pity, to an archive of mistakes. Abigail now carried the cumulative weight of regret and disdain brought down upon her by her current, pitiable state. Memories of mistakes made far before her own birth. In a way she had transcended herself at the moment of Mary-Frances's death, and this half-sacrificed life that she led was worse than drowning in the river; worse than being smashed into roadkill.

Abigail's crazy laughter and the sounds of her artful destruction alerted Curtis to the desperation of their circumstances and all he could think to do was sink down, deeper into all of it. An animal crouching into its own joints as it hid from the predator circling it. Curtis was now convinced he would never have any peace, he was broken. Mary-Frances had made off with everything: his heart, his mind and his well-being. His beloved robber would never rest until he did, lying in the dirt alongside her. The aftermath of Mary-Frances's death has caused a kinetic chaos inside of Curtis that yearned for the weight of black dirt to still it. After dealing with Beau he barely had time to collapse in the chair behind his desk before the garage's phone was ringing again. He pressed the palms of his hands into his eyeballs as they threatened to explode with the pressure. He hoped he had imagined the obnoxious trilling but there it was again. The sound of the world dragging him from his sanctuary. The sound was too much to ignore.

He lifted the handset, "Curtis's Garage."

"Curtis?" It was Liam sounding like a splinter of himself.

"Liam, is that you? What's wrong with you. Ya sound sick or something."

"I'm not sick. I'm jest havin' a lot a problems."

"Yea? What sorts of problems?"

Liam was in disbelief, "What kinda problems you think? You still haven't solved the issues with our business an' now people are showin' up at my house, tryin' ta get the money out of me. What in the hell Curtis? How could you do this ta me? Ya jest give them my address?"

"No. Course I didn' do nothin' like that. I's true I haven't figured out what to do about the unpaid bets, I've been busy. But I wouldn' jest give away your address like that. You know me."

"I dunno what I know anymore. How come those three jokers come knockin at my door then."

"Wait three of them? What'd they look like?"

"Oh… tall skinny. All three a them blonde an scruffy. I'm not sure I seen 'em before. They looked like brothers or somethin'."

"Shit. That would be the Gray brothers. They've always been givin' me trouble. They broke into my garage jest last week. Must a been where they found yer address. They couldn' get to the money themselves so they ran to you" Curtis began chuckling, "even though they were right there," then laughing. Laughing and laughing at the boys impotence. Laughing because his homemade safe had beat them.

"So yer tellin' me they broke into your garage an' stole my address? Goddamn it. It's not funny Curtis. My wife's fixin' ta divorce me over it."

"I'm sorry Liam. Don' worry about those idiots. They cain't do nothin'. Sorry they scared yer lil wifey. I'll put a stop to their shit." The laughter fled from Curtis's voice and he slammed the phone down. His face went deadly still, his stare grew long. His gaze drilled into the cement wall of the garage opposite of him. And there was Abigail on the other side of it, drifting unseen and silent; kept at bay by the thick walls of chaos that surrounded Curtis.

Chapter 30

Linville Falls 1973

With the axe raised above her head Mary-Frances paused. The unchopped piece of log before her had been dampened by the previous night's rain and dripped in a way that was almost lively, or slightly gory. Its blood-like sap was oozing from the scrapes on its bark right before her eyes. Behind her, her long early morning shadow stretched its thin legs eastward and the drops of dew that it cast over remained lifeless, unable to catch the sun and gleam. They sat like pearls of teeth in a closed mouth. A momentary chill seized Mary-Frances and the world around her trembled like a mirage about to disappear. She lowered the axe and turned to sit on the damp log. The hardier plants in her medicinal garden still pushed their way through the detritus that fell with autumn as it turned into winter. The boneset had long lost its blossoms but still stood proudly like stark, minia-ture trees- the tallest plant left.

As she gazed across her backyard and into the forest two cardinals tore from the fading world, shaking the branches of a douglas fir as they rose towards the sun together. It was the end of December and the landscape had been blanched by annual death. As the cardinals flew above the grey forest towards the sun, they were like two sparks of fire making their pilgrimage to the original source. Mary-Frances felt the coldness left in their wake move closer to her, it tried to burrow beneath her skin.

She breathed into her cupped hands, holding the warm air that she expelled close to the tip of her nose; cradling her own breath as though it was the most precious resource in the world, still happily unaware that it was. The bells of the Bent Branch Falls Pentacostal Church rang out, shimmering their tin song over the hillside. Mary-Frances could barely swallow, her throat was so dry, and despite this inner-drought, somewhere deep in her chest her illness germinated. The first seed of Mary-Frances's impending doom cracked open and the roots began to sink themselves into her flesh. The moment passed over Mary-Frances like a small cloud, a brief darkness. The church bells rang again and she lowered her heavy head into her hands. From underneath the nebulous song of the echoing bells came the sound of a drum beat.

Thump-thump. Suddenly Mary-Frances was back in her catholic high school, standing on the metal bleachers inside the school's gym. Thump-thump. She sunk down into the sea of scarlett sweaters and tartan skirts, hunching over as she scooted to the end of her row. She hopped off the bleachers and landed on the rubber floor as the rest of the girls started the final verse of the school's anthem. *With the greatness of god's love, thump-thump, with his blessing we stand tall each day.* She glanced up at her friend Bethany who gave her a quick nod before facing forward again and chanting along with the rest of the students. The path was free of teachers, so Mary-Frances slipped out of the gym, walked down the empty hallway to the side door, and left the school, closing the door softly behind her and listening for the metallic clank of the automatic lock.

Curtis was waiting for her in the school's drive, self consciously trying to avoid staring at Mary-Frances; brilliant as a cardinal blazing across the wide, cement steps towards him in her red school uniform. Already he had memorized the way that she walked: with a deer-like prance, resting her weight on the balls of her feet. She moved through the world with a precise and joyful rhythm, like that of a typewriter tapping out the whole history of manifest ecstasy. She caught his eye and took a goofy leap from the second to last stair. He was still smiling when she reached the truck and yanked open the door.

"Hi, there Curtis. Here," she reached in her pocket and handed him the chocolate milk that she had stashed away for him. "Figured ya missed these since yer not in school anymore."

He laughed and peeled open the cardboard mouth of the carton, "Probably the only thing I do miss about being in school."

Mary-Frances rearranged her backpack so that it leaned against the passenger door and scooted towards him on the bench seat. "Let's get outta here, if I get caught ditchin' class it's over fer me."

"Thought ya said it was jest an assembly," he raised an eyebrow at her.

"Yep, that's what it is. But it's all the same to those crazy teachers. If they find out they'll get on the phone to my parents and make it sound like I've blown off my entire education."

"Well, alright then" Curtis pushed the milk carton into a precarious cup holder hanging from his dashboard just above the broken stereo and yanked on the gear shift, puttering towards the exit of the school's parking lot and staring at her radiant left cheek.

"Where to?" he asked.

"I dunno, you decide. Take me somewhere beautiful."

In the months since their first date, Curtis had taken Mary-Frances to nearly all of his favorite places in the mountains. They had hiked to the top of Bears Ears, a pair of rocky outcroppings high enough to look over the entirety of Yancey County. They had fished at Rainbow Lake. They had eaten at the Smoky Mountain Diner with its rotation of different cobblers. The flavor of the day was always written out in crayon on a piece of paper stuck to the wall behind the cashier's head. It was peach, Curtis's favorite, on the day that he had taken Mary-Frances there, and he was sure this was a good sign. They had hiked to the bottom of the red rock gorge, whose river picked up a rose color as it ran over those rocks; it's waters streaming through the canyon like an unbreakable, pink ribbon. But there was one last place that Curtis had saved to the side out of a mixture of protectiveness and boyish hope. The place was the swimming hole at the bottom of Bent Branch Falls. In his daydreams, Curtis envisioned swimming with Mary-Frances naked. At the very least, he hoped she would be comfortable enough to swim in her underwear with him.

"OK, I know a place," his heart leapt as he turned right and headed towards the highway, "but this one's special. Ya cain't show anyone else."

Mary-Frances turned to smile at him, catching his eyes. She held his gaze like she had seen him hold a cut throat trout before throwing it back into Rainbow Lake, with a caution that rose from knowing that something isn't yours to take even though you couldn't resist reaching out to grab it. She liked the way that Curtis held the best things close to himself instead of showing them off. She wanted to be with a man who treated her like that.

"I won't show a soul. Cross my heart."

They headed up the small, two lane highway towards Bent Branch Falls, falling into their habitual silence. Already small talk had burned off between them and been replaced with stretches of silence punctuated by conversation that was both urgent and unnecessary: truth filled reports on their inner lives and past selves from the solitary atmospheres of their deepest thoughts.

"See that church? That's where my Ma drags me too every Sunday," Mary-Frances lowered her voice to a whisper, "I think she has a thing for the minister!" Then she burst out laughing.

"No she doesn'!'"

"I think she does! You should see the way she looks at him. I don' think it's god love in her eyes."

Curtis laughed and hunched further over the steering wheel. They wound their way into the mountains until the dense forest spit them out on the main street of Bent Branch Falls.

"I love this little town," said Curtis once they had passed through the two blocks that made up the downtown of Bent Branch Falls. He turned onto another county highway, "OK, it's not far at all now."

The pool at the bottom of Bent Branch Falls could not be made ugly by its brutal history, instead the eminent presence of death only sharpened its beauty. Curtis had heard about the prisoner's of Cherokee Natives that had been pushed from the cliffs above the falls and drowned in the strong eddy at their base. He and Elias liked to speculate about the amount of bones still at the bottom of the pool, unsure how long it would take for a human to completely erode while lying underwater. They always searched for pieces of the skeletons, what they liked to call the thin bones. These could've been the splintered remains of whatever had not dissolved into the river, the deteriorating memory of a human form, but they were more likely the bones of animals or tree branches transformed beyond recognition by the cold waters. Either way, it was more fun for the brothers to imagine them belonging to human beings from long ago. But Curtis would not tell Mary-Frances about this now, he didn't want to spoil anything.

Curtis parked the truck on a narrow pull off. He circled around the truck to open the door for Mary-Frances but she had already flung it open and hopped down.

"Aw sorry Curtis, I forget what a gentleman you are."

As they walked up the path together the conversation had somehow circled back around to Caroline and the minister. Mary-Frances was growing more and more animated, as though feeding off the kinetic energy of the falls, "And when she says his name she always looks out of the corner of her eye and bats her eyelashes like he could be standing right there over yer shoulder just cuz she thought of him."

"Does yer Pa ever notice?"

"Nah, I don't think he notices anything really, they're both kinda the dead-fish type. My Ma having a crush is probably the most interesting thing I've ever noticed about-"

Mary-Frances stopped when they stepped out of the trees right at the base of the waterfall. Mist shot through with prisms of light glassed over the cliffs behind it. Moss crept up the rock walls, rising from the pool. Mary-Frances was already bent over and unbuckling her shoes. She pulled her skirt tight around her upper thighs and waded into the water.

"Well, come on! Ya better come in here with me."

Curtis sat to yank off his boots, ball up his socks and roll up his pant legs.

"Oh come on Curtis, just take 'em off. Ya wanna go past ankle depth don't ya?" Mary-Frances turned to taunt him. "I'll do it if you do," she shook her hips at him teasingly and began walking back towards the shore, already unzipping the side of her skirt.

"You got yerself a deal," he laughed and began unbuttoning his pants. They stood in front of each other as they undressed. They turned and walked towards the water, hand in hand.

Mary-Frances remembered the relentless beat of the water-falls drumming all around them. Then the slightly less erratic beat of her heart as she pulled Curtis towards her and pressed her bare torso against his. *Thump-thump.* They're lips locked and they pulled at each other with increasing need. *Thump-thump.* She was opening to him, every part of her body waiting for him to come closer, to pass into her. *Thump-thump.* The noise seemed to be growing louder and Mary-Frances opened her eyes to see Abigail running out of the woods towards her.

"Mama?" She cocked her head to the side, surprised to find Mary-Frances sitting down. Then forgetting her momentary concern started dancing around excitedly,

"Mama, mama, mama! Look what I found," And her little fist bloomed open to reveal a heart shaped quartz rock sitting in the palm of her hand.

"Aw, look at that. It's even pink like a little heart."

"It's for you." Abigail deposited the rock in Mary-Frances's hand. It landed gently, with all the weight of a small heart.

"Thank you Abigail." Mary-Frances pulled her daughter into a hug, curled herself around the little warmth.

"It's cold out here don' ya think?" Abigail shrugged in response.

"Wanna think about it over a cup of hot chocolate?"

"Yes ma'am!" Abigail crowed, then took off running towards the house. Mary-Frances put a hand to her chest, trying to rub away the tightness that suddenly gripped it. She hated the thought of coming down with a cold now, after so much work had been pushed off during the holidays. She had been eager to get back to her routine chores by the end of Christmas day, but she couldn't deny the ache in her limbs and head, the irreconcilable coldness that had settled into her center. She sighed, brought the axe to the shed and hung it on its hook. The axe remained, faithfully and always on its hook, never to be touched by Mary-Frances ever again. As she turned and walked towards the house her shadow detached itself from her heels and was burned away by sunlight.

Chapter 31

Bent Branch Falls 1974

For as long as he could remember, Curtis loved the way autumn ignited the mountain side. Each year he waited impatiently for summer to burn so brightly that the trees burst into flame, as though they had absorbed so much sun in the hot months that they couldn't help but to remake themselves in its image. The summer after Mary-Frances's death crawled past particularly slow, in a grief induced malaise. Without Mary-Frances there was nothing for Curtis to do while he waited. He threw himself violently against the world's many rough textures, trying to create a spark, a distraction; anything. WIth the doors being constantly left open the house took on the same atmosphere as the outdoors and Mary-Frances's dip candles melted and dripped from the mantelpiece. Curtis could almost imagine that she had continued lighting them each night, then sitting down in the armchair to read like she always had.

It was nearing the beginning of August now and the immutable greenness of the landscape depressed Curtis. Green was the color of growing and living. Green was what made evident the fact that the rest of the world just kept moving forward after the day that Mary-Frances died, which was an intolerable miscalculation to Curtis. He wasn't moving forward and his obstinance challenged the fabric of time. He and Abigail's unnatural pursuit of a stillness at odds with everything that animated the world aligned them with death.

Curtis plucked a green glass bottle from where it was standing underneath his desk, on the garage floor. It was one of the many bottles of moonshine emptied by him and Jimmy over the years. He stared into his olive colored reflection and dialed Jimmy, then stood up with the phone pressed between his chin and shoulder and began pacing back and forth, turning when the length of the phone's cord ran out.

"Yep?" Jimmy sat down at his kitchen table to take the phone call, "Curtis, that you?"

"Yea it's me. Why do ya sound so surprised?"

"I dunno, just hadn't heard from you for a while is all. How ya been?"

Virginia sat on Jimmy's couch trying to discern the strange expression on her boy's face. She picked at a loose thread on her embroidered skirt, thinking to herself all the while that it would be best to leave it alone. It had been a peculiar summer in Bent Branch Falls, it was as though Mary-Frances's absence glided in silent circles over all of them, like a hoard of vultures waiting patiently. In her mind Virginia ran over the many untimely deaths that had occurred in the town over the course of her lifetime, reminding herself that each one had passed, eventually time would lift the shroud.

"I don' think so Curtis. Ya sure it's them?"

Virginia had politely lost the thread of her son's conversation but now regretted it as he seemed to grow increasingly agitated.

"Well, I don' know if you need to do anythin', they didn' get anythin' from you, right?"

Jimmy caught a glimpse of his face in the dirty window. His expression looked like the one he wore two decades earlier, as he watched Jo Fallon stretch a slingshot back and take aim at a squirrell. The squirrel was shaken out of blissful ignorance and began running across the tree branch that it sat on. Jimmy clenched his teeth, wishing he was brave enough to grab at Jo's arm, to stop the pointless killing. Jo was enamored with his new toy and assumed that Jimmy was as well,

"When you get one of these things, like mine, the trick is to stay two steps ahead of the animal, Jo advised him, "My brother told me that. Shoot where it's going, not where it is."

"Why do you want to shoot it anyway?"

"Why wouldn't I? Look, there he goes."

The squirrel plummeted from the tree, it fell straight down like a rock dropped from a bridge into the river. Jo let out a yell and some laughter then ran towards the tree. Jimmy turned to wipe his eyes then began to walk slowly towards the tree too, hoping the squirrel would somehow leap up and run away. His stomach clenched violently.

"Come on Jimmy, yer such a wuss." Jo ran back towards Jimmy to taunt him. He bent over and picked up a rock, a flint colored rectangle with sharp edges, and loaded it into his slingshot.

"If yer so sad about the squirrel, just wait til I shoot you." Jo aimed the slingshot at Jimmy and began circling him, never letting Jimmy leave the sights of his aim. Jimmy just stared at his feet and marched on. The grass disappeared near the base of the tree and the squirrel had fallen into mud. Its eyes were filled with the coppery glint of residual terror and there was a gash in its side where the rock had hit it. To Jimmy, its cherry pie insides were a sickening sight.

Nearly an hour later VIrginia found Jimmy, still standing at the base of the oak tree, staring down at the murdered squirrel. Jo had become bored and left long ago and the sun was setting. Jimmy's eyes were wet and lifeless. His nose was running with a viscous slime and his eyebrows were knit upwards, the same way they were now. Curtis was talking so loudly at the other end of the phone that Virginia could nearly make out what he was saying. Curtis had always given Virginia yet another reason to worry over Jimmy. Another stitch came undone with the tugging of her fingers and the bright red thread lengthened in her hand. As Virginia saw it, it was only the fact of not fitting in that bound Jimmy and Curtis together but beyond that, she refused to see any similarities between the two of them.

"Well don' ya think you could try an' talk to them?"

Curtis must be in some sort of stupid fight with somebody. Virginia decided she would ask Cora about it, she always knew what was going on in Bent Branch Falls. Virginia uncrossed her legs and pressed herself back, further into the narrow couch that was attached to the side of Jimmy's small trailer. When she visited Jimmy she couldn't help but feel that the trailer was all wrong, like a period placed in the middle of the sentence.

"I dunno Curtis, it doesn' seem worth it. Maybe you jest need to calm down."

The quivering edge of Jimmy's voice recaptured Virginia's attention and she lifted her head to meet her son's frightened gaze.

"Well, stay there. I'll be over." Jimmy dropped the receiver back onto the phone's cradle. He avoided Virginia's eyes as he grabbed his boots, floppy with the wear and tear of miles walked.

"Sorry ma, I gotta go over to Curtis's."

"Why? What's goin' on?

Jimmy sighed, "Somethin's not right with Curtis, he's not well. Anyways, he's thinkin' that the Gray brother's have been breakin' into his garage. So he wants to go over to their place."

"OK." Virginia tilted her chin towards the ceiling, "so ya think its true? Ya think they've been breakin' in?"

"I dunno. I mean, they probably would do somethin' like that. You know them. But it also seems to me like Curtis don' know up from down anymore."

Virginia submerged the impulse to drag her son home and keep him away from all of it underneath her collected exterior. Her frustration turned towards the trailer: the monolithic reminder that Jimmy was no longer her little boy the way that he once was.

"Well what's any a this got to do with you? Why don' you let that man take care of his own problems an' you can come have dinner with yer father and I?"

"Cuz I don' know if he's up to it, an' I dunno what Curtis is capable of doin' right now. It makes me worry that things could get outta hand." Jimmy bent over to lace up his boots, pretending to not see the grave expression that crossed his mother's face: a premonition as fleeting as the shadow of a rabbit running from a fox.

"Ma, it will be fine. Trust me."

Seeing that she had no other option Virginia conceded, "Alright, you know him better than anyone. Jest let me know if there's anythin' I can do. And when everythin' calms down you two can come over fer dinner if you want."

"OK thanks, I'll see you later." Jimmy left his mother still sitting on his couch. He was too distracted to walk her to her car like he usually did, his racing thoughts too all-consuming to make room for commonplace manners.

"Virginia remained on the couch while she dug her keys from her purse. She forced herself to leave slowly, assuming that if she did not see Jimmy as she left it would make it much easier to resist offering him a ride that she knew he didn't want.

As he approached the garage Jimmy caught a figure out of the corner of his eye, but it vanished into the mottled blur of dusk when he turned to look. He assumed it could be Abigail playing in the woods, if she played anymore. Her presence at his Mother's birthday party had been so somber that it was difficult to associate Abigail with childish activities like playing. Like a snake shedding its skin she had slipped out of childhood. After living through her mother's death, people were no longer capable of regarding her as a child. Somehow she slunk into an existence so detached from everything else that it was all her own: a small shadow cast by nothing.

Unmothered Abigail did not reappear as Jimmy reached the garage's door. The dank, smudgey smells of oil and wet cement hit him as he grabbed the door knob. But then something made him pause self consciously, he raised his fist to knock but quickly shook himself from this unfamiliar diversion and walked into the garage like he always did.

Curtis was hunched over, stuffing dirty rags into the mouths of half filled bottles that had been lined up on the floor of the garage, all of them the green wine bottles that had carried gifts of moonshine to Curtis. The realization fell to the pit of Jimmy's stomach, its roots burrowing into the lining even as he tried to shake it off. The smell of gasoline hammered the horrific knowledge of what Curtis was planning to do further into his head and blurred his vision. He could see drops of gasoline on the garage floor in between each bottle, stringing them together as though they were gemstones connected and hanging delicately from a chain, but wasn't everything? Wasn't all of existence dangling from the same thread? It dawned on Jimmy that the collapse had begun long ago while everyone was busy ignoring it, but the entropy was only increasing; the rate of destruction feeding on itself and growing quicker. Its energy only grew in heat and force.

"Curtis you cain't do that." Jimmy struggled to push the unfamiliar authority into his voice.

"Has ta be done Jimmy." Curtis paused and cranked his head at an unnatural angle, the yellow light in the garage sticking in his enlarged pupils as he peered over his hunched back at Jimmy, "I thought you were comin' over ta help."

"I am here to help. I'm here ta help you talk to the Gray brothers cuz that's how we're goin' ta solve this."

"Nope. I think we're past solvin' anythin' at this point. It's been two times that those boys have broke inta my garage, trespassed on my property. I haff ta put a stop to it. Ain't nothin' gettin' solved right now, it's just goin' ta get stoppped. Plain an' simple."

"No Curtis, this isn' the way ta do things and this isn' like you at all."

Curtis rose to his full height, "What do ya think you know about me? Huh? You think you know what I'm like all of a sudden? You don' know nothin'. You barely been around since Mary-Frances died. You don' know nothin' of what this place is like without her."

Jimmy stopped cold. His only friend had just declared him a stranger, and maybe he was. Sometimes he even felt as though he was a stranger to himself. Cold fish. Dead fish. He used to struggle with the mechanics of betrayal, thinking he could avoid it by cautiously figuring out who people were from a distance, but now he was beginning to think that it was impossible to know anyone. Does anyone truly get the luxury of a fixed identity? Perhaps it was all just good-natured self deception. Simultaneously the sensation of being an individual was unraveling for both Jimmy and Curtis. Curtis was moving beyond himself, being pushed forward by something truly awful. He would let it consume him.

"It's jest goin' ta happen no matter what. It isn't about me, nothin's ever been about me." Curtis balled his fists up as though hanging on to this conviction with all ten fingers, like he could pummel the world into making its confession: we are the puppets and it is our master. Jimmy turned on his heel, no longer determined to help Curtis but to stop him. In the open air outside of the garage Jimmy's anger and pain turned into fear, like a frozen rain falling through his body. Clean, sharp fanged fear. And suddenly he wasn't sure what to do. He had never asserted his will over anyone, he had always bent to everyone else. He turned down the road and began running to his parents house. The shame he felt at being unable to handle the situation himself felt like the shame of being unable to save the squirrel. But this time the outcome could be different, there was still time to change it.

Virginia had seen Jimmy approaching the house at a run and was already on the front porch when he reached it.

"What's going on?"

Jimmy gapsed, "I dunno, it's bad. I really think Curtis is goin' ta try an' burn down the Gray's house."

Virginia's hands dropped to her side and she immediately went into the house. Calling Cora was all she could think to do. Cora knew the Gray family well and always knew how to handle things. As she dialed the number to Harper's Grocery she struggled to imagine how she would explain everything that was happening. She exhaled and waited. Cora picked up on the third ring.

"Hello, Harper's Grocery."

"Cora it's Virginia, I need yer help with somethin'. I dunno who else to ask."

"OK." The emptiness of Cora's pause zipped through the phone line to Virginia as she struggled to decide if she sounded too dramatic. It was possible that over the course of these moments the situation was already diffusing itself.

"Look, ya know my boy Jimmy's good friends with Curtis." Cora clenched her jaw, expecting that the problem had something to do with Beau who had already been in a fight with Curtis once that day.

Virginia continued, "Jimmy's pretty convinced that Curtis wants to go an' burn down the Gray's place. Apparently Curtis and those boys have some sorta feud goin' on between them an' Jimmy cain't seem to talk Curtis out of anythin' at the moment."

Jimmy closed his eyes, languishing at the bottom of the hurt welling up inside of him. When had he become so ineffective?

Cora leaned against the grocery counter and lowered her head until it came to a rest on the tips of her fingers. If any of this was happening before Mary-Frances's death she would have laughed it off and told Virginia to settle down. But she had been at the funeral, she had seen Curtis, felt his resentment. She knew nothing about his family but it seemed to her that Curtis sliding backwards into a learned anger, a vitriol distilled for many generations. This newly uncovered part of Curtis was a stranger to everyone in Bent Branch Falls, nobody could assume that they knew what he was capable of any longer.

Chapter 32

Bent Branch Falls 1974

Could a life slip away unnoticed, like a shadow, as though it is not vital to our bodies but only collaborating with them to perpetuate itself? Or is it all that we will ever have, the only true parameters of the universe? Unsure of how to quantify the black hole that she was falling into, Mary-Frances had once assumed that death was a thing all its own, immovable and unavoidable. Though slowly she was beginning to suspect that death was a vast nothingness. Like the space over which the grim reaper's hood is draped- a face of emptiness. As she looked back over her life, considering its many tumultuous currents, it seemed more and more likely that death was simply a cessation of life. It is a hole that one can fall into while trying to avoid it. Its silence and darkness stem from scarcity; it is at its core, nonexistence.

But who can stand to think of something that is nothing? The contradiction is a torture that we grapple with by ordering flowers and headstones, building coffins and floating them along a final parade; making so many things out of the nothing that we can never know. The thought webbed itself over Mary-Frances's mind during her final days. Impossibly it hung, like a captured fly about to eat its predator. This reverie, as it threatened to turn inwards and gobble itself down, was interrupted when a finch hit the window. The thud of its flying force stopped short was followed by an unfinished trill. Mary-Frances raised her head up and her blanket slid downwards, from her chin to her stomach. She was immediately consumed by the symptoms of her fever. Chills moved like slow lightning through her. She fell backwards against the pillows, pulling the blanket up beneath her chin.

It was Abigail who answered the finch's painful call. When she returned to Mary-Frances's line of sight the stunned bird was cupped in her hands. It's legs dangled through her parted fingers. Its tail, cocked sideways, was incapable of steadying anything anymore.

"Mama look."

"I see babe, it's beautiful."

"I can see it breathing."

"Me too. Let's give it some rest and let it heal up. You know where we keep the birdseed right?"

"Yep."

"Ok why don't you put it outside with some seed and water OK? We'll help it get better."

"OK."

Mary-Frances closed her eyes against the demanding daylight as Abigail fixed the finch a small bed, made from a dish towel placed in a shoebox. The cusp of death is so precious like that, padded inadequately by the trappings of those who live without the knowledge of what lies beyond it. She laid the finch in its makeshift bed and it squinted up at her, its eyes gooey with confusion. Mary-Frances scrunched herself up and sunk even deeper into the pile of blankets that covered her. Abigail returned to the kitchen, found the lid of a jar and filled it with water from the kitchen sink, slopping half of it onto the floor as she walked towards the front porch where she had laid the dazed bird on the red dish towel.

Now that the possibility of death had entered her mind, Mary-Frances felt like a stranger to the life around her. Already the happenings of Bent Branch Falls were receding into a dusky static that pressed against the outside of the windows. It all peered into the living room where Mary-Frances lay, but like the finch, could not cross the threshold. The only vessel capable of bringing her the outside world in a way that didn't exhaust her was her radio. It sat on the coffee table, an arm's reach from where Mary-Frances lay. She switched between the three stations that came in, listening to melancholy country songs and sports, sometimes even giving in and listening to an impassioned preacher rattle through a sermon.

Her mind often wandered from the soothing stream of voices coming from the radio and flashed over her memories in feverish brilliance, like the rotating light of a lighthouse throwing the different chapters of her history into naked relief as it swept over her past. *You won't make a monster out of me.* These were the words that circled through her head, a catchy refrain to ward off her worst memories, to help her set her sights on all the goodness that had passed through her life. But still, while lying on her deathbed Mary-Frances couldn't help but think of her parents. She couldn't stop herself from sifting through her past, searching for something or someone to blame for their estrangement. The pregnancy that had torn them apart ultimately gave life to Abigail. Despite her innocence it was ultimately Abigail who would bear the weight of the past. This was something that Mary-Frances had always known but acknowledged for the first time as she lay on her deathbed.

Every coughing fit yanked on her worn down back muscles, in its throws her ribs felt like a loose scattering of broken branches clattering around inside of her. A destructive wind howled through her. Mary-Frances had never felt so weak before. Again the raw spasms shredded through her chest and she grabbed the washcloth lying on the coffee table, spitting blood streaked phlegm into its desecrated folds. When the episode was over she sunk back down into the couch. Every breath was a carefully measured effort; with an oppressive vigilance Mary-Frances attempted to breathe in just enough to get air without agitating her overburdened lungs.

Abigail quietly approached, picked the bunched up wash cloth off the table and replaced it, with the grave efficiency of an anesthetized nurse. Abigail had been washing and drying the two washcloths that Mary-Frances had been coughing into, facing the viscera of her mother's sickness unflinchingly. The small acts of caretaking that she could manage, refilling Mary-Frances's water glass, gathering hyssop and boneset from the garden, and switching out her rags, was all that Abigail could do to fill up the emptiness left in the wake of the illness. The days flatlined into a drab and burdensome stretch of unbroken time without Mary-Frances there to direct her through chores and activities. Abigail was also sunk into the deep pool of her mother's illness; it's numbing currents swirled over them, whispering away the rest of the world.

Just beyond the front door the finch lay, grappling with its own death. As he walked towards the house from his garage Curtis was preoccupied by Mary-Frances's illness, for the first time he was losing faith in her ability to heal. He should have ignored Mary-Frances's protests and called a doctor, he saw this now. As he climbed the stairs to the front porch he nearly stepped on the finch. A jolt, like falling in a dream, stopped him short. He crouched down to examine the struggling bird, its labored breath inflating then emptying its chest in unmetered rhythm. In a terrifying moment of clarity Curtis recognized Mary-Frances's breath in the small creature. All life animating the Kennedy land was becoming increasingly grainy and erratic, like a reel of celluloid film whose story was slipping away with time. Chunks of the background were disappearing, people moved through rooms with no logic or fluidity. Nausea filled their bellies simultaneously as though they were trapped on a broken rollercoaster. Together they careened forward with uncontrollable speed.

Curtis entered the living room adapting his movements to its quiet mood. Through the radio's rustling static the crooning voice of an oldies artist quietly rocked into the air. Curtis pulled the wingbacked, green armchair to the side of the couch, pushing the coffee table back to make room for it.

"Hey, baby how ya feelin'?" His voice was coated in a sticky sadness that he could no longer keep inside.

Mary-Frances squinted at him apprehensively, "I'm alright. I'm sure the sickness will break soon. Right now I'm just coughin' all the gunk outta my lungs." Curtis laid his oil marked hand over her forehead.

"Really, don' act all sad Curtis. I'll be here," but her voice faltered as she spoke and a single tear fell from her right eye.

"I know it. I Know ya will." Curtis ducked his head and stood halfway up so he could grab the radio off the table. "Ok then, ya mind if I put on that boxing match? Got a lot of bets on this one."

"Yea that's fine. We'll listen to it." Mary-Frances's head jerked back as her lungs filled suddenly, preparing for another gale of coughing. Curtis weathered the storm by pouring all of his concentration into turning the radio dial in small increments. The sounds of the outside world flew past them as though they were only spying on it, with their ears pressed against a closed door.

Abigail reentered the living room with the finch one more time. She stood quietly in front of her parents for a minute before asking, "Mama is it dead?"

Mary-Frances replied without opening her eyes, "yes honey, it's dead. But you knew that, didn't you?"

Of course she did. It was simplicity that gave the finch all of its grace, in flight and death. The finch expected nothing of death and so fell into it easily. Its existence winged off and over the final horizon with a lack of weight well suited for ending a life spent defying gravity. Abigail stood there, eyes dilated wide in an attempt to take in the unquantifiable nature of the finch's departure. Again, Mary-Frances was racked by a cough that seemed to get its voice from somewhere else. It sounded too demonic to be using the apparatus of Mary-Frances's own vocal cords to make its sound.

Abigail went outside to hide the finch's body underneath the porch's steps. A small line of blood had dried along its cracked beak. In three hours the emts from the county hospital would be there to take Mary-Frances's body to the morgue and her shadow would pass over the little bird before leaving her house for the last time.

Chapter 33

Bent Branch Falls 1974

After the fire burned down into ashes, the people of Bent Branch Falls had only their own hands to ponder. It was stupid really, they way that they had tried to ignore the smoke: a black twist streaming down the valley. As the uncontained house fire spread and leapt into a forest fire they let the animals disappear into the woods without following them. It took only three hours for the fire to creep from the Gray's trailer to the heart of Bent Branch Falls. But in those moments, rarified by impending calamity, the citizens of Bent Branch Falls, even Curtis- the origin, managed to convince themselves that they would remain untouched by the flames; as though something holy would intervene on their behalf. They held the unrealized miracle reverentially on their tongues, they waited quietly as the town's fate sealed itself around them.

In those final moments, with the fire in sight, Curtis and Abigail stood together in their driveway. Curtis had wound the garden hose around to the front of the house, attempting to protect the structure by soaking it with a stream so small it was nearly eviscerated in the hot air before it landed. For the second time that year they stood facing their small house, staring down a fresh tragedy that would bind them together while somehow managing to push them apart. In their memories the house would become the face of tragedy; the death mask of the time they spent living in Bent Branch Falls. Abigail shoved her bright orange kazoo into her shorts pocket and turned around to look at the red glow crawling ominously over the nearest ridgeline.

In the end everyone except Tallulah Gray ran for their lives. By the time the mob of townspeople that Cora and Beau had gathered together reached the trailer, it was too late. The flimsy siding was engulfed in flame, the window frames receding deeper into the fire like sleepless eyes. Jolene and her brothers were nowhere to be seen. Some speculated that they had abandoned their mother when the fire started, fleeing out the back door. It's also possible that they weren't home that afternoon, in the end Tallulah was the only one who could truly know. When Tallulah saw Curtis staggering up the road a few minutes before a ball of fire broke through her living room window and set flame to the carpet, she had turned away from his disturbing image and poured herself a final bowl of cereal. The frosted flakes glistened goldenly, their sugary glaze exaggerated by the tang's nuclear orange color.

With the startlingly violent arrival of the first molotov cocktail, Tallulah Gray felt an unnatural, numbing wave of resignation wash over her; a peacefulness that she hadn't felt since before Paul left. She sat down in her favorite armchair, her sweating feet inches away from a zagging line of flame. The burning curtains mesmerized Tallulah as she took a bite of cereal, the best she had ever tasted. As the fire progressed, encircling her, William Shatner sang *Taxi* on the television. He sang about torrential, San Francisco rain until his voice and image began to melt, running haphazardly like rivulets of water. He disappeared when the screen flashed and went black. WIlliam Shatner's image was pulled to the center of its own darkness as though he were performing on a dying star.

By the time Cora, Beau, Virginia, Camilla, Bud and Jimmy arrived, the structure had caved inwards. Though she already knew the answer Cora whispered, "Do ya think Tallulah's still in there?" then doubled over and vomited. Nobody moved to acknowledge the question, or the nausea its answer produced. The stories that were printed in the Caville newspapers would claim that nobody had alerted the fire department about the historic fire or its single victim until it crested the peaks surrounding Bent Branch Falls. At that point, someone in the next town over called the police. According to the stories in the papers, nobody knew how the fire started. *Nobody* was the name ascribed to the last inhabitants of Bent Branch Falls. Even in its moment of grave brilliance, the town went unacknowledged.

Curtis and Abigail waited, paralyzed by denial until the very last second. The heat rising from the ground had made a mirage out of everything, but their trance was broken when the crack of a falling oak tree broke through the sky above them.

"Get in the truck!" Curtis screamed and he and Abigail both started running for it.

As Curtis fumbled with his keys sweat sprung up between his knuckles. Every fiber of his and Abigail's bodies strained forward, out and away from the approaching flames while the unbothered engine kept its own typical time. One twist of the key and it turned over. One more twist and it let out an apathetic gasp. On the third twist it seemed to yell *fine!* as it roared to life.

Abigail and Curtis fled from Bent Branch Falls carried by four nearly melted wheels. The hot flash of the truck bed gathered ash and black branches as the forest fell around them. The truck ricocheted through the deep ruts of dirt roads- a red pinball. During their final and desperate scramble Abigail and Curtis clenched their teeth together in fear that a loose jaw would let their molars bounce and shatter against each other. Abigail contemplated the fact of their departure with unaffected resolve, Curtis with relief. The seatbelt rashed against the skin of Abigail's belly, the soft cotton of her shirt unable to provide any sort of comfort against the truck's violent lurching.

Acknowledgements

This book would not have been possible without the loving support of so many family members, friends, artists and communities. I would like to thank the following people:

Mom, Sal and all of my family members for your loving support.

To Delia, Alison and Sal: all three of you took the time to help me edit this book and shape it into what it is today. Thank you!

To Stain'd Arts and Azule Artist's Place for nurturing me with community and providing me with inspiration, time, and peace of mind.
Adelaide Books for all of your support.

About the Author

Andrea Dreiling grew up in Conifer, CO surrounded by the natural beauty of the Rocky Mountains. She loved reading from an early age and quickly became a card carrying member of the public library system. She earned her bachelor's degree in English/writing with a minor in ethnic studies from the University of Colorado Denver. After graduating she took time to travel to South America and eventually returned to Colorado and worked at a library for several years.

Andrea's love for the written word has led her to be a dedicated collector and supporter of zines and literary journals. She had the privilege of leading the Tiny Poem Picture Project with the support of Stain'd arts for a couple of years, and participating in several of their poetry readings and literary events. She has also published poems and short stories in publications such as *Teeth Dreams, Birdy, Stain'd, South Broadway Ghost Society* and *Fresh.Ink*.

Inspired by her love for Southern Writers such as Jesmyn Ward, Dorothy Alison, William Faulkner and Karen Russell Andrea traveled to Hot Springs, NC to complete a writing residency at Azule Arts before moving to Asheville, NC. It was here that she gathered the inspiration and ideas that made writing *The Burning People* possible. *The Burning People* is Andrea's debut novel. She currently writes articles and reviews for Paperback Paris and is working on her next book. You can visit her website at dre-writes.com

Made in the USA
Las Vegas, NV
20 November 2021

34831266R00156